Death Stalk

BOB LANGLEY

SPHERE BOOKS LIMITED
30/32 Gray's Inn Road, London WC1X 8JL

First published in Great Britain by
Michael Joseph Ltd 1977
Copyright © Bob Langley 1977
First Sphere Books edition 1978

Set in Intertype Baskerville

Printed in Great Britain by
Hunt Barnard Printing Ltd.,
Aylesbury, Bucks.

Death Stalk

ONE

At 10.20 a.m. on Monday 25th November, three days after his appointment as Director General of the BBC, Naunton F. Huntley took the lift to the third floor of Broadcasting House, and was met in the corridor by his assistant, Brumby Bayle. The two men strolled together to Huntley's office where they found his secretary, Mrs Grierson, sitting in a chair by the window, staring at them with a rigid expression. In the corner, covering her, was a man in a light nylon raincoat, holding a revolver. A second man, taller, heavier, similarly armed, crouched behind Mrs Grierson's chair, his gun pointed towards the open door.

'One move,' the man said, 'and you'll never live again.'

Naunton F. Huntley swallowed. He had spent his early years as an officer in the Parachute Regiment, had fought with Tito's partisans in Yugoslavia during the war and was no stranger to guns or the damage they could do. In more recent years, he had been obliged on numerous occasions to gamble his career on decisions which could easily have led to disaster. This too had taken a certain kind of courage, and he was not a man who frightened easily; but, taken by surprise, he felt confused and uncertain.

'What is this?' he murmured.

'Stand away from the door. Step forward three paces. Keep your backs straight and do it slow and easy. Then reach out with your foot and slide the door gently shut.'

Together, Huntley and Bayle obeyed, watching the gun, almost mesmerised. Their hands felt icy.

'You are Naunton F. Huntley,' the man said, 'Director General of the BBC?'

Huntley nodded, anger beginning to rise in his throat.

'Listen to me carefully,' the man said. 'Follow my instructions to the letter and no one need get hurt. We don't want to hurt anyone. That's not what we have come for. We'll do it if we have to, but we don't want to. Do as I say, exactly as I say, and everyone will come out of this alive. Can I count on your co-operation?'

Naunton Huntley stared at him without speaking. The man sighed.

'You are not making this easy for me, Mr Huntley. I am going to count on your co-operation. Should you fail to co-operate, then you, and at least one of your colleagues will be killed. Act sensibly, and you will still be alive this evening, and this lady here will be able to return to her family unhurt. Attempt to be heroic and it will be the last act you ever perform, and since I am by nature a vindictive man, you will not die alone.'

Mrs Grierson began to sob. Tears issued from her eyes, tracing uneven patterns down the steep curve of her cheeks.

'Ssh,' Huntley said soothingly. 'Don't worry, Mrs Grierson, everything will be all right.'

The man with the gun nodded approvingly.

'That's right,' he agreed. 'If everyone does as they're told, there's nothing to worry about. We are going on a little trip, Mr Huntley, you, my friend and I. We are going to take the lift down to the lobby and stroll into the street. We are going to do it casually, without haste, without any signs of tension and without speaking to anyone on the way. When we reach the pavement you will see a grey Hillman Avenger parked on the opposite kerb. You will cross the street in front of me and climb into the rear seat. Is that understood?'

Huntley did not answer.

'I said, is that understood, Mr Huntley?'

Huntley nodded briefly.

'Let me hear you say it.'

'It's understood,' Huntley growled.

The man with the gun turned his attention to Bayle. The man was big and heavy-shouldered. His face was pale and featureless, its surface smoothed out like moulded plasticine. It might have been a rubber mask, except for the network of tiny blue veins which traced the hollows beneath the cheekbones. Only the eyes seemed alive, and under their glittering stare Bayle felt his stomach lurch.

'You are Brumby Bayle, Mr Huntley's assistant?'

'Yes.'

'What are you called for short?'

Bayle looked at him in surprise.

'Just Brumby.'

'Well, Brumby, you will accompany us as far as the lobby. If anyone should attempt to speak to Mr Huntley on the way, it will be your job to discourage them. You will use the minimum number of words necessary, and you will do it with good humour so that their suspicion will not be aroused. When we reach the front door, you will stand on the step in full view of the street and watch Mr Huntley climb into the car. When the car has driven away, you will remain where you are for exactly three minutes. Do you have a watch?'

'Yes.'

'Time yourself. Three minutes, Brumby, to the second. My friend and I will be inside the car with Mr Huntley, and you may be tempted to sound the alarm, imagining yourself no longer in danger. Such an action would be extremely foolish since it would result in your immediate death. On the roof of All Souls' Church, a sniper with a high-powered rifle will keep you in his sights for three minutes after the car has disappeared. Should you make any unscheduled movement, should you attempt to step back inside the lobby, or to attract the attention of passers-by, you will be killed. Understand?'

Bayle licked his lips.

'Yes,' he whispered.

The man with the gun glanced quickly around the office. There were two doors, one leading into Huntley's private room in the rear, the other facing the window.

'Where does that lead?' the man asked.

'It's just a stationery cupboard,' Huntley said.

The man opened it up. Inside, there were boxes of headed notepaper, envelopes, typewriter ribbons, felt-tip pens and cardboard folders. It was dark, and smelled faintly of disinfectant. The man seized Mrs Grierson by the arm and dragged her to her feet.

'Inside,' he ordered.

She squeezed into the confined space, her cheeks pale and frightened.

'You will remain here until Mr Bayle returns for you,' the man with the gun said. 'You will remain silent until then. If anyone enters this office, you will make no sound to show that you are here. You will wait until Mr Bayle himself releases you. If you attempt to attract attention in any way, both Mr Bayle and Mr Huntley will be killed.'

He turned to Bayle.

'You tell her,' he ordered.

'I'm sure they mean what they say,' Bayle said. 'I'll be back to let you out in ten minutes. Until then, please keep absolutely quiet. I feel certain they won't hurt us as long as we follow instructions.'

The man with the gun closed the door and turned the key. He glanced at his companion and nodded gently.

'All right,' he said, 'let's go. And smile, Mr Bayle. You look like a man on his way to a funeral.'

They went out and along the corridor and through the fire doors at the far end. Mercifully, there was no one in the lift on the way down. They stood in absolute silence. Naunton Huntley could hear the rumble of the lift cable, interspersed with the softer clicking of his wristwatch. He was thinking about the guns at his rear, trying to imagine the sensation of being shot, wondering how it would feel, the impact, the searing pain, the bullets ripping into his flesh, severing tendons, organs, arteries. He could not

10

visualise that. He could not even begin to anticipate it. He could not, on this chill November morning, here in the familiar sanctuary of the BBC lift, accept that he might be on the threshold of death. He thought about other things instead.

That summer, he and his wife and their two children had rented a holiday chalet in Morocco. The chalet had stood in a snatch of sweetly-scented pine forest, commanding a splendid view of the beach and the grey rolling breakers of the Atlantic Ocean beyond. In the mornings, after breakfast, he used to take the children down to the seashore, down to where the sand was flat and wet and hard, and there they would play handball until the sun grew too hot for comfort. Afterwards, they would dash into the water and splash around in the rolling surf until lunchtime. On clear days, they could see the ragged hump of Gibraltar in the far-off distance. Arabs sometimes rode along the beach, white-robed Berbers on tiny burros, and once they had seen a whole camel train, the camels roped together, one behind the other, their humps laden with bundles of charcoal and straw. In the afternoons, when the sun grew too fierce to face, they would sleep inside the chalet with the windows open. Sometimes at night they had barbecues on the beach, eating their steaks with the night sounds all around them, and the gun-grey ocean in front of them, and the smell of pine and woodsmoke in their nostrils, and the lights of Tangier twinkling merrily across the bay. For some reason, Huntley thought about this as the lift trundled from floor to floor. And when the doors at last slid open, he came out of his reverie with a start.

The lobby was almost deserted. A handful of people waiting for appointments sat sprawled in the chairs which lined the opposite wall. Three security guards stood by the glass doors, watching the traffic slide past outside. At the main desk, a police sergeant with a florid face was chatting amiably to the two receptionists. He looked up as the four men stepped out of the lift, their heels clicking

11

on the marble floor. Huntley's mouth was dry as they crossed the lobby. He was not afraid, but there was a tension deep within him, an elusive drawing-out of nerves which always, he recalled, preceded a need for violent action. He felt as he had felt as a young man, waiting to go into battle, waiting for the order, not knowing if he would come out of it alive and, for the moment at least, not caring either, just wishing the waiting could be over. He saw the face of the nearest security guard, swaying in his vision. He saw the glass doors rippling in and out. Everything looked as if he was watching it under water. Even his movements felt like that, slow and ponderous, like the action of a film shown at half-speed. He could hear the big man behind him, walking so close that his breath left a warm circle on Huntley's neck. Someone called his name.

'Mr Huntley?'

He stopped. They were only two steps from the door. The security guard was already holding it open. He had been ordered to speak to no one. What now?

The police sergeant who had been chatting to the receptionists came strolling towards him, smiling shyly.

'Mr Huntley sir, you remember me, Sam Walker? I came up to your place when you had that break-in last year.'

'Oh yes, Mr Walker. How are you?' he muttered.

'Fine, Mr Huntley, I'm fine. I just wanted to say, I heard on the radio about you being the new chief here. I just wanted to offer my congratulations, sir.'

'Thank you, Sam, that is kind of you.'

The police sergeant went on grinning. Huntley was filled with a sense of the absurd. He wanted to break into maniacal laughter; it was crazy, all of it crazy, standing here in this mundane work-a-day atmosphere trying to make small talk with death only a coin's throw away.

'We were all tickled about it,' the sergeant said, 'that is, my colleagues and me. You remember Gerry Tooker? We had coffee together, the three of us.'

'I remember him,' said Huntley, his mind racing. 'How is he?'

'He's married now, Mr Huntley. He married a girl from the local nick.'

'Policewoman?'

'That's right.' The sergeant chuckled. 'He liked to keep it in the family.'

Huntley tried to smile.

'Please pass on my congratulations,' he said. 'Tell him I'm delighted to hear the news.'

Bayle coughed. He had been watching the exchange with an air of rising panic, acutely conscious that it was his job to see no one interfered. Now he felt something dig him sharply in the spine. His skin crawled.

'Mr Huntley,' he murmured, 'sorry to interrupt, but if you want to keep that appointment, we'll have to put a spurt on.'

Huntley nodded.

'You're quite right, Brumby.' He smiled at the sergeant. 'Sorry Sam, that's one of the handicaps of being in command. Your time is never your own. It was nice seeing you again.'

They shook hands.

'Nice seeing you too, Mr Huntley,' the sergeant grinned, 'I'll give Gerry your message. He'll be glad I ran into you. All the luck in the world in your new appointment.'

'Thank you, Sam. Goodbye now.'

Bayle breathed a sigh of relief as they stepped through the door and into the street. For a moment he forgot his instructions and was about to follow Huntley, but a hand on his elbow pulled him to a halt and he remained where he was, just outside the entrance, watching his boss and the two armed men pick their way through the busy mid-morning traffic. He could see the Hillman Avenger, but from where he stood was unable to make out its number plate. Despite the coldness of the morning, he realised his shirt was drenched with sweat. Cars zipped by; a bus, a mail van, a bevy of motorcycles. The sun shone, but it was a watery sun, without much heat. The buildings across the street looked as they always looked, busy, normal; he was overwhelmed by their normality. Was this really happening, or was it some kind of sick joke? Naunton F. Huntley being kidnapped? It seemed ludicrous, this bright November morning.

He watched Huntley and the smaller of the two men climb into the Avenger's rear seat. The big man, the one with the flat shiny face, slid behind the driving wheel. The car started up and eased gently out into the stream of traffic.

Bayle looked at his watch. His orders were to wait for three minutes before raising the alarm. But three minutes could mean the difference between Huntley living or dying. Now that the men with the guns had disappeared, some of their menace had disappeared also. Bayle stared at All Souls' Church across the road. Was there really a marksman positioned on that rooftop? He squinted, peering through the frosty sunlight. There was nothing, not a sign of movement, not a feature out of place. They were bluffing. There was no rifle up there, no madman waiting to shoot. They had to be bluffing.

He glanced at his watch. Forty seconds gone; two minutes twenty to go. Damn it, they were getting away. They were getting away, and he was standing here letting them go like a soft-brained idiot. How would he explain that later? *I believed there was a rifle covering me from across the street, officer.* He could just see the policeman's face. Incredulous, scornful. *A rifle, Mr Bayle?* He looked at his watch again. Two minutes to go.

The sergeant who had spoken to Huntley emerged from the door behind him. He began to stroll across the pavement towards his squad car, blowing his nose. In another few seconds he would be gone, and a vital lead would have been lost. Bayle glanced once more at the silent church. Its roof traced an unbroken line across the sky. There was no one up there. No one *could* be up there. Bayle licked his lips. He just had to do something.

14

'Sergeant,' he shouted hoarsely, 'for God's sake, Sergeant, the Director General is being kidnapped.'

They were the last words he ever spoke. The bullet took him in the chest, smashing through his rib cage, arcing downwards through his liver and spleen, churning the flaccid organs into shreds. Its impact hurled him backwards through the door. He heard the glass shattering, heard the sound of a woman's scream, hollow and shrill, fading swiftly like the whistle of a train entering a distant tunnel. Then the light faded, weariness filled him; he felt himself relax, sighing peacefully, and heard no more.

Extract from London *Evening News*, November 25th:

BBC CHIEF IN DEATH SNATCH

A man was shot dead on the steps of Broadcasting House today as the newly-appointed Director General of the BBC Naunton F. Huntley was snatched from under the noses of police and security men. The dead man was Huntley's assistant, 42-year-old Brumby Bayle, who was murdered when he attempted to raise the alarm.

The incident took place at 10.30 this morning, during the peak of the rush-hour traffic. Two men, said to be in their middle thirties, were seen escorting Huntley and Bayle to the main door of the BBC's radio and administrative building. Their relationship appeared to be cordial, but a policeman who spoke to Huntley at the time said later: 'He was pale and fidgety, and gave several indications of being under stress.'

Huntley continued to accompany the two men when they climbed into a grey Hillman Avenger, leaving Bayle standing on the Broadcasting House steps. As the car drove away, Bayle called out for assistance, and was shot by a sniper hiding on the roof of the adjacent All Souls' Church. An eye-witness said the bullet's impact was so fierce he was hurled bodily through the swing glass-doors, and died instantly. Both the assassin and the kidnappers escaped without trace.

A BBC spokesman said today: 'No words can describe the horror and revulsion felt by everyone in the Corporation at this savage and senseless crime. Mr Bayle has been with the BBC since 1951, and is regarded by all as a worthy colleague and a loyal friend. His death has been made more poignant by its sheer pointlessness.'

Mr Bayle leaves a widow and three children.

Police believe today's abduction is the latest in a recent spate of kidnappings, probably carried out by the same gang. The Director General's capture brings the total number of disappearances in the past month to five. On November 4th, Philip Goodman, an official at the Department of Energy was taken at gunpoint from his flat in Pembroke Villas, Kensington. Three days later, Birmingham businessman Michael Jacobs was dragged struggling from a crowded restaurant in full view of the manager and fellow diners. On November 14th, plumber Nelson Mackey disappeared from his home in the little Cumbrian seaside town of Thelton, and on November 21st, Sheffield wig specialist Marian Edwards was seized in the crowded city centre and driven off in a car which was later found abandoned. None of them has been seen since.

In each case, the description of the man leading the attack has remained the same. He is said to be six feet three or four inches tall, powerfully-built, with a face disfigured by scar tissue, probably the result of a fire accident or explosion. The police admit to being baffled as to motive. None of the victims knew each other, and so far no attempt has been made by the kidnappers to contact relatives or colleagues.

Letter to Controller BBC1, November 29th:

On December 10th, during the 9 p.m. BBC Television news, a piece of 16 mm film, lasting three minutes precisely will be delivered to the gates of Television Centre, Wood Lane. This film is to be slotted into the newscast and transmitted as a bona-fide item. No attempt to alter it, edit it, or even examine it is to be made before transmission. The film will be shown as a valid section of the news, and the newsreader will make no attempt to disassociate either himself or the Corporation from that validity.

To ensure that the correct professional standards are maintained, a BBC reporter will place himself at our disposal for the making of this film. The reporter will be William Mellinger, recently of the *Panorama* programme. Mr Mellinger will fly to Belfast on December 3rd where he will book into the Tara Hotel and await further instructions. He will not be harmed.

If the above demands are correctly adhered to, both Mr Mellinger and Mr Naunton F. Huntley will be released on December 21st. If, for any reason, the film should fail to be shown as ordered, Mr Huntley will be executed at noon on December 11th.

TWO

George Steiner sat in the BBC1 Controller's office and looked at the man who faced him across the desk. He decided that he liked what he saw. Since arriving at Television Centre less than an hour before, he had been passed from one simpering idiot to another, until he had begun to believe that the entire broadcasting world was made up of ridiculous young men whose principle concern in life was to strike postures of lazy elegance. George Steiner himself was far from elegant. George Steiner, as he was only too aware, having been informed of the fact on

numerous occasions by his wife, was embarrassingly
square. He was tall, although not outstandingly so. He
was broad, though not so broad as to stand out in a crowd.
He was fair, though not remarkably fair. He wore light-
coloured sports jackets with leather patches on the elbows,
grey flannel trousers and brown leather shoes of a type
which had gone out of fashion at the end of the war, and
were probably now only worn by George Steiner and a
handful of ex-army officers longing for the good old days.
Steiner, as his wife frequently pointed out, was just a hole
in the air, the kind of man you never noticed if he sat
opposite you on the tube, or bought his morning paper at
the same news-stall. Steiner, to his wife, and to most of the
dozens of people who came into contact with him every
day, scarcely even existed, a fact which, he had to admit,
had proved quite an advantage in his chosen profession,
for Steiner was a policeman, and a very good policeman
too : just over forty, he had already reached the rank of
Commander in the Serious Crime Squad, and his ability
to merge into the background, his knack for being under-
estimated by the opposition had succeeded in bringing off
more than one spectacular coup in his past career. But for
all that, George Steiner would happily have changed
things if he could. He did not particularly enjoy being a
square. He did not enjoy being cuckolded by his wife (a
fact he had suspected for more than a year now, but had
not been able to prove). He did not enjoy being patronised
by his colleagues. And more than anything, he did not like
being taken for granted by his superiors who, though they
recognised his qualities and had steered him indulgently
along the path to promotion, still kept him from the real
seat of power among the administrative offices of Tintagel
House.

Still, Steiner could not help being what he was. But
understandably perhaps, he had an instinctive distrust of
all wafflers and ditherers, which was why, sitting in the
plump Heyberdansk chair staring across the desk at the
man who was Controller of BBC1, he felt faintly re-

assured. There was a certain strength in that face, a blunt-
ness which he felt sure would match his own. The frustrations of the morning began to dissolve, and for the first
time since arriving, Steiner felt optimistic.

The Controller leaned forward, resting his forearms on
the blotting pad.

'How do we do this?' he asked. 'Do I talk, or do you sit
there and fire questions, or what?'

Steiner smiled.

'Well, I thought we'd just sort of kick it around between
us. Isn't that the phrase you use in this profession?'

'You've been watching too many American movies,
Commander,' the Controller said. 'Would you like some
coffee?'

'Wouldn't mind,' Steiner said. 'It's been a thirsty morning.'

The Controller pressed the switch on his intercom
machine.

'Miss Fontaine, get some coffee in here, will you. And I
don't want to be interrupted for the next hour at least. If
any calls come through, re-route them to Peter's office.'

'I understand, sir.'

The Controller flicked up the switch and sank back in
his chair. Steiner studied him thoughtfully. The man was
probably given to fits of impatience, he decided, especially
when surrounded by people who either did not know or
were not prepared to speak their minds. Steiner approved.

'Was Brumby Bayle a personal friend of yours?' he
asked.

The Controller rubbed his cheek.

'I liked him. I wouldn't call him a close personal friend,
if that's what you mean. I feel sorry for his wife. I can't
see why they had to do that, to kill him. What do you
think of the letter?'

Steiner smoothed out the sheet of paper on his lap. It
was typewritten – probably, judging by the typeset, on an
Olivetti portable. The envelope postmark was Belfast.
They would check it for fingerprints, of course, but he felt

sure the paper would be clean. They could examine the typeset itself, but there were thousands of Olivetti portables in the world, and trying to run this one to earth would waste time and valuable energy. He shook his head.

'I don't know. It's odd; no demands for cash, no political demands. Just one simple request. The screening of a film on BBC Television News. This must be the strangest kidnapping in history.'

'Not as strange as all that, Commander. Getting a film, an uncensored film on to a national BBC newscast could be quite a triumph for all sorts of extremist groups. The BBC holds a unique position throughout the world. Its reputation for accuracy and truth was built up and consolidated during the war, and that reputation still exists, both in this country and abroad. Even people who've made a fetish out of knocking the BBC still regard its nine o'clock bulletin as the finest news service on this globe.'

Steiner nodded.

'In other words, if you transmit this film on December 10th and can't release a statement regarding its validity until Mr Huntley is released on 21st, then whatever message the film puts forward, the world will accept as gospel.'

'That's about it.'

'So if I was some kind of crank who felt he had something to say, I couldn't ask for a better platform.'

The Controller smiled thinly.

'Beats standing on Hyde Park Corner with a sandwich board,' he said. 'The nine o'clock news picks up a nightly rating of twelve to fourteen million viewers. And that's on an ordinary evening. On December 10th, we're preceding it with a screening of the world title fight live, so you can bet on an audience figure of twenty or twenty-five million people. Half the population of this country.'

Steiner whistled.

'It was no accident then, that the kidnappers chose December 10th.'

'I doubt it.'

Steiner got to his feet and walked to the window. Outside, it was raining. The rain splashed the glass, distorting the gunmetal sky and the roof of the White City Greyhound Stadium across the street.

The Controller watched him thoughtfully. He decided he had been wrong about Steiner. His initial impression had been of a solid and rather dull-witted man who lacked imagination. Now he realised Steiner was putting on a front. His features, illuminated by the light from the window displayed a sensitivity the Controller had not noticed before. It was not an unattractive face, the Controller mused; he was sure women would find it attractive. The features were even, agreeable. It was just that it was an undistinguished face, unobtrusive, the kind of face you looked at and immediately forgot. Until you studied it closely. Then you noticed a hint of stubbornness, an elusive strength, and above all, a capacity for completely obscuring the thoughts which went on behind it. Even Steiner's chunkiness was false, created largely by the ill-fitting sports jacket he was wearing. Steiner was solid but not heavy; there was no superfluous weight on that big frame. He looked in trim, muscular certainly, but all of it under control, and the impression of a man going to fat was just another aspect of his façade. His hair was clipped short military-style, greying at the temples, but whereas the grey streaks would have given another man an air of sophistication, on Steiner they looked somehow untidy, unnatural even. He could have hidden them easily enough with a little discreet combing – could, in fact, with a minimum of effort have been quite a handsome man; but Steiner, the Controller knew instinctively, was not like that. Steiner did not give a damn about his appearance. He did not give a damn about a good many of the things other people put a value on. Steiner was a man who would go his own way, no matter what, and had probably spent his life being misunderstood and misinterpreted. Now, as he turned from the window, the shadows masked his face and he looked, once again, the dull-witted policeman.

Except, the Controller thought, that this time he knew better.

'Here's the situation we're faced with,' Steiner said. 'We have to somehow guess the content of that film before it arrives. If we can establish a motive, we're halfway to discovering who our kidnappers are, and more important, where they are. Have you any ideas on that yourself, Controller?'

The Controller pursed his lips.

'Could be a smear job.'

'How d'you mean?'

'An attempt to discredit the BBC. If we put out a news item which was grossly untrue and were then unable to issue a denial for eleven days, the damage to the Corporation's prestige would be incalculable.'

Steiner grinned.

'I think you're being a little over-sensitive,' he said. 'Once the situation was fully explained, I'm sure your most ardent critics would forgive you.'

'You're a more trusting soul than I am, Commander.'

'Not trusting. Logical, perhaps. I'm basing my opinion on human nature. These men cold-bloodedly murdered a member of your staff. Now that's quite a drastic measure just for a smear job. You'd have to have one hell of a chip on your shoulder to do a thing like that. No, I think for the moment we can dismiss the slur theory. Which leaves us two other possible fields of motive. Political and criminal.'

The Controller was surprised.

'Criminal?'

'Why not?'

'But they're not asking for money.'

Steiner walked back to his chair and sat down.

'There may be bigger pickings to be had elsewhere,' he explained. 'If the world believes a certain situation to be true, and only you know it isn't, who can say what capital you might make out of that. For example, supposing you were to broadcast that a certain company was on the verge of bankruptcy. By the following morning, the shares of that company would have reached rock-bottom. Anyone with his wits about him, and a bit of ready capital, could make a killing on the market involving millions, perhaps even billions of pounds.'

'There's a basic flaw in that argument.'

Steiner smiled.

'That's right. All we'd have to do would be to find out who bought all the shares, then nick him. Even if he did it illegally, using nominee buyers, we'd run him to earth sooner or later. But that's just one idea, plucked at random out of the air. There may well be others, more concrete, more reliable.'

The door opened and Miss Fontaine entered, carrying a silver tray with a coffee pot and china cups.

'Thank you Elaine,' the Controller said. 'Put it on the desk, will you.'

He frowned thoughtfully as he poured the coffee.

'I still think the political theory is a more likely one,' he murmured.

'So do I,' admitted Steiner, 'if only because of their ruthlessness so far. There was no reason to kill Mr Bayle. They were well on their way to escaping with or without his death. No professional criminal is going to step up his chances of arrest with an unnecessary murder if he can help it. With political fanatics however, you're in a different stadium. They're mad dogs. They'd do it almost by reflex.'

'So now you have to decide which political pressure group you're dealing with.'

'Right.'

'Couldn't you work that out by a process of elimination?'

'How d'you mean?'

'Well, Mr Huntley isn't the only man to be kidnapped in the past month.'

'No,' said Steiner, 'there are three more, and one woman, taken from various parts of the country.'

23

'Same gang?'

'Looks that way, judging from eye-witness reports.'

'Then there must be a link, some common denominator between them. Find that, and you've got your motive.'

Steiner sighed.

'We've checked and checked again,' he said. 'There's no connection whatsoever. They'd never met, they probably didn't know of each other's existence. They appear to have been grabbed at random, and from all walks of life. The kidnappers have made no statement regarding them, and no attempt to contact their relatives. This letter is the first break in the pattern.' Steiner paused, hesitating to ask the one thing that had been bothering him all morning. 'Tell me, Controller,' he said slowly, 'as far as you are aware, has Mr Huntley at any time in his past shown any affiliation towards a political group in or out of this country?'

The Controller shook his head.

'Never. Naunton isn't a political animal in that sense. If he was, it's unlikely he would have been appointed Director General.'

'Which leaves us with only one common denominator.'

'What's that?'

'The reporter. Mellinger. Why did they ask for him?'

'I don't know. That puzzled me too.'

'Who is he?'

The Controller shrugged.

'He no longer works for the Corporation. At first, I couldn't remember him at all. I got his file out, but that didn't tell us much. He was a contract reporter. That means we employed him on a free-lance basis as opposed to a staff man, and since he wasn't actually staff, no detailed records were kept. I discovered though that he worked as a film reporter on programmes like *Twenty-four Hours, Nationwide, Panorama* and, more recently, *Deadline*. Beyond that, I can tell you very little. However, I did ask the editor of the *Deadline* programme to wait in the other office. He remembers Mellinger very well. I thought perhaps you might like to chat to him.'

Steiner smiled. The Controller did not believe in wasting time.

'Thank you, Controller,' Steiner said. 'That was thoughtful of you.'

The Controller pressed the intercom switch.

'Miss Fontaine, send in Mr Horan, will you please?'

'Yes, sir.'

Steiner put down his coffee and got to his feet as the young editor entered the room. He did it deliberately. It would have been easy for Steiner to capitalise on the younger man's natural unease in his superior's presence. But when it came to initial human contacts, Steiner loathed any attempt by one side or the other to gain a psychological advantage. It had happened to him too often in the past.

'Come in, Donald,' the Controller said, 'Donald Horan, this is Commander Steiner of the Metropolitan Police's Serious Crime Squad.'

The young man smiled.

'Hello, Commander.'

They shook hands. Steiner was relieved to see that he was not one of the effete young men he had met on the lower floor. Horan was, he estimated, about twenty-nine or thirty. He was going slightly bald on top and his face had a Latin look, with dark skin, heavy features, and olive-black eyes. He looked like a man who knew his job, who knew what he was doing, and more important, what he had come to talk about.

'Would you like some coffee?' the Controller asked.

'No thank you, sir. I've just had some.'

The Controller smiled.

'The Commander here would like to ask you a few questions about William Mellinger,' he said.

Horan settled himself in the other chair.

'Just fire away,' he murmured, 'I'll do what I can.'

'Well,' said Steiner, 'it's nothing specific. I'd like you to tell me anything you remember about the man, anything at all. What was he like? What was his background? Did he have any strong political beliefs, things like that? Just talk, and I'll butt in with questions as we go along.'

Horan rubbed his chin reflectively.

'Well, William was always . . . difficult,' he said. 'I think that's the best way to describe him. He came to us from Fleet Street. He'd been working with the *Express*, I think, and before that, with some bi-weekly up in Yorkshire. He was a good reporter, but he didn't care for television much. He was always quoting Richard Dimbleby's remark "It's a long road to an ultimate emptiness." I must say there are times when I agree with him.' He cast a sidelong glance at the Controller, who smiled thinly. 'I think his basic problem was lack of discipline. He was pretty wild in those early days and didn't take to external control at all. We'd send him out on a story, and if he didn't think it was strong enough, he'd go off and find another one without checking in first. In other words, you might be expecting a film on, say, the future of tenant farmers, and he'd come back with an exposé on devious practices among local councillors. It may be impressive journalism, but if you're editing a programme and you're not prepared for it, it can knock hell out of your running order. We quarrelled a good deal during those early days of *Deadline*. William was married then, but he was away from home most of the time and playing around quite a bit on the side. Most of our reporters in the field were. It's a hazard of the job, I suppose. When you're stuck in a strange town or country for weeks on end, you've got precious little else to do. There's a hell of a mortality rate on marriages in our business.'

Horan leaned back in his chair, crossing one leg over the other. His face grew serious.

'William's marriage didn't break up though,' he went on. 'It never got a chance to. Two years after *Deadline* began, his wife and young son were killed in a car smash on the M.6, and after that something seemed to go out of him. He lost his wildness. He became withdrawn and morose. He stopped caring about the programme, and about his job.'

'Perhaps he felt guilty,' Steiner interjected.

'Guilty?'

'For philandering.'

Horan nodded.

'It's possible. In any event, three months after the crash, he asked to be released from his contract. I was sorry to see him go. He was one hell of a headache to have around, but he was a damned good pro and they don't grow on trees.'

'What's he doing now?' Steiner asked.

'He runs a mountaineering shop up in the Lake District. That was always his big love : mountain climbing, wandering around in the great outdoors, that sort of thing.'

'Did he have any strong political beliefs?'

'No. He was pretty much middle-of-the-road, as far as I can remember. He understood politics very well, of course, that was part of his job. But you could hardly say that he cared much one way or the other.'

Steiner frowned. From the sound of it, Mellinger seemed an unlikely choice for a kidnap gang. If the man had a reputation for being difficult, they could be creating a rod for their own backs. Unless . . . He glanced again at the letter in his lap.

'Seen this?' he asked Horan.

The producer nodded.

'Any idea why the kidnappers should specify Mellinger to act as reporter in their film?'

'None at all. It doesn't make sense. You see, William never really made it into the first grade. Most of the glamour jobs went to the first team, people like Julian Pettifer. William got the left-overs, the bread-and-butter reporting. Most of the time he specialised in outdoor stuff : mountaineering stories, potholing stories, deep-sea diving stories, that sort of thing. He did do one tour in Vietnam, another in America. And then there was that film piece he did for *Panorama* on the IRA. You may remember he refused to disclose his sources and went to prison for it in Dublin. It was just a token imprisonment – one day, I think – but the newspapers made a thing of it at the time.'

'The Provisional IRA?' Steiner asked.

'That's right.'

'Was he ever, as far as you know, in contact with other pressure groups either in Vietnam or the U.S.?'

'In Vietnam, I really couldn't say. In America, he did a number of stories which could come under that heading. There was one on the Black Power movements in Harlem. He also did a series of interviews with the followers of Charles Manson, just after the Sharon Tate murders. And he carried out an investigation into the Space/Industrial Complex.'

'What's that?'

'It grew up during the Apollo moonshots. America was spending millions of dollars on space research, and a number of senators had a vested interest in seeing that the space programme continued, regardless of cost. Mellinger's brief was to run those senators to earth, and put them in the hot seat.'

'So he could have made several powerful enemies there?'

'I imagine so.'

Steiner sat back, chewing his lip. Not a hell of a lot to go on, but he'd started out with less. At least he had Mellinger. He would have to play this right though. They didn't have time to fool around.

'At this point,' he said, 'our best bet appears to be the IRA. The film, presumably, is going to be made in Ulster. It could well be that the Provos trust Mellinger because he kept his mouth shut once before. Do you think Mellinger would be prepared to undertake one more reporting job, one which might even cost him his life?'

Horan shrugged.

'We could try. As I said, he can sometimes be difficult.'

'Got his address?'

'Yes.'

'I'll travel up and talk to him tonight.'

Horan hesitated.

'Commander, I think it might be a good idea if you let me do it. We've had our quarrels in the past, but I know that he trusts me. I feel he's more likely to respond to someone he already knows.'

Steiner stared at him for a moment, then nodded in agreement.

'All right, Mr Horan, we'll do it your way. You break the ice, and I'll talk to him tomorrow.'

He pressed his hands together, staring at the wall.

'Supposing we fail, Controller,' he said. 'Supposing we are unable to trace Mr Huntley before December 10th. What happens then?'

The Controller hesitated.

'Put crudely, Commander,' he said. 'Nothing.'

'You mean you'll refuse to screen the film?'

'I mean we must refuse. We are desperately concerned about Naunton of course, but the BBC has a responsibility to the people of this country. There can be no question of that film being transmitted.'

'So we have exactly twelve days to find Naunton F. Huntley, otherwise he dies.'

'That's about it, Commander.'

Steiner grunted. He looked across at Horan.

'I'm afraid a very great deal is going to depend on this difficult friend of yours, Mr William Mellinger,' he said.

THREE

For half a mile or more, the screenbank dropped almost vertically through lines of ragged spruce and pine. Below, thick forest clustered the valley floor like a carelessly spread handkerchief. In the hollows, granite outcrops nuzzled through the moorgrass and the bracken looked remarkably red. High on the sheer west wall of Pillar Rock, William Mellinger picked his way from crack to cranny, from groove to slab, moving slowly, choosing his route with care, reaching out for holds, feeling them, testing them, a big man, lean and slim-hipped with wind-tanned cheeks and wild unruly hair. He paused, sweating happily, and looked back to where narrow burns sparkled through clumps of bracken, brushwood, bog moss and bilberry till they joined the river far below. It was a day to be alive on, cold and fresh with a sky the colour of bright turpentine. The sun lit the hills, picking out their shadows and folds, sharpening their gullies and rolling across the craggy summits in patterns of dappled yellow and gold. Behind him, the ridge bobbed and dipped in a series of diminishing hummocks until finally there was only the sky, and a thin silvery ghostline that might have been the sea. On the far ridge, the peaks of High Style and Red Pike traced a ragged rampart towards the west, then fell hiccupping into the rounded domes of Startling Dodd and Great Borne. In the middle distance the hilltops rose from the trees in purple folds, tinged with grey where frost had streaked their tips.

He wiped his face on his anorak sleeve and began gingerly to inch up the network of blackened crannies, buttresses and jutting overhangs which swelled against the sky. This, he felt, was what he had been born for, the thrill of moving freely up a sheer rock face.

30

Tufts of grass clustered the ledges, and he could see the lines of ascent where constant passage on the well-used routes had polished the rock into shiny grey trails. He peered up. The cliff twisted and rippled above, vanishing into an indeterminate fusion with the sky. Across its jagged outline, fleecy clouds went scudding merrily westward. For a while, the going was mild, with lots of good hand and footholds, and he moved confidently, relishing the old familiar stretch of mind and muscle, the chill of the granite against his fingers, the wind in his face, the focusing of mind and body into one fundamental aim – to reach the summit – and above it all, the instinctive, almost imperceptible awareness of the increasing void below.

The frustrations of the summer, the selling, the book-keeping, the constant hordes of tourists, the day-to-day problems of the little mountaineering shop vanished from his mind. He was back where he belonged. Back on his good crags again, and as so often happened with climbing, he felt as if time had stopped, as if the world and all the bustlings of the human race had frozen momentarily while he gripped and straddled and shuffled his way up, letting his body do the work, reaching and pulling, pushing and scraping, heaving and humping, clumpety-clumpety clumpety-clump.

He reached a ledge with a good square foot of standing space and paused for breath. Below, the forest looked extraordinarily green. It crept up the slopes like a stealthy army, trying to take over. He could see the ragged line of Chapel Crags and to the west, the pale sheen of Ennerdale Lake rimmed with trees and flanked on two sides by bracken-clustered hills. There was a subtle change in the air now, a hint of things to come. It felt colder, fresher, and a cold wind was blowing in from the sea. The crisp late Autumn day was dissolving into the first intimations of early winter.

Mellinger peered up at the way he would go. There was a short easy stretch, and beyond it a difficult groove which ascended vertically for twenty or twenty-five feet. He began to inch his way upwards. It looked worse than it actually was; there were lots of good footholds, though he had to reach for them, splaying his legs as wide as they would go, and he was sweating heavily by the time he reached the top of the groove and paused for breath on a minute slab of rock. He was now approaching the crux of the climb, the most difficult stretch of all. From where he stood, he had to traverse across several feet of delicate granite into the foot of a steep chimney. There were no footholds of any significance, but a couple of good hand-ledges allowed him to swing across by the strength of his arms and get his left foot on the other side of the gap. At the base of the chimney, a large chockstone had jammed tight between the rocky walls. He wiped his palms on his breeches, hooked both arms around the stone and, grunting and hissing, heaved himself with immense lack of dignity to its top.

Above, the chimney rose straight as a plumbline for forty feet or more, corked by an ugly overhang. Mellinger stood perfectly still, putting off the moment of effort. His heart fluttered from the strain of the climb, and after eight months' inactivity he was uncomfortably aware of his exposure. A moment's indiscretion, a fractional slip and he would be off on a breathless drop to oblivion. He swallowed. The wind ruffled his hair. He pushed his left arm as far into the crack as it would go and began to shuffle upwards, his spine jammed against one wall, his feet against the other. He was gasping now, for he was shuffling straight up on a perpendicular grade and hand and footholds simply did not exist, though he did have some security from his left arm which he kept thrust deep into the chimney's throat.

After about thirty feet of painful slithering he spotted, on the outer rim of the right-hand wall, a tiny fold of rock. It offered no more than the most precarious toe-tip stance, but he knew it was the exit route to the summit buttress. It always seemed a crazy move to traverse out on to such a flimsy projection, but his only alternative was straight up until he came to a halt beneath the overhang.

He remained for a moment perfectly still, peering at the rocky nobble. There was no handgrip to speak of, only a slight declavity in the cliff's surface. Nevertheless, it gave him a fingertip pressure which steadied his body as he made the precarious move across, swinging out around the corner and on to the sloping granite wall. He had done it. From here to the top, the route was handholds all the way, and he scrambled breathlessly upwards until he was standing on the summit.

He stretched himself languidly, enjoying the satisfying sense of peace that climbing always gave him. Heavy clouds were beginning to roll in from the west, and already Great Borne and Banna Fell had been wiped out in a gloomy blanket of fog. The wind tugged at his hair and scoured his cheeks. He put a small cheroot in his mouth and reached into his anorak pocket for his matches. He was filled with a sense of lofty superiority, perched on his mountain stronghold with the valley and the river and the forest at his feet. This was something to savour, to devour. Eight months of drudgery, selling equipment to the tourists, and now this freedom. It was not to be rushed.

He sat for a while thinking about nothing, as dark clouds came rolling in thick and fast. He looked at his watch. It would soon be nightfall. Time to go.

He finished the cheroot and climbed to his feet as the sky came swirling in to snuff out the hills in a blanket of coaly grey. Going down proved a good deal faster than coming up. Nevertheless, the stars were out by the time he reached his car on the forestry road below.

He drove back to Derwentwater in the dark as the first half-hearted streaks of rain pattered across his windscreen. In the thirty-fourth year of his life, William Mellinger felt that somewhere along the way he had lost his sense of direction. It was not something he dwelt on deeply. Or was even aware of in a conscious sense, but he was plagued by a belief that he was only marking time, bobbing in the wind like a button on a thread. He had his shop of course,

3

the little mountaineering store which kept him run off his feet during the tourist season, and which left him with four months of freedom when the holidaymakers went away, and which was doing very nicely thank you if money had been his primary concern in life, which it wasn't. But it was hardly a vocation, Mellinger reflected. Still, he was lucky in many ways. He had the things he needed : the hills, the crags, they were all around him. And he had his friends, and he had his books and he had his freedom. He was his own man.

There was only the memory of Eileen and the boy to taunt him on cold lonely nights, like a vision from the past, piercing, aching, a nightmare fragment from a world he could never return to. But he had learned now how to handle even that. He simply didn't think about them any more. And perhaps, if he went on not thinking, in another year, or the year after, the pain would gradually diminish and he could begin to pick up the pieces of his life again. In the meantime, he had, as the psychologists would say, compensated perfectly. He had run away, but the running had been in the right direction. For the moment at least he was content in his Lakeland sanctuary, satisfied that no other action would have kept him so intact, so complete within himself.

He saw the lights of the little lakeside town loom up in front, and drove into the now-silent streets with an air of cheerful pleasure. It had been a white-hot summer that year, the hottest he could ever remember. Derwentwater had lain like a shimmering turquoise carpet, and the foliage had dripped over Walla Crag like lush Welsh rarebit. But now that the holidaymakers had gone, the air was filled with the delicious scent of winter, there was room to move about, to stretch out, to breathe and feel uncluttered, the little towns were mercifully peaceful again.

As he parked the car outside his shop doorway, he saw a figure standing in the hazy light beneath the street lamp. Mellinger would have recognised that lanky shape anywhere.

34

'Hello, Donald,' he called from the darkness.

The man moved towards him.

'Who's that?'

'Mellinger,' he said. 'How are you?'

He unlocked the door and stepped inside, knowing that Horan would follow, wondering what had brought him, now, after all these months, his old friend and enemy, his old boss with whom he had fought and argued and threatened and pleaded; he was like a ghost, or a creature from some distant universe, long-forgotten.

There was no light on the stair, and they picked their way cautiously, feeling along the banister like a pair of blind mice.

'I thought I'd surprise you,' Horan said with an air of disappointment, 'but you're never surprised.'

'I see in the dark,' Mellinger grinned, 'like a cat.'

He opened the door at the top and switched on the light. The room was filled with packing cases, and lines of bulky duvet jackets dangling from metal rails.

'Come on in,' said Mellinger. 'You *have* surprised me, Donald. It's been years.'

'Just one,' Horan grunted.

'Seems like years.'

The television producer stood on the landing, blinking rapidly. He felt unsure of himself, lost in this unfamiliar territory.

'This the shop?' he asked, peering at the packing cases and neatly-laid rows of haversacks and ice-axes.

'No, this is the storeroom. Shop's downstairs. I live over the top of it. It's a bit cramped, but big enough for me.'

They crossed the storeroom and went through another door into the flat proper. It was not so much a flat, Horan reflected, as a bed-sitter, with a bed tucked surreptitiously away around the corner. It was, as Mellinger had suggested, extremely small and narrow, but it was not the lack of space which impressed itself upon Horan but the lack of warmth, the lack of frivolity. The room was stark,

35

masculine – functional. Not a room to come back to, Horan thought to himself, and not, in any sense, a home. A pair of skis stood propped against the wall. An assortment of wet climbing boots were drying on the hearth. A rope, coiled, lay tossed across the sofa. Horan picked it up and laid it neatly on the floor. He looked at Mellinger who was busily lighting the gas-ring.

'You're looking well, William,' he said. 'The quiet life must agree with you.'

'Sit down,' Mellinger grunted, 'I'll make some tea. Have you eaten?'

'I had a snack on the way up. In Ambleside.'

'Well, I'm no great shakes as a cook, but I'll take you out to dinner, if you like. We could go down to the Borrowdale Hotel.'

'Don't worry about me. I'm not much of a trencherman.'

'That's right,' Mellinger grinned, 'I remember. You always ate like a bird.'

Horan sat down and looked dismally around.

'It's nice here, William,' he lied. 'You've got it very nice. But it's a bit . . . well, it's a bit stark. Something's missing.'

Mellinger turned and stared at him.

'Yes,' he said coldly, 'there is something missing.'

Horan swallowed. He could see the pain plainly in Mellinger's eyes, and cursed himself for his own stupidity.

'Sorry, I didn't mean that,' he murmured.

'It's okay.'

'No, I am, really. I thought after a whole year . . . '

'A whole year,' Mellinger snorted, 'Christ.'

The gas flames cast crimson shadows across his cheeks, hiding the eyes in pools of murky grey. Horan watched him in wonderment. After all this time, a simple remark, a simple unmeaning remark could still rip the man to shreds. Horan would never have believed it. This man, of all people. Horan studied him thoughtfully, his lips pursed.

'Are you happy here, William?'

'Ecstatic.'

'How's the business going?'

'I've just closed for the winter season. I've got four months to do whatever I like in. Climb, travel . . . even thought I might write a book or something.'

'Never miss the box?'

Mellinger smiled.

'You're joking.'

'Not even a teeny bit?'

'Donald, I wouldn't get on that merry-go-round again for a half-share in a Kimberley diamond mine.'

Horan shook his head.

'You were good, William. What a waste.'

'Good?'

'You know you were.'

'What does good have to do with it? It's a fucking sausage machine, always was.'

'You fought it too much. You should have gone with the tide like the rest of us.'

'No thanks.'

Horan rubbed his palms along his trousered thighs. He liked Mellinger, always had, but for some reason he never felt at ease in his presence. He was surprised to find that it was still the same, even now, when they no longer had to depend upon each other, when there was no programme to get out, no deadline to meet, nothing to quarrel over. The uneasiness was there and it was strengthening. Mellinger was no longer the man he knew. He had changed. In some elusive way, he had changed.

'You're different, William. I never saw you like this. You're . . . quieter.'

Mellinger smiled thinly.

'Older.'

Horan grinned at him.

'Yes, you were a wild man then.'

'My heart was lighter then. Come on, Donald, don't muck about with me. What are you doing here? You didn't come just to inquire about my health.'

'No.'

'A job?'

'In a way.'

'Stuff it.'

'Not a proper job, William. What I mean is, not a full-time job. A special.'

'Film?'

'Yes.'

'I'd be rusty as hell. Haven't even looked at a television set for more than a year.'

'That doesn't matter. This is no ordinary film.' He hesitated. 'I may as well tell you. You could easily get killed.'

Mellinger stared at him.

'What?' he said.

'It's dangerous, William.'

'Are you bullshitting me?'

'No,' said Horan, 'sit down, I want to talk to you. Just sit down.'

Mellinger sat, and Horan went through it all in detail, beginning with the kidnapping, which he felt sure Mellinger had already read about, going on to the letter with its curious stipulation, and ending with Steiner's plan to use Mellinger as bait. Throughout it all, Mellinger sat and listened without expression. His eyes never left Horan's face. Horan talked earnestly, nervously, uncomfortably aware of Mellinger's gaze and yet, in spite of it, unable to decide what his reaction would be.

'That's about the size of it,' he finished off lamely. 'If you refuse to go, Huntley dies. If you agree to go, you could both die.'

Mellinger took a deep breath and rubbed his cheek.

'You don't know what the film is about?' he murmured.

'No.'

'And you don't even know who's financing it. The IRA's only a guess.'

'It is a fairly inspired guess, William. You've dealt with them before. Why else would the letter ask for you?'

Mellinger grunted.

'What's Steiner's plan?' he asked.

'You fly out to Belfast and check into the Tara Hotel as stipulated. You wait there until you're contacted by the kidnappers, and you go wherever they take you. You'll be under surveillance all the way, from the second you step off that plane. You'll also be carrying a small bugging device as an added precaution. As soon as you've led the police to wherever Huntley is, they'll move in.'

Mellinger twisted his face.

'Screw that,' he said.

'William.'

'Listen, they may not seem much to you, the things I have here. But I'm happy. Understand me? I'm not about to chuck it all down the drain on some crazy James Bond mission.'

'I'm sorry, William, but you're Huntley's only chance. If you refuse, then he's done for. It's a rotten choice to make, but you're stuck with it.'

Mellinger crossed his arms, hugging himself as though cold.

'What's Huntley to me?' he growled. 'I don't even know what he looks like.'

Horan said softly: 'You will though, William. If we don't get him back, you'll remember him the rest of your life.'

Mellinger swore and Horan nodded understandingly.

'I don't envy you, William. I don't know what I'd do if I was in your position.' He stood up and looked around. 'Where are the teacups?'

'Top drawer.'

He found them and set them out. Now that he had got it over with, he felt less uneasy, as if Mellinger's indecision had given him a certain psychological advantage. The kettle boiled and he made the tea with care, first warming the pot and emptying it, then dropping in the teabags and topping it up again.

'Got any sugar?' he asked.

'In the cupboard. Bottom shelf.'

Horan busied himself with the tea things, laying them out with meticulous care. By the time he was ready to pour, he knew Mellinger had reached a decision.

'Listen,' Mellinger said. 'This is as far as I'll go. Okay, I'll fly to Belfast and check in at the hotel, but that's it. When the kidnappers make contact, the police move in. I'm not going on any country drives with a bunch of armed fanatics.'

Horan pulled a face.

'That's a bit dodgy, William. We don't know who the contact will be. If the police pick him up and fail to make him talk, it could mean the end of Huntley.'

'That's his lookout. They've *got* to make him talk. That's theirs.'

'Well . . .'

'I'm not finished. I don't want to be sitting all alone in that hotel room chewing my fingernails either. I want official protection.'

'Bodyguard?'

'Preferably two. And armed.'

'You could blow the whole thing sky-high.'

'I'm no hero, Donald. If you want Huntley back, you'll have to do it my way.'

Horan thought for a moment. It sounded reasonable enough. He was no policeman dammit, but Steiner would just have to play along. After all, it was Mellinger's neck in the noose, not Steiner's. He nodded.

'Seems fair.'

'Okay you're on.'

Horan picked up the teapot, shook it gently, and began to fill the cups.

'I'll be mother,' he said.

FOUR

On 3rd December, William Mellinger packed his bags, drove to Manchester and caught the afternoon flight to Belfast. In the Ulster airport, waiting for his suitcase to be unloaded, he studied the faces around him. A little knot of clergymen stood chatting beside the newspaper kiosk. A pair of paunchy businessmen, grey-haired and sporting Rotary badges, laughed uproariously at some joke or other. A workman with a badly deformed spine swept imaginary dust in the opposite corner. There was no sign of police surveillance, no sign of anything at all extraordinary, so either, Mellinger decided, they knew their job, or someone had slipped up badly. The second possibility was too awful to contemplate so he put it from his mind. On the way into town however, he could not resist peering through the taxi window at the stream of cars trailing in their wake. They looked innocent enough, he told himself, and it was after all, early evening, the time when most people were making their way home from work. He felt faintly reassured.

Ahead, the dying sunlight cast pools of pastel pink across softly rolling hills, and cupped in their lap Belfast looked almost ethereal, misty and mysterious, out of place with the grassy slopes around. Mellinger felt his heart beat faster. It had been five years, he estimated, since he had last visited this city. Then, it had been like a city at war, torn apart by sectarian tension, with street barricades, riot mobs and, in certain areas, kerbsides littered with burnt-out shells of private cars. He had stayed at the old Grand Central Hotel where a sign in the lobby had warned guests that all services would cease at six p.m. to allow the staff to get home in safety. Now, as they slid

41

down Royal Avenue and swung past the City Hall Belfast looked like a city anywhere in the world at five o'clock on a December evening, brimful of people, traffic, noise and bright lights.

At the hotel, the receptionist gave him his key with an air of professional boredom.

'202,' he said. 'Second floor.'

There was, apparently, no porter service. Mellinger took the lift and walked along the corridor feeling vulnerable and alone. It was, he knew, a crazy thing he was doing. To come back here, to this city of fear, to set himself up as a target for nameless terrorists, was insanity enough. To rely, for his survival on people he did not know, was even worse. William Mellinger did not have a great deal of confidence in other people. In eleven years of reporting in the field, he had learned to rely almost solely upon himself. To some extent, he supposed, that had been the underlying cause of his discontent. In Television you relied on teamwork, and by his very nature he had been and always would be, a loner. He had compromised, sometimes willingly, sometimes not so willingly, but he had done it. And he was compromising now, except that this time it was his life that was on the line. He just hoped Steiner and his friends from Special Branch knew what they were doing.

He reached his room and stepped inside, fumbling for the switch. Something hard ground against his spine.

'Mellinger?' he heard a voice say softly.

He froze, his hands turning cold.

'Mr William Mellinger?' the voice repeated.

'Yes,' he hissed.

'Switch on the light, Jackie.'

The light flashed on and Mellinger blinked, his alarm fading into surprise. Two men, both in their shirtsleeves, both carrying weapons, studied him closely.

'It's him okay,' one of them said.

They slipped their pistols into waistbelt holsters, and the first one stuck out his hand.

'I'm O'Connor,' he said. 'That's Jackson. We're your bodyguards.'

Mellinger felt relief flood through him. They were an oddly-assorted pair, O'Connor short and chunky with a beefy face and receding blond hair, the other, Jackson, thin as a giraffe, his cheeks pale, his hands long, slender and artistic.

The room was typical of a type of hotel room Mellinger knew well: air-conditioned, centrally-heated, soundproofed, draught-sealed – soulless. There were two beds, a built-in wardrobe, a TV set, an automatic drink dispenser and a tall double-glazed window overlooking the square outside. He drew back the curtain and peered out at the stream of traffic. The square, he was relieved to see, was extremely well-lit. Its tarmac surface glistened under the street lamps. On the opposite corner stood a police station. Its doors were heavily sandbagged, guarded by troops with automatic rifles. Mellinger felt reassured.

As he watched, a pair of armoured cars zipped by, disappearing from sight in the direction of the Shankill Road.

'Better draw the curtain,' the man called O'Connor advised.

'You'll make a pretty target, outlined in the light.'

Mellinger felt tired. This whole thing seemed a melodramatic farce. He thought of his little flat above the mountaineering shop on Derwentwater. It was no palace, he knew that, but he felt secure there, he belonged there.

He threw his suitcase on the bed, and began wearily to unpack.

'What happens now?' he asked.

'We wait.'

'Just sit?'

'You'll get used to it,' O'Connor grinned.

Mellinger went into the bathroom and brushed his teeth. He stared at his face in the mirror. His cheeks looked pale and worried. Fear showed plainly in the lines around his eyes and in the set of his mouth. He was no hero for God's sake, never professed to be. There was a difference between physical courage, the pure gutsy-get-up-and-do-it kind of physical courage, and this. This decoy thing was something else : slow, nerve-rending . . . emasculating.

He pushed the plug into the bath, and turned on the tap. From the other room, O'Connor called : 'What are you doing?'

'Taking a bath.'

The two policemen looked at each other.

'What happens if they come while you're in there?' O'Connor asked.

'They'll catch me with my defences down,' said Mellinger.

Outside in the street, George Steiner turned up his rain-coat collar and shivered in the chill December wind. A handful of leaves fluttered aimlessly along the kerbside. Rainwater lay between the lamp-posts like pools of shiny tar. He looked at his watch. It was eight o'clock. He heard footsteps on the pavement behind him, and up came one of the Special Branch men clutching a vacuum flask.

'Coffee?' he offered. 'It's none too strong, but at least it's hot.'

'Thank God for that,' Steiner grinned. 'I was beginning to think you'd find me in the morning, frozen solid like Lot's wife.'

'Lot's wife wasn't frozen,' the Special Branch man said, 'she was turned to salt.' He stared at the oblong of light which they knew to be Mellinger's room. 'Anything happening?'

Steiner felt blessed warmth seep through the plastic cup into his hands.

'Nothing,' he muttered. 'He came to the window just for a second, then he drew the curtain. There's not been a flicker since.'

'Traffic's dying down,' the Special Branch man observed. 'It'll be quiet soon. That should make our job easier.'

Steiner voiced the anxiety that was in him.

'I keep telling myself nothing can go wrong,' he said.

'Nothing can,' the Special Branch man maintained. 'We've got that hotel sewn up tighter than a pimp's purse. There are men front and back, in the lobby and on the roof. Even if they do manage to break in, they'll sure as hell never get out. Every road into this square is guarded by armed paratroopers. The entire area can be sealed off in three seconds flat.'

George Steiner nodded without answering. He did not tell the Special Branch man the thing that was really worrying him. Largely because he did not himself know the thing that was really worrying him. It was just that something didn't sit right, something was out of place, and no matter how hard he tried, Steiner couldn't put his finger on what. Oh, the square was staked out admirably, he had no qualms on that front. But the kidnappers after all must be aware that some attempt would be made to trip them up. They knew it, they would be ready for it, and what was more they were operating on their own territory, which gave them an advantage from the beginning. They had nerve too, one hell of a nerve, setting up a rendezvous within thirty yards of a police station. Either they were deliberately flaunting their contempt for the law, or – and this was what worried Steiner most of all – they knew something the police didn't know. Steiner had to admit he could not see how even the most enterprising criminal could break through this security net, but the worrying thought still persisted that none of them, neither himself nor the Special Branch, were aware of the true situation. It was like trying to treat the symptoms of a baffling illness without knowing its cause.

'Is there a call box nearby?' he asked, draining the plastic cup and giving it back to the Special Branch man.

'There's a phone in the station. You can call from there.'

'This is personal,' Steiner said. 'I'd rather not.'

45

The Special Branch man shrugged.

'Well, you'll find one two blocks down to your right, just around the corner of Oxford Road. That's if the vandals haven't smashed it to bits again.'

Steiner thanked him and began to stroll down the deserted street. He walked with his hands in his pockets, collar turned up against the chill, filled with the sense of unease that walking alone in Belfast by night invokes.

Steiner hated not being in control. This was the Special Branch's show, and he could see the sense of that. They knew the area, they knew the IRA. But he worked by instinct, always had, a deeply-ingrained instinct he had never fully understood but which, by some remarkable sequence of fate had managed to pay off time and time again. Now that instinct filled him with an ominous foreboding. Somewhere along the line, he felt convinced they had missed the key to the whole puzzle – the link – the link which *had* to exist between the various kidnap victims. If they could find that, they would find the motive, and if they could find the motive, they would at least know which ring they were fighting in. But this – this blatant show of force was too obvious. Steiner was sure the men they were dealing with had something up their sleeves, and he felt uneasy.

He found the phone box and dialled his home. There was no reply. He stood with the receiver to his ear, and for a moment forgot Mellinger, the Special Branch and the IRA as all the old uncertainty about his wife came flooding back. Where was she? It was Thursday, and normally she did not go out on Thursdays.

He hung up, took out his address book and called a second number. The line burred. After a moment, he heard a click at the other end, and a woman's voice said brightly : 'Yes, who is it?'

'Clara?' George Steiner asked.

'That's right. Who's this?'

'It's George. George Steiner.'

46

'Oh hullo, George. This is a surprise. I thought you were in Ulster.'

'I am. I'm calling from a phone booth.'

'Something wrong, George?'

'No, no, nothing. I just thought . . . well, Janie said she was calling round to see you tonight, and since there's no answer at home I thought she might be there.'

'Janie?' He could hear the mockery in her voice. 'She's not at home, George?'

'No,' he murmured miserably.

'I wonder where she can be.'

Bitch, he thought and cursed himself for phoning. This was just the kind of situation Clara loved. He could imagine her telling her friends at Luc's in the morning.

'Well, she's not here, George.'

'No,' he murmured lamely. 'Well, I just thought . . . it was worth a try.'

'Perhaps she got lonely. You know how lonely she gets when you are not there. Perhaps she went down to Angelo's. Why don't you phone her again when the pubs come out?'

'Yes, I'll do that,' George Steiner muttered, and hung up.

He strolled back miserably towards the square. Sometimes he felt it was better not to know the truth, and yet, if she *was* betraying him, then sooner or later he had to know. But knowing meant making decisions, taking action, direct irrevocable action. He couldn't bear that. He loved his wife. He couldn't bear to live without her.

He was thinking this, walking slowly with his hands deep in his pockets when the awful thing happened, and by the time he reached the square, it was already over.

William Mellinger lay on his bed and stared glumly at the hotel ceiling. The two Special Branch men, O'Connor and Jackson had taken to playing Scrabble. Mellinger wondered how they could do it, could switch themselves off like that, carrying on with the mundane functions of

47

life as if there was nothing in the world to worry about. He lay smoking cigarette after cigarette, listening to the murmur of the TV set, the occasional laughs and exclamations of the Scrabble players and thinking about his life, not in a despairing way, but with an almost detached interest, reflecting on the way things had turned out. He was thinking in particular about Eileen, the girl he had married; unwillingly, if the truth were known, after he had got her pregnant in the back of a Cortina estate car, not realising or caring at the time that she was not experienced enough to be on the pill and not having the heart to abandon her when the inevitable happened.

He shifted on the bed, as the memory brought with it the inevitable sense of pain. He had just started in television then, a fresh young reporter who believed fervently in the importance of communication, and who talked with a nervous intelligence about things which later became too embarrassing to think about. Television had seemed like a bold new instrument breaching all frontiers and he had felt privileged to be part of it, had believed, fervently believed, that he had been born for it and had felt that he would somehow help to fashion it, for his longings, his ambitions had seemed too intense not to be gratified. Lying on the bed, his mouth twisted into a wry grin. He put out his cigarette and reached automatically for another. Outside, rain pattered lightly on the window pane. He lit up and inhaled deeply, letting his mind drift back. Eileen was a dark slender creature. She had an exuberance, a lack of guile, an inability to deceive which Mellinger had found enchanting. And he had loved her all right, even in those early days. But he had been so hungry for life and experience that somehow his marriage had become only secondary in importance. It had been a crazy kind of life, he reflected, frantic, frenetic – glamorous even, if you could call endless nights in endless hotel rooms glamorous. Still, the job did have a certain gloss to it. At least other people thought so, particularly women, and there had been plenty of those around. They had

48

been a facet of life on the road in those early days; women, and sly guilt-ridden weekends in small hotels in Clacton, Harrogate, Morecambe.

Mellinger sighed. The movements on the TV screen cast reflections across the ceiling. He lay watching them, smiling thoughtfully. It was hard to think back to his wife and not feel loutish on this cold and dreary night. Yet I could not have loved her any better, he thought. And it was true. But by the time their boy was born, it was already too late. By then, he was on the merry-go-round and nothing in the world could get him off. He was committed – to an insatiable machine that chewed up people as quickly as newsfilm, to women who somehow or other started out as casual lays and graduated to complex relationships, to a code of conduct that had become almost a pre-requisite of the business he was in. He was trapped, going through the motions like a computer, so that when the crash came, when he heard the news that his wife and boy no longer existed, the bottom had blown completely out of his life. That was the way it was, he thought; you went along knowing you were trapped on some perilous collision course, and when the collision came from a totally unexpected quarter, you were shot to hell.

He had stopped that merry-go-round as easily as he might have stopped it any time, if he had only tried. But by then it was too late. By then he was into the chasm and there was only the emptiness around him, and the left-over remains of his life to kill.

He inhaled slowly, letting the smoke curl from his nostrils in a slender stream. It had been a mess all right, a stupid futile mess. But the crash would have come regardless. He could not be held responsible for the crash. And he had not done so badly in pulling the threads together again, taking the shop, making it go, recreating a new life from the ashes of the old.

He sighed, putting out his cigarette. The TV set rattled monotonously on.

'Hey,' O'Connor said, getting up from the Scrabble

4   49

board to twist the knob, 'Tommy Cooper, he's good.'

He grinned at Mellinger.

'My wife can't stand him, but I think he's bloody marvellous.'

Mellinger nodded and O'Connor studied him curiously.

'You used to be in this game, didn't you?' he said.

'Telling jokes?'

'No. The telly. Documentaries, that sort of thing. I saw you once on *Panorama*.'

'That was a long time ago,' Mellinger sighed.

'Yeh, you were doing a thing about the American moonshots.'

O'Connor stood at the bottom of the bed, smiling down, his round face shiny with sweat. He wanted to talk.

'Listen, tell me something. How does a man get into a job like that?'

'Luck,' said Mellinger.

'Takes a good education though, I'll bet. University, and all that.'

'Not necessarily. Some people graduate from newspapers.'

'Like you?'

'Yes,' said Mellinger, 'like me.'

'I've got a cousin who works in TV,' O'Connor said conversationally, 'Malton, Jimmy Malton. He's on the other side though, Harlech. Works in the props department.'

Mellinger shook his head.

'Don't know him,' he said.

O'Connor perched on the side of the bed, crossing his legs.

'He's got a job against the world, that man,' he murmured. 'He works a day, they give him a day off. One day on, one day off, call that work?'

Mellinger grunted.

'Must have changed since my day,' he said.

O'Connor studied him sceptically.

'You did all right, though,' he insisted. 'Travelling all

50

over the world : expense accounts, famous friends.'

'It was just a job.'

'Oh yeh.'

'A job like any other job.'

'Not like ours. You weren't short of a bob or two.'

Mellinger looked at him.

'When the alarm went off in the morning, it sounded just the same,' he said.

O'Connor grinned.

'I'll believe you, thousands wouldn't.'

Mellinger stared at him curiously. The round face looked bright and happy. The man seemed oblivious to their reason for being there.

'Aren't you . . . ' Mellinger muttered. 'Don't you ever get tense?'

'You mean now?'

'Yes.'

'Oh, we're tense all right, Jackie and me. We've just learned not to think about it, that's all.'

'I don't know how you can sit there, playing Scrabble.'

O'Connor shrugged.

'Why not? They'll come in their own sweet time. No sense getting paranoic about it.' He grinned reassuringly. 'Listen, you've got nothing to worry about. This hotel is sealed up tight. As soon as they knock on that door we'll have 'em.'

'Don't you think they know that?'

'What?'

'They must know bloody well you'll have some sort of trap set up. They'll be ready.'

O'Connor sniffed.

'They can be as ready as they bloody like. We'll have 'em, just wait.'

Mellinger stared at him for a moment, then got up and went into the bathroom. He felt strained and tired. He looked at his watch. Ten past eight. He filled a glass with water and drank it thirstily. In the other room, he could hear O'Connor laughing. In an almost vague and disorientating way, he felt the floor begin to vibrate beneath his feet. It seemed to buckle, thrusting upwards as if the boards were coming apart at the seams. Suddenly, for no real reason he could determine, the glass was out of his hand and the room had tilted, the ceiling no longer above his head but facing him, slightly askew and blurred at the edges. Then he felt a rush of white-hot air as the building shook to a thunderous explosion, and above and beyond the roar he heard the tall double-glazed bedroom window shatter into a million pieces and thought incongruously; lucky I drew that curtain. The sound rippled away, and in the silence Mellinger heard a voice – my God, was that human? – screaming in pain and terror. He realised he was sprawled on the floor. The glass he had been holding had shattered, and now his hand was bleeding. He peered at the scarlet drops with a strange fascination. They were dripping on to his trouser leg. His leg was sticking out in front of him, but like the rest of his body, seemed somehow detached, as if he had no control over its movements or position. What's happening? he wondered.

Almost simultaneously, the bathroom walls seemed to tremble, swaying in and out like strips of india rubber, as a second explosion, more shattering than the first, pealed backwards and forwards, escalating into an ear-splitting thunderclap which subsided slowly as pieces of the bathroom ceiling began to rain on Mellinger's head.

Stunned, he clambered shakily to his feet, dusting plaster from his hair. He heard people running panic-stricken down the corridor outside. From somewhere below came the screams of frightened women, the cries of people in pain and the crackle of flames. The bathroom door burst open and O'Connor dashed in, pistol drawn. He seized Mellinger by the shoulder.

'Into the bedroom, quick,' he gasped. 'We've been bombed.'

Mellinger obeyed without a thought. The second man, Jackson had been hurt by a piece of flying glass. His cheek was cut open and he was gripping his pistol in one hand while he attempted to staunch the bleeding with the other.

The shrill scream of the fire alarm rang down the corridor. The two Special Branch men looked at each other.

'We'll have to use the fire escape,' O'Connor hissed hoarsely.

'Screw that.'

'It's our only chance.'

'What if they're watching? They'll grab Mellinger.'

'No. They'll expect us to make for the lobby. It's closer.'

Mellinger stared at him, swivelling his mind back into focus.

'You mean,' he said, frowning, 'this is just a diversion?'

'Looks like.'

'But if we stay here, we'll get roasted.'

'He's right,' O'Connor muttered.

Jackson thought for a moment.

'I'll whip downstairs and see how bad it is,' he said. 'If everything's under control, we sit tight and wait for Simon. If not, we take the fire escape.'

'Okay,' said O'Connor, 'be quick. And when you get back, sing out loud and clear before coming through that door.'

Jackson nodded. He slipped outside and was gone.

O'Connor looked frightened. He paced up and down, clutching the pistol like a man expecting to be attacked from all sides. Mellinger sat on the bed watching him. The noise in the corridor gradually subsided and soon most of the action appeared to be taking place downstairs. He could smell the pungent scent of cordite and drifting smoke.

'Sealed up tight, did you say?' he growled sarcastically.

'We'll be all right,' O'Connor said.

'What the hell's happened to your friends?'

'They'll be here.'

'They're taking their own sweet bloody time.'

O'Connor glared at him.

53

'Relax. No one's coming in here unless he wants a bullet in his throat.'

Mellinger scowled back. He could hear the flames plainly now, crackling and spitting, obliterating even the shouts in the square outside. Damn it, he should have known better. Placing himself in the hands of total strangers had been an act of insanity. He'd asked for it, all right.

'How long do we wait?' he demanded.

'Long as we have to.'

'What if Jackson doesn't come back?'

'He'll come.'

'If he doesn't, we'll be cooked.'

'Shut up,' O'Connor growled.

He was hostile, trying to hide his nerves with a show of aggression. He slipped his pistol into its holster and wiped his palms on his pants. Mellinger looked at the window. The curtain was fluttering in the wind, ripped to shreds by flying glass. Outside, he heard the whine of an ambulance and the hollow ring of a police loudspeaker urging spectators to stand well clear. Again, the pungent scent of smoke drifted into his nostrils, this time stronger than ever.

'This place is burning up,' Mellinger exclaimed angrily. 'Let's get down that fire escape while we've got a chance.'

O'Connor looked stubborn.

'We stay here,' he ordered.

'You stay,' Mellinger snapped. 'I'm a free agent, and I've stayed long enough.'

He got to his feet and O'Connor moved in to block his escape. As they stood there, both of them wondering what to do next, the door suddenly burst from its hinges with a grinding crash. For a moment, Mellinger could not believe what had happened. In front of his astonished eyes, framed between the doorposts, stood the biggest man he had ever seen. He had a face that was not really a face at all. It looked as if someone had fashioned it out of sculptor's clay, and had then carefully smoothed out the features so that the nose and lips, cheekbones and eyesockets all merged one into the other. The skin was smooth and shiny. Only the eyes seemed alive. They glittered out from that mummified expanse like the eyes of a wild animal. The man was dressed in a grey pullover and cotton slacks, and as far as Mellinger could see, carried no gun. This fact impressed itself simultaneously upon O'Connor who made a frantic snatch at his holster. With a speed Mellinger would not have believed possible, the big man slid across the room, his arm lifting and falling in a dizzy blur. O'Connor's pistol was only half-drawn when the first blow broke his arm. There was a sickening crunch of bone, and O'Connor screamed in pain as the revolver clattered from his useless fingers. He doubled forward, gasping for breath and a second blow squashed his nose, blurring his vision, filling his mouth with blood. Strong fingers gripped his hair, forcing his head down. Then his brain exploded as the big man's knee caught him full in the face. Dazed and whimpering with pain, he tried to pull back, ducking and weaving like a boxer, clutching his wounded arm with his free hand. The big man moved again. One huge paw seized O'Connor by the throat, lifted him bodily into the air and held him wriggling like a helpless terrier. The man stared at Mellinger, his eyes icy.

'Do exactly as you're told,' he hissed, 'and you might walk out of here.'

The sound of the voice brought Mellinger to his senses. He glanced quickly around for O'Connor's gun, but he was already too late. The big man slid his free arm around O'Connor's spine as if they were about to dance together, and with a neat economical wrist-flick, snapped O'Connor's neck. Mellinger watched in horror as the detective's body tumbled lifelessly to the floor.

The man jerked his head.

'Let's go,' he ordered.

Dry-mouthed, Mellinger stared at the powerful shoulders and wild grey eyes. He stared at O'Connor's broken

55

frame sprawled obscenely across the carpet. Traces of vomit were drying swiftly on the detective's lips, and a few flecks of blood scattered his shirt. He looked crumpled, like a mutilated plastic doll.

Mellinger went.

FIVE

George Steiner sat in the police station and watched the stretcher cases come in. The front lobby had been turned into an emergency field centre where a team of doctors and nurses were working frantically, giving first aid, while ambulances ferried the injured to hospital. Women and children, cut by flying glass, huddled speechless along the white plastered walls, waiting for attention. A boy, sobbing hysterically, was being comforted by a police woman; his face was lathered in blood, and beads of scarlet dripped from an ugly gash along his arm.

'What's the casualty roll?' Steiner asked.

Culpepper, the Special Branch man, tall, portly, with pitted cheeks and thin brown moustache, pulled a face.

'Four dead. At least. Four more injured by the first blast. Another ten by the second. That's a conservative estimate.' He was watching a woman whose left arm had been ripped off, receiving a blood transfusion from a young Indian doctor. The doctor's face muscles were rigid with shock.

'We've seen plenty of it in Ulster,' he added, 'but it's something you never get used to.'

'IRA?'

'It's got all the hallmarks.'

'What about Mellinger?'

Culpepper pursed his lips. He looked embarrassed.

'Gone,' he said. 'I'm sorry, Commander.'

'He couldn't be trapped in the wreckage?'

'No chance.'

'The building's blazing like a November 5th bonfire. How can you be sure?'

'Because the second floor is still intact. Our men have already been up there. The kidnappers took Mellinger out through the kitchen and into the sewer at the rear of the hotel.'

Steiner stared at him, frowning.

'What sewer?'

Culpepper pressed his lips together again. He did not like explaining this, explaining how they had bungled.

'There's a disused sewer tunnel leading from the hotel yard down to the river Lagan. It was dug eight years ago when they planned to build an expressway between the city and the airport. As it happened, the expressway never got built; the tunnel was closed up and everyone forgot about it.'

Steiner stared at him angrily.

'Including Special Branch.'

'Yes,' Culpepper sighed. 'Including Special Branch.'

George Steiner got to his feet and began to pace the floor. He was almost choking with frustration. Such a stupid and incongruous oversight. They had sealed off every possible escape hatch except the one that led to freedom.

'Well, the IRA certainly didn't forget about it,' he snapped. 'No wonder they chose the Tara Hotel. Why, for God's sake, didn't somebody check the lay-out of the place before we moved in?'

Culpepper didn't answer. He was surprised at the venom in Steiner's outburst. Steiner had seemed such a gentle man. Gentle, and inelegant. His creased suit, his lack of concern for appearances had given him an almost gawkish quality and the Special Branch man had been surprised at first that this was the great George Steiner, the commander whose name was already a legend throughout the force. Now he began to see Steiner in a different light, and Steiner's passion told Culpepper something of his secret. Steiner cared.

He watched the Commander flop into his seat, looking depressed.

'It's not over yet,' Culpepper said. 'There's still one possibility. A flimsy one, I admit, but at least a possibility.'

'What's that?'

Culpepper got up.

'Come on, grab your coat.'

'Where are we going?'

Culpepper grinned.

'To gaol,' he said.

They drove across the now-silent town, stopping at four successive army roadblocks on the way, and as they travelled Culpepper explained what he had in mind. Two days before, he said, they had picked up a notorious gunrunner, an American called Hackett whom they had been trying to nail for more than a year. Hackett had been running arms into Ulster on a converted naval MTB, and in spite of continual efforts to catch him had managed to carry on a highly lucrative business until the day before yesterday. Acting on a tip-off, British Navy gunboats had trapped Hackett in a small bay on the Antrim coast and captured both him and his crew together with eight Czech RPG-7 bazookas, a sixty mm mortar tube, seventy mortar bombs, and two hundred thousand rounds of standard 9 mm ammunition.

The point, Culpepper explained, coming to it at last, was that Hackett was not merely a gunrunner, but also a trusted ally of the Provisional IRA, and a personal friend of at least three members of the Provo Council in Dublin.

Steiner stared at him in the darkness.

'What are you getting at?'

Culpepper shrugged.

'We owe you something,' he said. 'What happened tonight was our fault, and nobody's trying to claim otherwise. We want Hackett badly, but if you think you can use him – well, he's yours.'

58

'You mean ... a deal?'

'Why not?'

'Can you do that?'

Culpepper smiled thinly.

'Listen, this isn't London. There's a war on, didn't you know? We can do anything we damn well please, as long as we're discreet. Maybe Hackett can get you Mellinger back. Maybe he can find out where Huntley is. Maybe, if we turn him loose, he can give you some kind of lead – anything.'

'And maybe he'll run, and keep on running, until he's back in the U.S.A.'

Culpepper grinned.

'Yes,' he said, 'maybe.'

At Crumlin Road Prison, they sat in the Governor's office and waited for Hackett to be brought from the cells. When he came in, Steiner studied him with interest. He was a small man, slightly built, with dry brittle hair and a sullen disposition. He was dressed in denim trousers and a crumpled denim jacket. His cheeks were pale, his eyes puffy with sleep. Evidently, he had been fetched from his bed.

'Well, Hackett,' said Culpepper briskly. 'You're in a real mess this time.'

The small man spat on the floor.

'Screw you,' he growled.

Culpepper smiled.

'You can spit all you want, it won't help you one little bit. You're about to be prematurely retired.'

'This is a put-on, pig man, you can't do much to me.'

Culpepper's face was inscrutable.

'Think so?' he answered evenly. 'We're going to toss the book at you, Hackett. If there's one thing none of us can stand – that is, my colleagues and me, it's foreigners who stick their noses into business which doesn't concern them, thereby causing us great upset and annoyance.'

Hackett sneered.

'I'm not sitting in this rathole longer'n I have to.'

'Hackett, you've been sitting in one rathole or another all your life, but this is one you'll have to get used to.'

'I didn't kill nobody,' Hackett scowled.

'Killing's a matter of degree. How many killings did your merchandise perform?'

'Guns don't kill. People do.'

'I've heard that argument before. This time it won't wash.'

'Like hell it won't. You can't nail much on me.'

Culpepper smiled thinly.

'All we've got, Hackett,' he promised. 'Every little thing that's been looking for someone to lean on. Look at it this way. You should have retired years ago. We'll be doing you a favour.'

'Stick your fingers up your arse.'

'I'm talking about a twelve to fourteen year favour, Hackett.'

Hackett went pale.

'You'd never pull it off,' he snarled, his brown eyes flickering nervously. Culpepper's smile broadened. It was a chilling smile, devoid of humour.

'Oh, but we will,' he murmured. 'What age are you now? Forty eight? Not too many good years left, have you? Still, there's one consolation. You won't have the future to worry about. By the time you get out of here; you'll just about qualify for an old-age pension.'

Hackett stood in silence, watching Culpepper balefully. Steiner could tell that his brain was bright and alert. He knew that Hackett's aggressiveness was only a front. Hackett felt trapped. Trapped and scared. Culpepper knew it too.

'Unless,' he mewed casually, 'unless you manage to change our minds about your character.'

Hackett frowned.

'What the hell are you talking about?'

Carefully, Culpepper explained. He told Hackett about the kidnappings. He told him about Huntley, and about Mellinger. He told him about the stake-out at the Tara

Hotel, about the bombings, and about Mellinger's subsequent disappearance.

'Get Mellinger back for us,' he said. 'Find out where he's being kept, and more important, why, and we'll drop all charges.'

'You're crazy.'

'You don't believe me?'

'What the hell difference does it make if I believe you or not? If I do that, the next time you see me I'll be in a ditch with my brains blown out.'

'It's up to you, Hackett. The possibility of a quick death, or the certainty of a slow one. Help us, and we'll help you. Refuse, and you go back to that cell to rot.'

Hackett chewed his lip, studying the two men thoughtfully.

'How do I know I can trust you? I've already been formally charged.'

'We could lose your file. It's happened before.'

'Come to that, how do you know you can trust *me*. I could just as easily run for the border.'

Culpepper folded his hands.

'I'm counting that you will, Hackett,' he smiled. 'If there are any answers to be found, that's where they'll come from. Take a trip to Dublin, look up some of your old friends. We'll drop the charges as a sign of good faith. If you find anything, come back, and we'll give you back your boat on condition that you promise to leave Ireland for good. Is it a deal?'

Hackett stared at him in silence for a moment. His face was blank, as if he could not believe his good fortune. He nodded slowly.

'It's a deal,' he said.

Next morning, December 4th, Hackett rented a hire car and took the road south towards Newry. It was a beautiful day, the sky bright and cloudless, the air tempered with a soft end-of-season warmth that made it seem more like spring than early winter. Hackett felt good, better, he decided, than he had felt in that windowless cell in Crumlin Road Prison with the bleak prospect of years of incarceration ahead. Now, unexpectedly, his whole future had changed, and as he drove south listening to the morning pop music on the car radio, he made plans with the pleasure of a man who had just been, surprisingly, reprieved from death. Back to the States, he thought, that was the first step. He'd been away too damn long anyhow. The Florida Keys maybe. He had always had a hankering for the Keys. There was a good living to be made for a man who knew how to handle a boat – and who didn't care too much about the risks he took. Well, he had proved himself on that one, by God. He had taken the risks all right in the past year or two. A thousand to one some of them. Crazy risks. Suicidal risks. He had been out of his mind, of course, but that was the name of the game. In Hackett's world, there were only two ways to live. You played it straight, and took whatever society had to offer, or you took what you wanted and paid for it with your guts and your nerve. And the risks had paid off all the way, until now. Now – he hated to admit it – now, they had him by the balls. In his profession, a man without a boat was like a cowboy without a horse. He had to have that boat. With it, he was back in business. Without it, he was just another joker, hungry for a buck. The Irish run was played-out anyhow. He had pushed it too goddamned far; that had been a mistake, which he knew and would not make again.

Not that he had any intention of betraying the IRA. No way. It was not so much a question of loyalty as simple economics. Opening up in new territory meant fresh contacts, and even in his profession, fresh contacts sometimes required references. A background of treachery could prove to be an embarrassment in the future. No, there was no question of betraying the IRA. But maybe he wouldn't need to. They owed him a favour or two over the past couple of years. Maybe if he just explained things right, they would help him get his boat back. He was counting on it.

He crossed the border south of Newry and stopped for lunch at a little pub outside Dundalk. When he had finished eating, he went into a phone booth and made a call to Dublin. Afterwards, he drove on south until he reached a quiet stretch of roadway, then he turned off along a narrow cart-track which meandered lazily through the flat surrounding fields. When he had travelled a mile or so, he parked the car on a grassy verge, secreted himself in a clump of bushes a dozen yards away, lit a cigarette, and waited. An hour passed. No one came. Satisfied, Hackett got to his feet, stretched himself luxuriously, and began to walk down the track, moving diagonally towards the main road. It was two o'clock in the afternoon, and the sun was high and bright, casting slivers of gold between the trees and across the sharply-etched furrows of the rolling fields. He heard the sound of a cock crowing, and rounding a bend in the track came upon a little whitewashed farmhouse, its roof sagging with age. A bicycle stood propped against the door, and without hesitation Hackett slung one leg over its saddle and pedalled swiftly off towards the distant hum of traffic.

When he reached the highway, a group of schoolboys were playing rugby in a nearby field. He leaned the cycle against the wire fence, and raised his thumb hopefully at the steady stream of cars and lorries. Within ten minutes, he got a lift from a farmer who dropped him five miles down the road where he was picked up by a travelling salesman who took him all the way to Drogheda. Here, he boarded a bus to Dublin itself.

It was half-past four in the afternoon when they swung into Grafton Street and stopped outside Trinity College. Hackett got off, found a phone booth and dialled a number.

A voice said : 'Yes?'

Hackett said : 'This is the Spanton Foodliner Company. We are conducting a national survey, and wondered, have you tried our products yet?'

The voice said: 'I'm afraid I can't answer that. You will have to wait until our housekeeper returns.'

Hackett hung up. He was too early. He still had a little time to kill, which could be useful. Hackett felt certain he had not been followed. His little diversion south of Dundalk had satisfied him of that, but he was by nature a cautious man. His meticulousness, his attention to the smallest detail had saved his life on more than one occasion. Now he spent an hour drifting around Dublin's city centre, twisting backwards and forwards, re-tracing his steps, getting on buses and getting off two stops later, wandering into restaurants and dodging out through the rear door, ambling with the students in St Stephen's Green, mingling with the end-of-day commuters in Merrion Square. He felt, as he always felt during such complicated manoeuvres, vaguely ridiculous, but he went through the motions anyhow. Better to feel stupid now, than even stupider later.

By the time six o'clock arrived, darkness had fallen and the sky was high and bright and filled with stars. This time when he made his phone call, the answer came back: 'Our housekeeper has just returned. If your representative would care to call, I'm sure all your questions will be answered.'

Hackett hung up and took a bus to a small council estate on the outskirts of town. The house he went to looked no different from forty others in the same street: a small semi-detached with sloping roof, utility garage and a handkerchief lawn dotted with plastic gnomes. Hackett knocked at the door, which was opened immediately by a man he knew simply as Big Sean. In the hallway, he was made to stand with his palms against the wall and given a thorough body search. He knew the search was not for weapons – he was hardly likely to start shooting surrounded by Provo gunmen – but for police bugging devices. The frisking over, he was taken into the kitchen and given a cup of coffee. Perched on a small stool, waiting to be called upstairs, Hackett felt the old uneasiness sweep through his stomach. He hated these formal meetings. They seemed de-humanised somehow. As if they were all playing a game, an elaborate and deadly game, for although he wanted to laugh at the drama of it, he knew that failure to play his part could well cost his life. They killed without a moment's thought these Provos. He stared at the men who surrounded him in the kitchen, young men mostly, in their late teens and early twenties. They seemed like young men anywhere, earnest and friendly; but Hackett knew that one word from upstairs, and they would take him without a second's hesitation out to some remote stretch of highway and blow out his kneecaps, or his brains. That's what fanaticism did for you, he thought. A criminal, out for profit, might indulge himself in remorse or compassion. But these men had their consciences conveniently taken care of. Everything they did was for the cause. Hackett shuddered. He felt like a gladiator awaiting the lions.

Eventually, Big Sean popped his head through the doorway and Hackett was taken upstairs to a large double bedroom. The curtains had been meticulously drawn and the bed pushed back to make way for a foldable table to be set up adjacent to the opposite wall. Behind it, six men sat facing him as he stepped through the door. They looked ordinary, conventional men, the kind who would never stand out in a crowd. Their ages varied between twenty-five and fifty. Three of the faces he knew : they had drunk together, had joked together, and they had in fact, all of them, entertained him at their homes on more than one occasion. But now, as he stood before them, they gave no sign of recognition. They were sombre, quiet and businesslike.

Haltingly, Hackett told them his story, beginning with his capture and proceeding through his internment to his meeting with Culpepper and Steiner the night before. He told them what he knew of the kidnappings, the bombings at the Tara Hotel and Mellinger's disappearance. He

5

lingered for some time on Culpepper's offer, explaining what it could mean to him in terms of freedom and the return of his boat, then he recounted his journey down, including the abandoning of his car and the various diversionary tactics en route. They listened in silence until he had finished. The room filled with a rancid humidity. Hackett could hear the roar of the gas heater blaring away in the corner. He felt naked and exposed.

'Wait outside,' one of them said quietly.

He stood on the landing talking to Big Sean and trying to hide his nervousness while the panel discussed his story. Then once again he was taken into the room, and tense and fidgety, stood before them like a man facing his last judgement.

The spokesman of the panel was a man he knew well, a man he had always been proud to refer to as his friend in Ulster Republican circles. This man leaned forward, resting his elbows on the tabletop, his face as remote and expressionless as that of a total stranger.

'We are puzzled by your account,' he said, and Hackett's heart jumped. Everything he'd told them had been the truth dammit. Maybe something didn't tally. Maybe the goddamned Special Branch had set him up. The possibility made his knees quiver, but the spokesman's next words calmed his fear.

'We read about the kidnappings, but didn't realise they were being attributed to us. As far as we are concerned, they are not the work of the Provisional IRA. We agree that the Tara bombings could easily have been carried out by one of our Belfast units, but we've had no confirmation of that.'

The man paused, and stared at Hackett with what seemed, to the American, the imperturbability of an animal slaughterer.

'We are aware,' the man went on, 'that the Provisional IRA is in your debt, and are prepared to help you, if we can. We suggest that you remain here while we contact our Ulster units and see if we can throw any light on

Mellinger's disappearance. If we fail, then we further suggest that you forget about returning to Belfast and make your escape to the United States, or wherever else you may wish to go, as quickly as possible.'

Hackett took a deep breath and swallowed gratefully.

'Thank you,' he said.

Steiner stared at the bedraggled figure of Hackett standing before him in the office. After three days of absence, the American looked more woe-begone than ever. His cheeks were pale, his chin and throat coated with beard stubble. His eyes were red-rimmed and watery, they scowled down at Steiner and Culpepper with thinly-disguised contempt.

'Say that again,' Steiner whispered.

Hackett sighed. He was nearing the end of his tether. Three days with the IRA in Dublin, and his nerves were close to breaking point. He should never have come back here. He should have taken the Provos' advice and got out while he had the chance. But he needed that boat, and though he had failed to turn up Mellinger, he did have something which might be bargained for.

'They didn't do it,' he said.

'That's crazy.'

Hackett frowned.

'I'm just the errand boy,' he murmured, 'I'm telling you what they told me.'

'The Tara bombing?'

'They deny that too.'

Steiner sat back in his chair, letting the tension seep from him in a hiss of exhaled breath. He looked at Culpepper across the desk. Culpepper pulled a face.

'They could be lying.'

'No,' Steiner sighed. 'They've got no reason to. If they really did have Mellinger, they'd want to shout it from the rooftops.'

He sat hunched in his seat, weary and resigned. If it wasn't the IRA, someone had gone to a great deal of trouble to send them careering off in the wrong direction. Now which way did they turn?

Steiner drummed his fingers on the desk, while Hackett watched him in silence.

'Don't you want to hear the full story?' Hackett asked.

Steiner looked at him.

'There's more?'

'Much more.'

'Go on, Hackett,' Steiner snapped. 'Don't play games with me.'

'Well, the man in the newspapers, the one with the funny face . . .'

Steiner sat up straight.

'What about him?'

'On the night of December 3rd, a guy answering that description paid a Derry farmer ten pounds for leaving a small aircraft in one of his fields.'

'Any idea what kind of aircraft?'

'No, just small, he said; possibly a Cessna.'

'What about the farmer?'

'All I know is he's a Republican sympathiser. He thought this joker belonged to the Provos so he asked no questions. The guy left the plane in the early evening and came back for it around midnight.'

'He took off in the dark?' Steiner hissed.

'He got the farmer to light the field with his Land-Rover headlamps,' Hackett said. 'It was risky as hell, but he did it anyway.'

Hackett paused. This was the news he had to bargain with and he wanted the policeman to appreciate its full significance.

'Get this,' he said. 'The farmer remembers he was carrying something when he returned. It was a bundle, wrapped in sackcloth. Could've been a man, either dead or unconscious. Could've been Mellinger. The farmer was specific about that. The bundle was the rough shape and density of a human frame.'

Steiner sighed.

'We've been duped,' he said.

Culpepper nodded, watching him with sympathy.

'Looks like, George.'

'It's been nothing but a con job.'

'Right.'

Hackett stared at them both, not reassured by what he saw. He had counted on his news making them more amenable, putting them in an understanding mood. Instead, they looked tired and despondent. He coughed delicately.

'I done what you asked,' he explained. 'I went to Dublin, I put myself at great risk. Maybe I didn't find your man, but I stopped you sprinting along the wrong track. Now what about my boat?'

Culpepper glared at him.

'Why the hell should we believe you?'

Hackett's eyes narrowed. A sense of uncertainty shook him, but only for a moment.

'You believe me okay,' he said softly.

Culpepper swore.

'Wait outside,' he snapped. 'If and when I'm satisfied you're telling the truth, you'll get your boat. Get out of here, you snivelling little bastard.'

Hackett reddened in anger, but one look at Culpepper's face told him this wasn't the time for a showdown. He went out without a word and closed the door behind him. Culpepper looked at Steiner.

'I'm sorry, George,' he said gently.

Steiner shook his head.

'I was never happy with it from the beginning. It seemed too neat, too pat. They'd thought the whole thing out, move by move, and we trotted behind as obligingly as you please. They wanted us to think it was the Provos. They wanted us to waste our time and energy chasing moonbeams south of the border. Jesus, they must be laughing up their bloody sleeves by now.'

'Don't blame yourself, George.'

Steiner got up and studied the map of Europe on the wall.

'Harry, how far could a Cessna with a full fuel tank fly?'

Culpepper shrugged.

'God knows.'

'France? Spain? Switzerland?' Steiner drew an imaginary circle on the map with his forefinger. 'They could be anywhere inside that circumference. A hell of a haystack to lose a needle in.'

Culpepper folded his hands across his stomach.

'Not such a small needle, though, George,' he said. 'You can check out all listed landings with the necessary European authorities, and don't forget, you know quite a bit about our man already. You know what he looks like. You know that he kills without mercy, and with great expertise. You know that he has experience in the handling of explosives. You know that he's familiar with the streets of Belfast, familiar enough to be aware of the existence of the sewer tunnel behind the Tara Hotel when Special Branch didn't. And you know that he can pilot a small aircraft. That's not bad for starters.'

Steiner smiled thinly.

'There's something else I know, Harry. This film, this newsfilm; it will be precisely three minutes long, and ready for transmission when it is delivered. What does that suggest to you?'

Culpepper thought for a moment, then shook his head.

'Nothing,' he admitted.

Steiner sat down again.

'Film is the most complicated part of television there is,' he explained. 'Once you've shot one, it has to be processed and edited before you can put it on the screen. Now a film that's going to be slotted into a live news programme must have been processed and edited already, right?'

Culpepper stared at him with respect.

70

'So our kidnapping friends will need access to the necessary equipment?'

'Not just the equipment, Harry. They'll need the services of someone who's trained at processing and editing too. I'm putting my money on Plastic Face. He's been running this thing like a one-man show so far. First, I'll run a check on all film and TV companies, national and regional, and get a list of personnel who've been employed in film processing and editing since the industry began. Then I'll get a list of everyone holding a current pilot's licence in the U.K., and see which of the names cross-check.'

'Bingo,' Culpepper grinned. He studied Steiner with admiration. It was a long shot certainly, but still the only game in town. Culpepper did not need to be told how the detective had got his reputation.

Steiner picked up the phone.

'Could one of your boys get me on the afternoon flight to London?' he wondered.

Culpepper got up.

'I'll do it myself,' he said.

Steiner phoned his office in Tintagel House and asked for Detective Superintendent Barry Fawkes. Fawkes was Steiner's assistant. The switchboard girl told him Fawkes was out of the building, but promised to get him to phone Steiner directly he came back. Forty minutes later, Fawkes returned the call.

'I'll be in London by this evening,' Steiner said crisply. 'Here's what I want you to do.'

He gave his assistant a list of complicated instructions, repeating some of them in detail while Fawkes scribbled them down. Steiner's voice had lost its weariness. His setback with the IRA was already forgotten. He sounded alert and sure of himself. He finished speaking, and hesitated.

'Barry?' he added.

'Yes, Guv'?'

'Don't let Janie know I'm coming, will you?'

71

Fawkes sounded surprised.

'Okay, Commander, she's your wife.'

Steiner hung up. He sat for a moment with his hand on the receiver. He felt helpless, caught in a world that seemed somehow beyond him, at which he could only guess. Well, the guessing would soon be over. He could not go on like this, not knowing, filled with suspicion and hurt pride. He remembered Clara's voice on the telephone. It had been mocking. Scornful. Was that how he seemed to his friends? A figure of ridicule. He sighed and dialled his home.

'Hello,' a voice said.

'Janie?'

'Oh hullo, George, how are you?'

'I'm fine. What about you?'

'Oh, I'm fine. You know.'

'I phoned the other night, Thursday. There was no reply.'

'What time?'

'Eight-thirtyish.'

'Well, I told you George, I went to Clara's, I told you about that.'

'So you did,' Steiner said evenly, keeping his voice relaxed, 'I forgot. Listen, this thing seems to be dragging on for ever. It now looks as though I won't get home before next weekend.'

'What, another week, George?'

'I'm afraid so.'

'What will I tell Pamela? We're supposed to be going to her party on Friday night.'

'You'll have to bow out gracefully. Do the best you can.'

'Oh, George.'

'Sorry love, it's not my fault.'

'Okay then, I'll give her a call. When will you be back?'

'Sunday probably.'

'Look after yourself.'

'You too.'

'Goodbye, George.'

Steiner said goodbye and hung up. He sat looking at the telephone for a long time. He was thinking deeply. When at last he picked up the receiver again, his face was hard and set.

'Get me a taxi to the airport,' he said.

SIX

William Mellinger came back to life from somewhere very far down. He was swimming under water, lost in a murky seaweed-green universe. He struck out for the surface, watching the light change, watching it filter through different shades of grey, losing its density, growing paler, lighter – then all at once his eyes were open and he was staring, puzzled, at the cracked uneven plaster of an ancient ceiling. His stomach lurched and he swallowed, holding on to himself with an effort. Waves of nausea swept his body, making the walls ripple in and out. He sat up. He was on a narrow bunk in a tiny oak-beamed room. The walls were uneven, as though at some time in the distant past the building had sagged to one side, probably through age. In places, the plaster had crumbled away revealing heavy grey stone beneath. The floor too was stone, and there was no carpet or rug to speak of, just a soiled tattered bath towel draped along the foot of the door to keep out the draught. A second bunk stood against the opposite wall. Its blankets were rumpled, as though someone had recently slept there. A mug with coffee dregs in it stood on the floor below the pillow. The rest of the furniture was crude and primitive: there was a table, roughly-fashioned, a handful of rough-hewn wood chairs, and a tiny stool. Sitting on this stool was a man in shirtsleeves with a thin pointy face and iron-grey hair. His right arm was suspended in a sling around his neck. He was watching Mellinger, fascinated.

Mellinger swung his feet out on to the floor, and his brain seemed to tilt like a schooner deck. He groaned and clutched his forehead.

'Feeling shaky?' the man asked.

Mellinger looked at him.

'Where is this place?'

The man shrugged.

'Goodness knows. Some God-forsaken part of the globe, I expect.'

'Who are you?' Mellinger demanded.

The man smiled.

'Naunton F. Huntley, Director General of the BBC. What about you?'

Mellinger felt bile gathering thickly in his throat. He swallowed it back. He could not remember when he had felt so ill.

'Mellinger,' he whispered.

'Mellinger who?'

'William Mellinger. They sent me to fetch you back.'

'I see,' the man said. He smiled again. 'I hope you don't mind my saying this, old man, but you haven't done a very good job of it so far.'

With a supreme effort, Mellinger pushed himself to his feet. The room spun wildly around him. My God, he thought, I'm going to faint. He saw the ceiling sweeping down like a breathless shroud, and his stomach lurched alarmingly.

'Steady,' Naunton Huntley whispered, stepping over to put one hand on Mellinger's shoulder. 'You've been on your back for nearly two days. They brought me in the same way, pumped full of some drug or other. I'd better warn you I had the runs for twenty-four hours after I came round; you'll probably be the same.'

Mellinger stared at him, focusing his gaze with an effort.

'They?' he echoed weakly.

'Well . . . Kyle. That's what he calls himself. He's the only one I've seen so far. There are others though. I've heard them talking.' He lifted his eyebrows hopefully. 'You don't have a match by any chance?' he asked, 'I've not had a smoke for more than a week. I think I must have lost my damned lighter during the kidnap.'

'Top pocket,' Mellinger mumbled.

'Oh thank you, Mr Mellinger,' Huntley said gratefully. He offered Mellinger a cigarette, but Mellinger shook his head. He was staring at the window. It was a very small window, no more than six inches square, and through it Mellinger could see a sweep of tawny hills and the distant gleam of a mountain tarn. Clouds hurtled across the sky, and as Mellinger watched, the wind changed, sweeping the moorgrass left and right like the skin of an angry beast.

'You've no idea where we are?' Mellinger whispered.

'None,' said Huntley, 'except that it's lonely, and we're surrounded by mountains. But mountains look pretty much the same almost everywhere in the world. We could be in the Pyrenees, the Maritimes, or even the High Atlas in Morocco. Take your pick.'

Mellinger shivered.

'Too cold for Morocco,' he said.

Huntley chuckled.

'You've obviously never been in the High Atlas, my boy.'

He inhaled deeply, letting smoke curl lazily from his nostrils.

'I must say, Kyle seems to trust you,' he muttered. 'No harness.'

For the first time, Mellinger noticed the length of chain attached to Huntley's left ankle. It was eight or nine feet long and stapled securely to an iron ring in the wall. He frowned.

'How long have you been trussed up like that?'

'Since I got here. It's rather ingenious really. I can move around quite freely, go to the bathroom, help myself at the food table and things like that. But no matter how hard I try, I can't get rid of this ankle thing.'

Mellinger stared at him curiously. He was getting control of himself at last. The awful sickness still persisted, but some of his initial dizziness had begun to disperse. He peered at Huntley's right arm, suspended in its sling.

'What happened there?' he asked.

'Oh, I made a stupid mistake. I imagined – God knows what gave me such a ridiculous idea – that I could overpower Kyle and steal his key. I waited until he brought my evening meal, then hit him with the stool as he came through the door. It was an idiotic move. The blow had no affect on the man whatsoever. He broke my right arm to teach me a lesson. Did it with his bare hands, quite expertly too. He's good at that sort of thing.'

Mellinger nodded grimly.

'I've seen him in action,' he said. 'What is he?'

'No idea, old son.'

'What's he after then?'

'I thought you might be able to answer that.'

It occurred to Mellinger that Huntley would know nothing of what had happened since his kidnapping. In fact, he would probably know nothing of what had happened *during* his kidnapping since even his assistant's death had taken place after he had been driven away. So Mellinger sat and told him the full story while Huntley listened in silence, his face grave and attentive. When Mellinger had finished, Huntley shook his head.

'Poor Brumby,' he said. 'What a senseless waste. They didn't need to kill him like that.'

Mellinger was silent for a moment, letting Huntley absorb the progress of events. Then he asked: 'Have you any idea what this film is about?'

'My dear Mr Mellinger, I haven't the faintest idea about anything. All I know is, I was kidnapped, I was brought here and I've been here ever since. I have seen no one, other than the man who calls himself Kyle, and he's not much of a talker, as you'll discover.'

Mellinger stared again at the broken arm. He could see the fingertips peeking out between two rude splints.

'Who set it?' he wondered.

'Kyle did. Very efficiently too. In fact, he seems to be efficient at most things. That's the problem.'

'Have you asked him why he brought you here?'

'Of course, my dear fellow, repeatedly. But extracting information from Kyle is like drawing teeth. He's not human, you know: not living flesh and blood like you and me. He's an animal, or a robot rather, cold and clinical and very very deadly.'

Mellinger got to his feet again. He was feeling better every minute. The dizziness was fast receding, and now there was only the threat of vomiting to worry him seriously. He breathed deeply, sucking air into his lungs.

'We've got to get out while we've still got a chance,' he said.

He turned to the window, examining the tiny catch. It was stuck fast. He gripped it with both hands and twisted hard. It wouldn't budge. Huntley sighed.

'I've tried all that, Mr Mellinger,' he said, 'countless times. Even if you did manage to get it open, we'd never squeeze through such a narrow space.'

Mellinger sat back. Huntley was right. Only a monkey could get through there, and judging by the window frame, the walls were at least a foot thick. There had to be another way. He stood up, peering around. The heavy oak beams looked riddled with woodworm.

'What about the ceiling?' he whispered.

Huntley licked his lips.

'I don't know. It's a thought. Probably some sort of loft above.'

'And above that, the roof. Let's give it a try.'

He stood on the bed and tapped the ceiling tentatively with his fingertips. It sounded hollow.

'Pass me that chair,' he ordered.

Huntley wasn't listening.

'Someone's coming,' he hissed urgently.

Mellinger jumped to the floor just as the key turned in the outside lock and the heavy door swung slowly open. He felt something cold touch his throat as he stared for a second time at the man who had snatched him from the Belfast hotel. Standing there, he looked like some strange species of animal, his massive frame almost filling the space between the doorposts, his heavy blunt head moving slowly from side to side as he carefully surveyed the room. Mellinger shuddered; that was a hell of a face, he thought – flat and shiny, with deep furrows in it where the cheeks should be, but not really what you could call a face at all, not a human face. It was a face that stopped you in your tracks, a face to have nightmares over, chipped and bloodless and somehow – Mellinger felt his stomach lurch as he thought of this – as indomitable as a centurion tank. There was something unstoppable about this man. Mellinger remembered how smoothly he had dealt with poor O'Connor, how he had wrung the detective's neck as easily as he might have killed a chicken. The light from the window cast shadows around the thin cruel mouth, illuminating the eyes, and for the first time, Mellinger realised that the man's dry lifeless hair was not his own. It belonged to an ill-fitting wig which clung to his skull like a woolly cap. And what was more – Mellinger could not imagine how he had missed this – the face was devoid of both eyebrows and eyelashes. As Mellinger stood digesting this fact, the man jerked his head towards the open door.

'Let's go,' he grunted.

Mellinger glanced at Huntley and stepped outside. A cold wind hammered his cheeks. They were in some kind of paddock or ancient farmyard. He could see a stretch of crumbling concrete, with what appeared to be a battered fountain in its centre. Beyond it, the sagging hump of an old barn swelled against the sky. Beyond that, the ground rippled into the sweep of the rolling hills.

The big man locked the door carefully and began to cross the paddock, making for the barn. Mellinger hobbled after him, trying to keep up. His sickness was strengthening. He swallowed.

'Where are we?' he hissed against the wind. The big man did not answer. He continued walking, as if Mellinger did not even exist. Mellinger noticed a puckered scar on his neck, high and to the left, above the shoulder. He looked as wild as the landscape around him.

Mellinger gasped for breath as waves of nausea swept from the pit of his stomach.

'I feel sick,' he croaked, holding on to the fountain for support. The man stopped.

'Rest awhile,' he murmured.

Mellinger squatted weakly on the fountain's rim. The landscape was spinning and the sky seemed to come down and wrap itself about his head like a ball of cotton wool.

'What the hell did you pump into me back there?' he asked.

The man looked at him, his eyes cold and expressionless.

'You'll be okay,' he grunted, 'you've got three days to recover.'

'Then what? What happens in three days?'

'You do what you were brought here for. You film.'

Mellinger held on to his stomach, breathing deeply. He stared at the man's hands, fascinated. They were huge and corded. Mellinger could see the strength in them, could feel in his fancy those solid fingers twisting his neck as they had twisted O'Connor's, or bending his arm as they had bent Huntley's. He remembered too how fast the man had moved at the Tara Hotel; it wasn't natural for such a huge frame to move so quickly.

'Who are you?' he demanded.

'My name is Kyle.'

'I mean who *are* you?'

The man shrugged, not bothering to answer. He seemed almost to retreat into himself. Mellinger tried another tack.

'Where is this place?'

'Farm, used to be.'

'But where?'

Again no answer. Mellinger glanced around.

'Supposing I decide to make a run for it?'

For the first time, the man actually smiled. His flat dead face seemed to split open as if a fracture had run across its surface. It was a chilling smile, and Mellinger shuddered.

'You can laugh all you want,' he said defensively, 'but this is my kind of country.'

'I know,' the man called Kyle said. 'That's why you're here.'

Mellinger stared at him.

'Because of the mountains?'

'That's right.'

'You mean we're filming in the mountains?'

The man nodded.

'What kind of film?'

'Come with me and I'll show you.'

The man led Mellinger to the barn, unlocked the door and swung it open. Mellinger peered inside, blinking in the unaccustomed darkness. The barn was roomier than he'd thought, and when he got used to the change of light he saw that it wasn't a barn at all, but a second cottage, not unlike the farmhouse itself.

Crouched in the shadows were four people. They looked pale and frightened, and their clothes were crumpled as if they had been slept in. Each of them was chained around the ankle, just like Huntley. Mellinger frowned.

'Who are these people?' he asked.

Kyle did not answer. Mellinger saw the look of hopelessness in the four pasty faces.

'Who are they?' he demanded angrily.

Kyle swung the heavy door shut and carefully locked it. His face was expressionless.

'They are our protagonists,' he said softly. 'In three days' time, we will film them as they die.'

It was raining when Steiner got off the plane at Heathrow. The runways glistened like black tar, and little coloured lights flittered through the darkness like fairy lamps on a Christmas tree. A cold wind scattered leaves across the concrete as he turned up his collar and joined the trickle of passengers filing into the bright chrome-and-glass comfort of the terminal building. A hollow tannoyed voice was announcing the departure of the 10.20 flight to Paris. Feet clattered on the marble stairway. There was a sense of movement, and life, and that subdued excitement which never failed to communicate itself to Steiner in big international airports.

He found Detective Superintendent Barry Fawkes waiting for him in the baggage room. Fawkes was a pale-faced man of thirty-four with stringy blond hair and heavy sideburns. He looked more like a disc jockey than a detective, though Steiner never said so, for although he did not approve of his assistant's appearance, that deceptive charm had proved a distinct asset on more than one occasion. Fawkes was smiling as Steiner walked in through the door.

'You shouldn't have bothered,' Steiner said. 'I could've caught the bus.'

Fawkes shrugged.

'No sweat. I was on my way home anyhow. I wanted to give you these.'

He was clutching a thick wad of files.

'How'd it go?' Steiner asked.

'Slow. You've got to give 'em time, Guv'.'

'We don't have time,' Steiner growled. 'Us, them, the poor bastards wondering if they'll still be alive after December 10th.'

Fawkes twisted his face as they pushed through the swing doors and headed for the car park.

'They pulled out all the stops, Guv'nor. I thought they were very co-operative, considering.'

Steiner turned the files over in his hand. They were large and heavy.

6
81

'Looks like we've got a lot of sorting out to do,' he said. Fawkes nodded.

'That first one contains a list of every licensed pilot in the country,' he explained, 'I ran into a spot of bother with it however. You see, licences only relate to specific types of aircraft. In other words, you might have a licence to fly a twin-engined hopper, but that doesn't mean you can pilot a 707.'

Steiner gave him a dry look.

'What d'you take me for, an idiot?'

'Yeah, but it could work the other way round, Guv'. What I mean is, the man we're looking for could be registered as an airline pilot, but still be able to fly the smaller stuff. Also, pilot licences aren't like driving licences. You've got to renew them every year, and if you don't you're right back to the starting line. See what I mean? Maybe our man deliberately allowed his to lapse.'

'So?'

'So I got a list for the past ten years.'

'Good lad,' said Steiner approvingly. 'What about the film companies?'

'I did what I could. Some of the lists are already in, the rest I expect to get tomorrow. I ran into a snag on that one too. Some of these TV firms send their films out to be processed by specialists like Kodak.'

George Steiner swore.

'The editing too?'

'Oh, that's always done at base. I got the names of every man and woman employed in film editing since the ITV companies opened up. I'm expecting more from the BBC, Granada and Grampian sometime tomorrow morning.'

'Been through them yet?'

'Well, just hurriedly, Guv'.'

'Anything cross-check?'

Fawkes shook his head.

'Sorry sir, not a damn thing.'

In the car from the airport, Steiner sat with his little

pencil torch and studied the lists in detail. He was pleased to see that they were comprehensive, with a summary of each man's earlier background and, in the case of those who had moved on, a note on where they were thought to be now. Fawkes however had been right. None of the people mentioned appeared to have held a pilot's licence in the past ten years. Steiner folded up the papers and put them carefully away. He would study them again in the morning when the final register came through.

He sat back and peered through the window at the streets of London zipping gloomily by. Rain coated the windscreen, distorting the images beyond. The wipers clicked away, carving out half-moons of clarity. Ahead, the road wound through the suburbs like an oily slug, lost in the damp black night. Steiner felt weary and discouraged. Something told him his long-shot wasn't going to work. The people they were dealing with were too bloody clever. They had worked it out like an intricate jig-saw puzzle, piece by piece, and Steiner knew that anyone who could go to such lengths just to make them believe they were chasing the IRA would hardly slip up on an elementary point like a pilot's licence. Still, it was often the little things, the seemingly unimportant shreds of evidence which led to the breaking of a case, and his mind went on ticking over as Fawkes swung the car around the Chiswick roundabout. To make a film for television, he thought, you had to have decent equipment. Might be worth checking the camera companies to see what gear had been purchased recently. Or stolen. But deep down, the worrying thought still plagued him that they had missed the point, the crux, the answer to the fundamental question, why those six? The Director General was easily explained; he was the lever by which the kidnappers hoped to get their film screened. But why Mellinger? And why the other four? Somewhere there had to be a link between them. Yet they came from different walks of life, their businesses, their interests, even their personalities were totally diverse. None of them had ever met. It was crazy, he thought. But that inborn feeling that had been with him all his life and on which he utterly relied told him there was something they had missed, something obvious.

Ahead, traffic lights flashed and Fawkes slammed his foot on the brake.

'Fancy a pint, sir?' he asked. 'Still twenty minutes to go.'

Steiner shook his head.

'I'm whacked out,' he said.

'Straight home then.'

'Yes.'

He peered at Fawkes, whose pale face looked even more colourless in the flat light of the street lamps. He liked Fawkes. He trusted him. Beneath that boyish grin, the man was tough as old teak. He had never let Steiner down yet, and Steiner believed that he never would.

'You didn't say anything?' Steiner muttered.

'What about, Guv'?'

'To Janie.'

Fawkes looked at him quickly.

'I've not seen her.'

'Good.'

'You said to keep mum, Commander.'

'That's right, Soldier.'

The lights changed and Fawkes started the car again. Steiner peered through the rain at the gleaming pavements and the rows of shiny iron railings. A group of young Africans in colourful tribal togas scurried heads-down through the downpour. Two girls with umbrellas stood at the kerbside waiting to cross the street. The car swung north towards Kensington High. Steiner watched the rain. It matched his mood. There was a dullness in his head, but it was not a headache. Despondency seeped through him. He looked at the candle-lit restaurants, at the couples waiting for taxis beneath their shiny canopies, and something seemed to break inside him. It was an awareness, an acknowledgement of what he had come for: truth, revelation. Did he want that? The responsibility of knowing? No, by God he did not, but there could be no turning back now, for he had come like Ulysses to seek vindication or revenge.

They reached Steiner's street.

'Home sweet home then,' Fawkes said with a smile.

'Drop me here,' Steiner ordered.

'I'll take you to your door.'

'No, let me out on the corner.'

Fawkes looked at him, frowning, but he stopped the car without a word. His face gleamed like a sliced cheese. His eyes were inscrutable. He said : 'Get a good night's sleep then Guv', I'll see you tomorrow.'

'Yes, first thing,' said Steiner. He hesitated before slamming the door. 'Thanks for picking me up,' he added.

Fawkes shrugged.

'What are friends for?'

Steiner watched him drive away, then turned, walking quickly through the driving rain. There were pools of water in the gutters and between the lamp-posts. Soggy cigarette packets littered the kerbside. Parked cars shone like polished glass in the drenching downpour. Steiner could feel his heart thumping. This was the moment. He had longed for it, and dreaded it. Truth, it had a dangerous ring, that word. Truth meant pain, decision, action. He felt very tired. Forty seconds to go, he estimated, in forty seconds he would know once and for all, and his life would either go on as before or be ultimately and irreparably altered. He did not wish to reach his door. He dreaded what he would find there. More than anything, he wanted to walk on by, to go elsewhere, a pub, a restaurant, anywhere. He wanted light, and life, and movement. He wanted a place to phone from, to announce his coming, to issue a warning so that the world, his world, would not be shattered. Supposing, he thought, she wasn't even there. She might have gone out. Then it would all have been for nothing. There would be no truth, no revelation, and no responsibility either. He still would not know. Not for certain. My God. His ears sang. The rain pattered on his face, blurring his vision. Don't let her be there, he thought. He prayed she would not be there.

He let himself in through the front door. The hall was quiet. No unidentified coat hung in the closet. That was a good sign. This was his home, a home he had built and paid for with the sweat of his brow, a home he almost owned now, and would own if he could keep up the payments for another five years. The familiarity of it wrapped itself around him like a comfortable shawl. He crept into the living room, and his heart sank. She was here. He could smell the whiff of her perfume on the air. He knew that perfume, knew its tang, he had bought it for her himself.

The room was in darkness, the curtains drawn. The big Victorian sofa had been pulled forward towards the fire. The cushions were rumpled, and one of them lay on the white fleecy rug, its fluffiness crushed where a body – or bodies – had lain across it. On the little card table, a pair of empty glasses stood rim to rim. In the ashtray, two cigarettes, half-smoked, lay side by side in a mocking taunt.

Steiner felt his stomach cringe. She was here. She was not alone. He knew it as surely as he knew he had to climb that stair.

He turned and walked back to the hallway. He went up two steps at a time, taking care to miss the third from the top which sometimes creaked, moving like a stalking tiger, silent and deadly. On the landing, something pale caught his eye in the darkness. He picked it up. It was Janie's blouse, a white lacy thing that did little, he remembered, to hide the curves beneath. There were more clothes lying at the foot of the bedroom door: a hastily-dropped skirt, a pair of tights, a bra – and two beautifully-tailored men's shoes decorated with elaborate finesse, the toes so lean, so slender, it was hard to believe they could fit a masculine foot. George Steiner felt the coldness sweep

86

his entire body. Something raw caught in his throat. With elaborate care he laid the blouse, neatly folded, over the banister rim. Nothing existed inside him now : not jealousy, nor hate, not even anger. Only the icy coldness of realisation. The games were over. Guessing, suspecting, it was all over. He was here, he knew, and he was cold.

He entered the bedroom quietly, more quietly than he had intended, for there was no further need for stealth. The evidence was complete, the case closed. But somehow the door opened without a sound – or perhaps the sound was there but they, the lovers, were too occupied to hear, for they were at that moment of union when passion is strongest, she poised above him, furiously impaled, her alabaster skin gleaming, her buttocks twitching and shuddering under the exquisite agony of sexual climax, he sprawled on his back, lips compressed with effort as he strove to delay his finish. Steiner stood looking down at them and something, his shadow perhaps, caused the man to open his eyes and look into Steiner's. They reflected everything Steiner expected to see there : surprise, alarm, panic, dismay. The man stopped moving, and his thin aesthetic body went rigid, corpse-like, as though frozen by some dire supernatural circumstance, and Steiner's wife, seeing for the first time the trepidation on her lover's face, turned to Steiner with a little choking sob. For several seconds they remained like that, an obscene tableau, the couple on the bed still joined together, Steiner cold and expressionless, filled with icy fury, watching them. He had never seen this man before. That was a blessing. He did not know what he would have done if it had been a friend, or worse still, a colleague, but the man was a stranger, skinny as a cucumber, pale, aesthetic – effeminate really – with long womanish fingers (a curious choice, Steiner remembered thinking later). But he hardly noticed the man except in the most detached way, for his eyes were fixed firmly on his wife's, knowing that for the first time in their eight years of marriage he held the advantage, enjoying it perversely, cruelly, angrily, knowing too that this was the last time they would be together in such intimacy. For a few seconds longer he stood there, watching the twin spots of colour on her pale tortured cheeks, the lank hair, shiny with sweat, strung across her forehead, the plump freckled breasts gleaming softly in the pale dusky light, the look of utter despair staring out from her wild frightened eyes. Then, with a deliberate effort, he turned and stepped swiftly from the room. He crossed the landing and entered the spare bedroom where his clothes were kept. He was holding himself in place with an effort. Every movement he made seemed to be done in slow motion. He wanted to escape, to get away from this house which could never again be called his own. Its familiarity no longer cushioned him, he felt stifled, smothered – it was time to go. He slid the heavy suitcase from the wardrobe top, opened it, and began to pack. He put in shirts, socks, slacks, shoes, shorts, vests, shaving gear, and the paperback Eric Ambler he was halfway through reading. He had almost finished when there was a creak on the landing, and Janie stood framed in the bedroom door, her slim-hipped full-breasted body hidden beneath a fluffy housecoat and a pair of loose leather-thonged sandals.

'You said you wouldn't be back till Sunday,' she hissed accusingly, and Steiner almost smiled to himself. It was typical of Janie that, cornered, she would try to gain the advantage by going in to the attack. Steiner did not answer. He closed the suitcase lid and snapped the fastenings shut. Janie was quiet for a moment. He sensed some of the fight go out of her. Seeing aggression would get her nowhere, she decided to change her course. Her eyes looked large and moist in the landing light.

'George,' she whispered, 'where are you going?'

Steiner did not answer. He took a dry overcoat out of the wardrobe, and began to pull it on. Janie watched him in silence. A muffled sob sounded deep in her throat.

'You can't blame me, George,' she whispered. 'Not entirely. I was lonely. You were never here, George.'

Steiner buttoned his coat and picked up the case. She looked at him with an air of panic and remained in the doorway, blocking his path.

'He means nothing to me, George, nothing at all. He never did, not even in the beginning. You've got to believe that.'

Steiner looked at her calmly. He did not feel calm, however. Now that the first shock of confrontation was over, he wanted to charge angrily back into the other room and tear that bastard limb from limb. But he forced himself, outwardly at least, to look calm.

'Get out of the way, Janie,' he said.

She put her hands against the doorposts.

'I won't let you go,' she stated. 'Not until you listen to what I have to say.'

Steiner sighed. He put the suitcase on the floor, took hold of his wife by the hips and tossed her, kicking and screaming on to the spare bed. The sound of the scuffle brought her lover running across the landing. He had managed to pull on his trousers, but was bare-footed and naked to the waist, his girlish ribcage glistening with sweat, and his eyes were bright with a mixture of fear and alarm.

'What's going on in here?' he shouted. He peered past Steiner's shoulder at the sprawled-out figure on the bed.

'You bastard,' he hissed, and seized Steiner's lapel.

Something snapped in Steiner's brain. He gripped the narrow wrist. The bone felt as frail as a bird's. He squeezed hard, sinking his fingertips into the gristly flesh. The man's eyes moistened with pain as he sank, lips writhing, on to his knees. Steiner looked down at him, the anger almost uncontrollable now. He held on, squeezing hard, and contemplated smashing his knee into that thin aesthetic face. In the end, he decided against it. The man, after all, owed Steiner no loyalty. If there was any guilt, then it had to be his wife's. There seemed to be no strength whatsoever in that fragile arm. Hitting him would be demeaning. Steiner let him go, stepped over the

89

shivering body and walked slowly down the stair. He had reached the front door when Janie ran on to the landing and called his name.

'George, don't go, let's talk it out, for God's sake. Is that too much to ask?'

Steiner hesitated for a moment with his hand on the latch. Then he stepped outside and closed the door behind him.

At the corner of the street he hailed a cruising taxi.

'Where to, Guv'nor?' the driver asked, flicking on the meter.

Steiner slumped in his seat, the suitcase propped beneath his elbow. He looked out at the falling rain. Wisps of fog hung between the street lamps. He felt hollowed-out inside, bitter and disgusted.

'Take me to an hotel,' he ordered.

SEVEN

The hills rolled in every direction, starting with the plain, deep green and cluttered with bracken, rising slowly into the first tentative swell of the nearmost hummocks, and finally erupting into a series of jagged peaks and shark-tooth ridges. The sky was a brilliant blue, with just a handful of fleecy white clouds shifting westward like grazing sheep.

Ahead, cliffs of deep brown granite lunged out of a hillside tossed with moorgrass and wiry heather; along its rim, trees, stunted and wind-tossed, leaned hopefully towards the east.

William Mellinger paused for a moment and rested his spine against a boulder, watching Kyle's huge, deceptively spry frame pick its way up the tricky screeslope which fell

90

from the tip of the nearest mountain to the sandy belly of the dried-up river below. Mellinger was sweating freely, glad to be out on this bright blustery autumn morning, glad to be back among hills again, though in truth he did not know which hills. Could be Norway, he thought. They had that feel about them. Deep grassy clumps, heather-clad slopes, a sense of space. And the air smelled thin, clear as chilled wine. Still, it was only a guess. Huntley was right. Mountains looked similar the world over.

He watched Kyle ahead with a sense of hate. The sight of that muscular figure took the edge off his enjoyment. Kyle seemed tireless, a man devoid of fatigue, oblivious to discomfort, a walking, breathing machine for God's sake, not a man.

It was now two days since Mellinger had woken up in the farmhouse, and since then, every hour had been spent in Kyle's company. Kyle slept in a little bungalow at the rear of the farmhouse, and he had insisted that Mellinger slept there too, for although the big man seemed to regard him as being on a different level to his other captives, he took no chances on any attempt at escape.

They had fed on smoked deer-meat and dried berries, which had not been as bad as Mellinger expected for though the venison itself was stringy and needed salting, the berries, which had looked at first glance like balls of dried rabbit dung, had been surprisingly palatable. He was curious how Kyle came to know so much, a man who quite literally could live off the land, providing not only for himself, but for six other mouths too; that took knowledge, a great deal of knowledge, and a great deal of skill.

Kyle was no ordinary man, even without his strength; he belonged to this country, he seemed part of it, an integral part. Take him away and something would be missing. He slotted into place like the mountains themselves.

Mellinger could not work out how Kyle had brought him here, for if there had been a road to the farmhouse it had long since been overgrown with moorgrass, and now only the plain and the rising hills broke the monotony of a landscape as desolate as the surface of the moon.

It was the evenings Mellinger hated most. Kyle did not believe in small-talk, had no interest in it, and seldom answered if spoken to. Worse than that, he seemed oblivious to darkness. When nightfall came, instead of lighting the hurricane lamp which stood on the bungalow table, Kyle sprawled motionless in his chair while shadows gathered in heavy grey folds. He could sit like that for hours, not moving, not speaking. Only his eyes, wide-open, indicated he was still awake. Mellinger hated to be beside him. The hours dragged and he fidgeted incessantly, always aware of this mountain of bone and muscle which crouched in the gathering dark, always grateful when enough of the evening had passed to allow them to turn in to their respective bunks.

He had so far been unable to glean any further information either about Kyle himself, or about the film they were to make, beyond the fact that it involved the deaths of the four people he had seen in the barn. They were undoubtedly the other kidnap victims. The question which plagued Mellinger was, what should he do? The thought of taking on Kyle hand to hand was ludicrous, he knew that. In those massive hands, he would break like a twig. He had considered once or twice hitting Kyle from behind with a rock or a lump of wood, but the memory of Naunton Huntley's broken arm discouraged him, if Kyle began breaking his bones he would be in no fit state to help anyone, much less himself. There had to be another way. Escape, possibly. But where? He did not know how far he would have to travel to safety, or what Kyle would do to his other captives once he realised Mellinger had gone.

The effects of his drug had, happily, long since worn off and he felt almost himself again, especially here among the good wild hills, glad to feel his body responding to the old familiar stretch of muscle and limb. But he was still no match for Kyle. My God, that man. Had he been born like everyone else, out of a union of love or passion? It seemed hard to believe. Kyle showed no evidence of being human, not truly human. He was like a species set apart, dependent on no one, proud of his strength, proud of his self-sufficiency, and totally incapable of normal emotion.

Suddenly Kyle turned and waved him forward, indicating with a slight downward movement of his hand that Mellinger should keep silent. Mellinger forgot, for the moment at least, his worries about tomorrow. He slid across the screeslope, taking care not to disturb the boulders. The wind tugged at his hair. He caught the scent of heather and peat. A steep ravine curved away to his right, matted with scrub and tangled bracken.

When he reached Kyle's side, the big man pointed to a snatch of wind-scoured trees whose roots clutched at the earth like thirsty tentacles.

'Deer sign,' he whispered softly.

Mellinger stared. He could see nothing. Even the grass seemed undisturbed.

'Where?'

Kyle knelt down and pressed his fingers against a tree trunk. A tiny sliver of bark had peeled away, leaving the underwood naked to the wind. Mellinger would never have glanced twice at such a flimsy scratch, but Kyle ran his fingertips along its length and said authoritatively: 'Young buck. He's been rubbing his antlers.'

He felt lower and studied it carefully. Mellinger frowned. He felt out of his depth, caught in mysteries he could only guess at. Christ, I'm out of touch, he thought. Once, he might have been at home here, a hunter stalking his prey. He doubted it. Hunting had never been his game, and besides, there was nothing to see. Only a slight declivity in the grass, and a few bits of crushed fern tossed haphazardly around.

'He lay here,' Kyle whispered softly. He touched the earth with his hand. 'Still warm. Can't be far. Probably following the ridge.'

'How can you tell?'

Kyle moved forward two or three paces and indicated a

narrow imprint in the soft peat. It might have been anything, a furrow caused by a rolling stone, a twig torn from
the dirt by the wind, anything : it was not even complete –
just the tiniest of indentations, almost indistinguishable
between the grass clumps.

'Just been made,' Kyle whispered. 'Moisture hasn't had
time to seep in.'

He peered along the ridge, eyes narrowed against the
wind. The hills swelled into a series of jagged breakers,
their lower flanks almost obscured by a flimsy haze, sun-
tinged in the early morning. To their left, the ground
sloped into a steep-sided valley clustered with pine forest
and threaded by the snail-trail of a gurgling river.

'If you're right,' said Mellinger, 'he must be well ahead
of us, and making for the summit.'

Kyle shook his head.

'A young buck will always circle to the left, particularly
with pine trees down there. He'll head for the woods and
the water. Come on, we'll be waiting when he gets there.'

Kyle zig-zagged off the scree and down the steep valley
wall, moving, Mellinger thought, like a bloody mountain
goat, ignoring the precipitousness of the path, ignoring
gravity, ignoring every damn thing. Look at the bastard
go, he thought. Mellinger watched him in wonder as he
weaved his way through a labyrinth of peat hags. Even in
the mountains, Kyle seemed superhuman, nothing stopped
him, nothing slowed him down.

Mellinger began to follow, trying desperately to catch
up, dodging between the gritstone outcrops till he reached
the peaty trough, then scrambling between the great folds
of slimy bog until, breathless and shivering with exertion,
he joined Kyle on the forest rim. The big man looked at
him and put one finger to his lips.

'He's beaten us to it,' he whispered softly.

Mellinger swallowed. This is crazy, he thought. They
had no weapons, nothing to hunt with. How could they
track down a live deer and kill it with their bare hands?
It was beyond the laws of nature. Kyle turned and ducked

swiftly beneath the thickly-entwined branches, moving with such a liquid gentleness that he seemed no more than a puff of wind. Mellinger followed as best he could, trying to avoid dried-twigs or anything at all which might crack underfoot and give their presence away. He heard birds pouring out a graceful discord. It was good to hear them beneath these pine and spruce boughs, to know he was not alone and that it was still not too late in the year for birdsong. The wind whipped the trees and the branches swayed about his head. He scarcely noticed, so concentrated was his attention. Watch that twig there. Mind the bracken, it'll rustle like fury. Miss that pine cone.

Ahead, the ground sloped into a steep grassy hollow, surrounded by clumps of dying fern. Kyle stopped, and as Mellinger approached, he signalled gently with one hand. There in the clearing, half-obscured by the trees and shafts of filtered sunlight, a roe deer stood nibbling tentatively at the grass. It seemed oblivious of its danger, lost in a world of winter peace and sanctuary.

Kyle signalled to Mellinger to stay where he was. Without a sound, he vanished into the undergrowth. Mellinger stared in amazement. Despite his massive size, Kyle seemed able to drift at will, and without disturbing a blade of grass. Where, Mellinger wondered, had he learned such tricks? He was like a Red Indian brave from centuries back.

In the forest, the deer grazed happily on. Even the ferns were undisturbed. Mellinger sat sniffing the air, keeping his gaze fixed firmly on the clearing ahead. The thought of escape entered his mind once more, but he dismissed it instantly. Where would he go, for God's sake, to escape a creature like Kyle who could move through the hills as fast as a horse, trail a deer with the instinct of a tiger, and kill with his bare hands. No . . . escape, at least for the moment, was out of the question, and Mellinger remained where he was, mouth dry, eyes fixed on the soft brown hide of the animal ahead.

Suddenly the deer stopped grazing and lifted its antlers,

nostrils poised. Something had disturbed it. Mellinger waited, holding his breath. For a full five seconds it stood like that, frozen into immobility, then, with a toss of its bunny white tail it turned and lunged for the woods. Too late. Almost in the same instant, a figure emerged from the ferns, arching high in the air and coming down hard on the animal's spine, one massive arm knotted firmly around the throat, the other fastened tight in the furry antlers.

Mellinger felt his heart swoop as he watched Kyle spread his feet and slowly and deliberately twist the animal's head to the rear. Christ, the strength of the man – it was horrible to see – that poor helpless animal doomed to die in front of his very eyes. The four thin legs thrashed helplessly in the air as Kyle exerted pressure, holding hard, the muscles on his arms bulging through his thin army combat jacket. Poor beast. It didn't have a chance. There was nothing to give it purchase, nothing to get a grip on. Kyle had it in a killer's hold. The deer thrashed like a wild thing, feeling the moment of death approaching. It was done for, its breathing shut off, its windpipe flattened. There was no cough, no final cry. Just a last despairing convulsion, then stillness. Kyle let it drop to the ground. He knelt swiftly, slid his knife from his belt and carefully sliced its jugular. Lifting the inert body as lightly as if it had been a rag doll, he let the blood pump into his mouth like a peasant drinking from a wine-skin. Mellinger moved out of the forest, watching him in disgust. He had never seen Kyle look more primitive, more sub-human than at this moment. The big man stopped drinking and looked at Mellinger with blood dripping from his chin. He held the deer aloft, inviting Mellinger to join him, but Mellinger shook his head. Kyle shrugged and tossed the lifeless carcass across his shoulder. He cleaned his knife by plunging it into the soil, then re-sheathed it and began to climb from the forest, moving diagonally up the hill towards the scree. Mellinger followed. He felt sick inside. They needed food, of course they did, he knew that. But not like this. Kyle's method of killing upset him, and the sight of Kyle drinking blood had been like a fragment from some long-forgotten childhood nightmare.

He stumbled up to Kyle's side, filled with a sense of blank despair.

'Tomorrow,' Kyle said conversationally, 'we begin the film.'

Mellinger was startled. It was the first time in two days that Kyle had actually volunteered information, the first time in fact that he had bothered to speak without first being spoken to. Now Mellinger forgot the deer and his brain began to race as he asked, casually: 'You still haven't told me what it's about.'

No answer. Mellinger wiped his face on his shirtsleeve.

'You weren't serious about . . . about killing those people?'

'You know I'm serious.'

'But why? What have they done to you?'

Kyle grunted.

'It's because of what they've done to humanity that they must die.'

Humanity? Mellinger stared at him wryly. Kyle and humanity seemed poles apart. They went on scrambling upwards, Kyle moving as delicately as a ballet dancer, seemingly oblivious to the weight across his shoulder, Mellinger following close behind, keeping up with an effort. His brain felt light. He concentrated on the roughness of the slope.

'At least tell me what they're guilty of,' he said at last. 'It must be something bad, I mean really bad, for you to want to kill them like that. Tell me, and let's discuss it. Who knows, perhaps they're innocent.'

Kyle laughed humourlessly, and Mellinger sighed. As they stumbled on he stared again at Kyle's ridiculous wig: it was not even a decent fit, and to make matters worse, a threaded seam showed quite plainly along its parting. Whatever reason the man had for wearing it, it certainly wasn't vanity.

'What purpose can this film possibly serve?' Mellinger demanded.

'It'll be a warning,' Kyle said. 'They'll be the first, but not the last.'

Mellinger ignored his remark.

'I take it you've got the necessary equipment,' he said.

Kyle nodded.

'An Eclair A.C.L. with a ten to one. Plus an infra-red lens for shooting at night.' He glanced at Mellinger. 'The filming's my job,' he said. 'Your job is to report.'

'On the murder of four innocent people?'

Kyle frowned.

'Not murder,' he said. 'Retribution.'

Mellinger shook his head in disgust. He knew enough to realise he was not talking to a rational man. Kyle's reluctance to converse, his clipped sentences, his dogged rhetoric suggested an unbalanced mind. Mellinger decided to proceed more cautiously.

'Listen,' he said, 'I'm sure you've got your reasons but you must see this whole thing is ridiculous. Those people down there, they've done nothing; they're very ordinary, they lead ordinary lives. They're not politically motivated, they're not evil, or perverse, or potentially dangerous. They're just very ordinary.'

Kyle glanced at him.

'Have you ever met them?'

'No.'

'Then how can you say that?'

'Because I've studied their backgrounds, that's why. I went through the newspaper cuttings before I travelled to Belfast.'

Kyle's face was inscrutable. They moved on to the scree and slid across it to the winding ridge. Beyond, the plain lay in an unending vista of grey and brown, dotted with cloud shadows and the almost indiscernible sprawl of their farm.

'They will be an example,' Kyle said, 'for others.'

Mellinger almost groaned. The man was insane. Nothing disturbed him, nothing penetrated that hard impervious shell. He could not be talked to, pleaded or reasoned with.

Mellinger hesitated.

'How do you . . . how do you plan to do it?'

Kyle shrugged.

'Like the deer.'

'With your hands?'

'It's better that way. There is contact. A bullet is too impersonal. I want them to know that they are dying, and who is killing them.'

Mellinger spat angrily into the dust.

'At least the deer had a chance,' he snapped. 'He could've run.'

'They will have the same chance,' Kyle said calmly. He paused and stared out across the hills, the wind plucking at his wig. 'Look,' he murmured, 'it's good here, a good land. A place to feel free, with clean air, and emptiness. When you learn to survive in country like this, then the land itself is kind. It provides for all your needs. It takes you to its breast like a mother. That way – westward – lies a village. Safety. It is nineteen miles. I will give them one hour's start. If they can reach it, using the land to help them, then they will have earned their freedom and have learned something on the way.' He looked at Mellinger. 'I do not believe they will survive however,' he added, 'for they are weak and useless and deserve to die.'

Mellinger studied him in disbelief.

'A hunt?'

'That's right.'

'You're going to hunt them like animals?'

'Would you prefer I killed them like chickens in a coop?'

Mellinger shook his head helplessly.

'But they're city people, all of them. You can't turn them loose in country like this. They won't have a chance.'

'They'll have you,' Kyle said softly. 'You will be their guide, you could lead them across the mountains to safety.

You said yourself this is your kind of country.'

'But I thought . . .'

Kyle smiled thinly.

'Don't worry, you won't be harmed. I need you for later, after the filming's finished. We'll record the commentary on ¼ inch tape. I'll tell you what to write, but some of it you must write yourself. I want you to explain how it feels to be hunted, to die slowly in the wilderness, helpless and lost. Afterwards, when the film has been shown, you and Huntley will be free to go.'

Mellinger stared at him in silence, appalled by the inevitability of Kyle's plan, a pattern so neat, so preordained that he felt within himself it was bound to happen. A hunt. With human prey. Across a landscape as inhospitable as a Dali nightmare. He looked at the thick corded hands and remembered how they had crushed the throat of the little roe buck. Kyle would kill them one by one, four innocent people, because of some fancied discourtesy in his twisted mind. And only he, Mellinger, stood in his way. It was a monstrous responsibility to shoulder.

Kyle hoisted the carcass into a more comfortable position.

'Let's go,' he said, 'it's time for you to join your new companions. If you're going to write about them, it's important you taste the full extent of their terror.'

EIGHT

George Steiner walked down the corridor to his office, an angry man. His experience of the night before, his confrontation with his wife, had left him restless and irritable. In the hotel afterwards, he had lain for hours staring at the ceiling and when, towards dawn, he had at last slipped into unconsciousness, so exhausted was he that he had slept through his morning call and was arriving now nearly two hours late, angry both with himself and the world in general.

As he stepped into the outer office, the faces at the desks peered at him curiously. The room was a hotch-potch of confusion, as it always was at ten-thirty in the morning : papers, crumpled and torn, lay scattered around the linoleum floor : cardboard cups, with coffee dregs still inside them, dotted the desktops : the other detectives, most of them in shirtsleeves, dialled phones, scribbled notes on official forms or simply leaned back in their chairs and watched the rain hammer monotonously at the double-glazed windows.

Barry Fawkes, a sheaf of folders in his hand, looked at Steiner with surprise.

'Mornin' Guv'nor. Christ, you must've had a hell of a night – you look like death.'

'Never mind the bright remarks,' Steiner snapped. 'Those lists in yet ?'

'You're in a mood all right.'

'Hey Harvey,' Steiner barked, 'get me some coffee in here, will you ? I've got a head that's lifting off.'

Harvey, pot-bellied, pink-cheeked, forty-two, made a sign like pulling a lavatory chain. But he got to his feet nevertheless, shuffling off with a sigh in the direction of the canteen.

Steiner stepped into the little glass cubicle which served as his office, and tossed his coat across the spare chair. Fawkes followed him in, still wielding his sheaf of files.

'You sure you're all right, George,' he muttered nervously, studying his superior's gloomridden face.

'Top of the world,' Steiner snapped. 'What've you got there ?'

Fawkes put the files on the desk.

'The last of the names,' he said. 'They came in this morning.'

'Good work,' Steiner grunted.

Fawkes shook his head.

'You won't think that when you look at them. Nothing checks.'

'Are you sure?'

'Sorry Guv'. It was a great idea, it just hasn't come off.'

Steiner swore, disappointment flooding through him. He had been counting on those lists. He sat down at the desk and reached for them resignedly.

'Let's have a butcher's,' he sighed. 'Sometimes you never know what you're looking for till you've found it.'

'I've been right through them, Guv'.'

'I know, I know: I'll just give them the once-over to set my mind at rest. Anything in on the aircraft?'

'I'm still following that one up.'

'What about the equipment manufacturers?'

'They're phoning back this morning.'

'Okay, let me know if anything develops. In the meantime, keep everybody out of here apart from Harvey with the coffee. If there's anything at all in these files, I don't care how small or insignificant it looks, I intend to bloody well dig it out.'

'Okay Guv' it's your morning.'

Fawkes closed the door behind him, and for the next sixty minutes George Steiner went through the lists from the TV companies, checking each individual name against the pilot licence file. It was boring time-consuming work, and his mind inevitably kept drifting back to the memory of his wife. He saw her naked, frozen in that moment of climax he had witnessed the night before, head back, lips drawn tight in an expression of ecstasy. A shiver touched his neck, a serve-you-bloody-right barb from times when he had been harder on himself, and when the world and everyone in it had seemed part of a clearly-defined pattern of right and wrong, where issues, consequences and events were sharply-enough etched to reach some kind of conclusion and understanding. Now that world had hit him smack between the eyes. The image of his wife danced in his brain. His concentration was shot to blazes. He felt relieved when Barry Fawkes peered in again, his pale cheeks tinged with colour.

'Couple of things you might find interesting, Guv'.'

'Uh-huh?'

'First, an Eclair film camera was stolen from an ITN news crew operating in Belfast three weeks ago.'

'That so?' said Steiner.

'Two nights later, an image intensifier was taken from the same team near Crossmaglen.'

'An image what?'

'Image intensifier. That's an electronic attachment which picks up any minute source of light – a star, a cigarette end, even a reflection in a pool of water – and magnifies it many times over. The army use them for shooting at night. They assumed of course that the theft had been carried out by the IRA and that the intensifier was now being adapted for use by terrorist snipers.'

'And isn't it?'

'Well, here's the thing, Commander. This image intensifier was designed for shooting film stories in the dark.'

Steiner sat back in his chair. It could be pure chance, but he didn't think so.

'That *is* interesting,' he said.

'I thought so, Guv'. It's a special infra-red lens, made for fitting on to an Eclair A.C.L.'

'Anything else?'

'Well, reports are still coming in from Europe. All the registered landings in France and Holland have been accounted for. I'm still waiting for word from Spain, Germany and Switzerland. However, listen to this: "On August 17th, a Britten-Norman Islander was stolen from MacLaren's Air Company at Mulgye in Scotland." An Islander is a small twin-engined job built specially for rough country. It can land and take off on a beach, a field, almost anywhere at all that's reasonably flat for twenty or thirty yards. MacLaren's run a passenger and freight service in the far north. It's one of the most remote regions in Britain, nothing but hill country and a few scattered farms and villages. To tell the truth, the service wouldn't pay if it wasn't sponsored by the Highlands and Islands Board.'

'Who lives up there?'

'Sheep farmers, shepherds, a few forestry workers.'

'That all?'

'That's all now. The S.A.S. used to use it as a training ground up to four years ago.'

Steiner started.

'Who?'

'You know . . . Special Air Service.'

Steiner frowned, his mind racing. Why had he pricked up his ears at the mention of the S.A.S.? He spread the papers out in front of him and quickly scanned the names. Yes, there it was. 'Jonathan Kyle: ex-Special Air Service. Joined Tyne Tees Television, Newcastle, worked processing and editing departments, left after fourteen months. Present whereabouts unknown.'

Steiner thoughtfully rubbed the back of his neck. He got to his feet and strode into the outer office. Fawkes followed, puzzled.

'Hey Gerald,' shouted Steiner, 'weren't you in the S.A.S.?'

A stocky fresh-faced detective, mid-thirtyish, looked up at Steiner and shook his head.

'Naw,' he said. 'Marines.'

'Ever have anything to do with them?'

'Those bastards.'

'Didn't like them, huh?'

Gerald shrugged.

'Aahh, they were all right. It's just . . . ' He grinned. 'Well, jealousy, I suppose. They were the cream, weren't they, the fucking elite.'

Steiner stood looking down at him thoughtfully. An idea was formulating in his brain. He sat on the edge of the desk.

'Tell me about them,' he commanded.

104

Gerald shrugged.

'What's to tell? They're the top secret branch of the British army. Nobody knows anything about them, certainly not me.'

'Secret, hey?'

'Yeah. The newspapers call them the James Bond soldiers. That's a good description. The S.A.S. are the army's secret agents.'

'What are they used for?'

'Christ knows. They're a law unto themselves. Story is, they're the first ones into a trouble spot and the last ones out, but that's only a story – they never discuss their operations.'

'Haven't there been nasty rumours that they're a kind of British Gestapo organisation?'

'Oh, that's just journalistic mud-slinging. They were founded by Stirling in North Africa in 1941, primarily for carrying out raids behind enemy lines. At the end of the war they were disbanded, but later reformed and were used for jungle operations in Malaya during the fifties, and then in Oman, Indonesia, Borneo, and against the rebels in Aden.'

'Ulster too?'

'Yes, that's common knowledge. The rest is only hearsay.'

'Tell me about the hearsay.'

Gerald grinned.

'Well, you can get it from any newspaper file, but they're said to be the most highly-trained unit in the British army. They're toughened up like prize-fighters, and I mean not just physically, but mentally too. They're trained to withstand torture, interrogation, and to keep on going when every last shred of strength and will-power has been shot to hell. The story is, their initiation course is so tough that only a tenth of the volunteers who start out manage to see it through. They specialise in fieldcraft, survival, tracking, infiltrating enemy lines, unarmed combat, mountain warfare, that sort of thing. They wear no badges, and what's more aren't subject to the rules and regulations the rest of the Army has to abide by. I remember how they used to arrive at our camp in the dead of night and refuse to identify themselves. If any of our officers got shirty with them, they'd more or less tell him to get stuffed. They were arrogant bastards, hard and cocky and sure of themselves, but I've got to admit it – they were a crack mob.'

'What about flying?'

'Huh?'

'Could a member of the S.A.S. be taught to fly without being officially registered as a pilot?'

Gerald looked puzzled.

'Hell, I don't know, George. I don't think flying comes into their regular schedule, but I imagine a man could be selected for special duties and then taught to fly. If that was so, then I reckon they'd try to keep his name off the official register. They're shit-hot on security.'

'How would we find out?'

'Get in touch with their H.Q. at Hereford. Mind you, I'm not saying it'll do any good. Extracting information from the S.A.S. is tougher than drawing teeth.'

Steiner turned to Barry Fawkes.

'Get on to Hereford,' he ordered crisply, 'and talk to their commanding officer. See what you can discover about this Jonathan Kyle. In particular, we want to know if he was ever taught to fly a plane, and if possible where he's living now. If they give you any trouble, put the call through to me.'

'Okay, Guv'.'

Steiner got up. He knew the call was just another long-shot but he'd based his whole career on long-shots. What was more, with only five days to go to D-Day, he could think of no other way to turn. He moved to the map of Europe which covered more than half the office wall, and stood studying it thoughtfully, eyes narrowed.

'I wonder where those bastards are,' he whispered.

Gerald shrugged, but did not answer. Steiner thumped the map with his fist, making the wall tremble.

'Wherever it is,' he said, 'sooner or later they've got to make a mistake. And when they do, we'll be waiting.'

It was eight o'clock in the evening, and the little bar on Birmingham's Grey Street was almost empty. Ted Riggins, the publican, stood behind his counter and watched his only group of customers weaving drunkenly in the corner. Jesus Christ, how could people get that soused in less than an hour-and-a-half? Four years he had spent building up his pub's good name, and still you got the odd out-of-towner who came in looking for a fight. And Ted Riggins had no doubt at all that there was going to be a fight. He had seen it the instant those two had walked in, a hard-faced pair, young and tough as nails. Probably fresh out of prison, if he was any kind of judge. Criminals certainly, he knew the type. In his early years, Riggins had worked as a barman in the East End of London and he'd seen them all in his day: the Krays, the Richardsons, and some of the tougher boys who were far too smart ever to allow their names to appear in the press. He had become a dab hand at recognising villains, and not only recognising but categorising them too. This pair he placed way down the list. Toughies yes, but strictly the hired help variety. Probably heavies employed by some local gang. And out to celebrate a windfall, judging by the determined way they were knocking back the booze. Things might have been okay if that damned kid hadn't come in. Well, it wasn't so much the kid as his girlfriend. She was a real looker, long-legged, high-breasted, and with a crazy tangle of hair falling all the way to her shoulders.

The villains had spotted her the minute she'd entered the door, and for the next half-hour had stood casting sneering glances at the booth where she and her boyfriend had seated themselves. Amazingly, the kid seemed oblivious to the situation. Riggins had toyed with the idea of warning the couple to get out, but dammit business was business; he couldn't afford to turn custom away. Besides, if anyone should leave, then by God it ought to be this pair. But the two men showed no signs of leaving. They went on filling themselves with drink, peering and sniggering. In the end, Riggins supposed, they had finally grown bored. Or tired with just looking. As calm as you please they had gone over and introduced themselves. Just like that. And the idiot kid still hadn't recognised the danger signs. Now the four of them were sitting in the booth, chatting away like old friends. It was only a matter of time, Riggins knew, before that conversation erupted into violence. He had seen it all before.

With a sigh, Riggins leaned up off the counter and went into the office. Might as well tip off the Old Bill now as later. Not that they could do anything before the action started, but at least, with a little warning, they might be quicker off the mark.

Ted Riggins hated contacting the police at the best of times. Once they got it into their heads that your pub was a hot spot, they were more bloody trouble than they were worth; always popping in to check on your clientele, or to see if you were serving after closing time. Riggins had worked hard to get away from that kind of harassment, and having built up his reputation he hated to tarnish it by reporting the possibility of a brawl. But the alternative might be even worse. Smashed-up furniture or a badly-injured customer could close him down for a week.

He had the phone in his hand when he heard the girl scream and realised he was already too late. From the other room came the tinkle of glass and the unmistakable grunts of combat. With a resigned sigh, Ted Riggins replaced the receiver and walked back into the bar. The girl was crouched in the corner of the booth, her pale face contorted with terror. Her boyfriend lay sprawled on the floor between the tables, and the two thugs were taking it in turns to kick him, not with anger or passion but coolly and deliberately, choosing their time, picking their target.

Ted Riggins knew better than to interfere in a fight like

108

this. He had seen too many publicans finish up in a hospital bed for defending their customers too enthusiastically, and he never forgot old Charlie Stacey who had tried to rescue a young man from a group of Scunley's commandos, and had spent the rest of his life in a stinking wheelchair. No, Ted Riggins had no intention of getting involved, at least in the physical sense, but he ran through the back office and into the street, shouting for help. The pavements were empty, the traffic slid implacably by. He raced around the corner, and by a miracle a police patrol car was cruising sedately along the line of the kerb. Riggins waved his hands and it slid to a halt. Four faces peered out at him through the windows.

'Fight,' he stammered hoarsely. 'Two bastards've got a kid in the bar there. They're bloody murdering him.'

The constables did not wait to ask questions. The doors burst open, they scrambled into the street and disappeared at the double into Ted Riggins's pub. By the time Riggins found the breath and energy to follow them, the ruckus was already over. The two tearaways, faces bloodied, were squatting on the floor beside the bar, silent and subdued. One of the constables was trying to console the girl who was sobbing hysterically. A second was down on his hands and knees, studying the senseless figure of her boyfriend.

'Better get an ambulance, Les,' he said to one of his companions, 'he looks in a bad way.'

He glanced up at Riggins.

'What happened?' he asked.

Riggins told him the story and the young policeman listened in silence. When Riggins had finished, he said: 'We'll need it in writing. I'll come back later, once we've got this lot sorted out. Make the boy as comfortable as you can, will you. The ambulance should be here in a jiffy. In the meantime, we'll take care of these two jokers.'

He glared at the two men in front of the counter.

'Up,' he commanded shortly.

They scrambled to their feet and stood, silent and contrite, staring at the ground. Sods, Riggins thought. Now that they had been arrested, they looked as harmless as a couple of boy scouts. The constable however, was unimpressed.

'Outside,' he snarled.

The two villains shuffled forward. Their heads were bowed, their faces, smeared with their own blood, displayed no expression whatsoever. As they passed the window sill, Riggins saw one of them slip something into his artificial plant. He frowned. What the hell was that? Drugs? Obviously something they didn't want the Old Bill to discover. It had to be drugs. Ted Riggins swore under his breath. That was all he needed, for Christ's sake. Heroin in his plantpot. That could close him down for good.

He watched the constables hustle their prisoners through the door, and peered swiftly around. The young man was still senseless on the floor. The fourth policeman was sitting with his arm around the girl, holding her tight as she sobbed against his shoulder. Her entire body trembled with the force of her weeping. The policeman was trying to comfort her, and dry her face at the same time.

Ted Riggins stepped to the window sill. He slipped his hand inside the plantpot. His fingers closed on something solid. It was a cigarette lighter. He turned it over, frowning. Something on its side caught his eye; an inscription. He held it to the light. The inscription said:

WITH AFFECTION AND ADMIRATION,
FROM THE ROYAL TELEVISION SOCIETY
TO NAUNTON F. HUNTLEY

NINE

The door slammed. Mellinger heard the key turn in the lock, and for a moment he stood where he was, accustoming his eyes to the sudden change in light.

The barn, or what had once been a barn, was surprisingly cosy inside. Although the walls were built of bare stone, a huge fireplace in the corner gave the room a sense of cheerful warmth. No barn this, he thought, at least, not any longer. Someone long ago had converted it into a comfortable dwelling house with a wooden stairway leading to a small shadow-clustered loft, a table, a few scattered chairs, some ancient crockery and – as the single ornament – a painted wagonwheel suspended from the ceiling like a chandelier : it looked out of place somehow, an affectation. The floor, like the farmhouse itself, was built of stone.

The log fire cast a flickering light across the hearth, picking out the shadows, casting orange patterns across the four people who crouched within its glow. They, like Huntley, were firmly shackled but, like Huntley, the chains on their ankles were sufficiently long to allow them access to what Mellinger assumed was the bathroom, and to the line of bunks which stood against the opposite wall. It had all been meticulously thought out. The captives, kidnapped one by one, had been secured in such a way as to allow them mobility without including freedom. A clever touch, they could move as they wished, but always within the boundaries which Kyle imposed.

Mellinger stepped forward, feeling the heat from the fire strike his face and chest. He needed no introductions to tell him who the captives were. In some strange way, each seemed to reflect his background in his appearance. The tall weedy man with the world-weary face had to be Philip Goodman. His pale cheeks and slightly-ruffled civility suggested a lifetime of business luncheons, board meetings and cool decisions behind locked office doors. The fleshy man with the scraggy eyebrows would be Michael Jacobs, the Birmingham manufacturer. His thick neck and chunky shoulders carried an air of purpose and determination. He looked like a man who had dragged himself up from nothing by sheer willpower. The thin anaemic one with the stubby nose and receding hairline was probably Nelson Mackey, the Cumbrian plumber. And of course the girl, blonde, big-eyed, with a strong explicit body, had to be Marian Edwards.

They were watching him, all of them, with a guarded hostility. He knew they were ready to hurl themselves at his throat, to make him suffer as they themselves were suffering, for unlike Kyle, he had no charismatic strength to discourage them.

'Who the bloody hell are you?' snapped Michael Jacobs.

'My name is William Mellinger,' he answered calmly.

Jacobs rose, small, fat and belligerent.

'Kyle's man?'

'I'm his prisoner. Like you.'

'Liar,' hissed the girl. She was watching him with a look of glittering hate. Her hair was loose and tangled, giving her a slightly unhinged appearance. Her lips, full and sensual, were drawn flat against pale even teeth. The force of her emotion was so intense that Mellinger almost shrank from it. He looked at her.

'It's the truth.'

'Then why aren't you chained?'

'No point,' said Mellinger, 'Kyle knows I won't try to escape.'

'He does, eh?' echoed Goodman, rising to stand beside Jacobs.

'He knows there'd be no sense in it,' Mellinger said.

112

On the floor, Mackey, the plumber, laughed humourlessly.

'Christ, just give us the chance.'

'Yes,' Jacobs grunted; he tugged at his ankle chain. 'If we could slip out of these, I'd like to see that bastard try and catch us.'

'He intends to,' said Mellinger. 'Tomorrow.'

'What do you mean?'

'He's turning you loose.'

For a moment he thought they had not heard him. No sound penetrated the walls of the old grey barn. Only the crackling of the logs in the grate, and the rustle of the girl as she climbed to her feet broke the stillness. The firelight cast a crimson backcloth which illuminated the outlines of the people standing before it. The farthest corners of the room were hung with darkness. Only here was there light, and warmth, and movement. Mellinger waited. Something like a sigh broke from Goodman's lips.

'Are you serious?' he whispered.

'Absolutely.'

'Free?'

'Not free, loose, there's a difference.'

Mellinger hesitated. This was the moment he had been dreading. He knew it was cruel to wait, to put off telling them even for a second longer, and he hated Kyle then, hated him more strongly than at any point since his capture, for it was not by accident that Kyle had given him the burden of explaining. Slowly, hesitantly, he sketched in the events of the past few days bringing them up to date for, of course, none of them knew about Huntley, or about the letter, or for that matter about himself. They listened without a word, absorbing everything in silence, but when he reached the bit about Kyle's plan to hunt them to their deaths, he saw fear spring into their eyes. That bastard, he thought. If he terrified Mellinger, how much more terrifying would he seem to these four who had spent weeks in his company? By the time he had finished, Mellinger's throat felt choked, his hands icy.

'My God,' Goodman breathed. His voice was strangely hollow in the stone-walled room.

'I'm sorry,' said Mellinger.

Goodman rubbed his cheeks with his hands.

'So he's going to hunt us down like animals.'

'That's right.'

Mackey, the plumber, gave a little choking sob.

'I knew we would never get out of this alive, I knew it.'

'Don't talk like that,' snapped the girl.

'But he's going to kill us all.'

Mellinger stared at him, frowning.

'Do you know why?' he asked, 'Why you four? There's got to be a reason.'

Goodman shrugged.

'There *is* no reason.'

'There must be,' Mellinger said. 'There must be something you've all got in common. If we could work out what it is, maybe we could talk him out of it.'

The girl shook her head helplessly.

'But we'd never met before . . . before this. None of us have anything in common, anything at all.'

'Can't you see?' Goodman insisted, 'whatever Kyle thinks he's achieving in that twisted mind of his, that's why he chose us. Not because we're in any way similar, but because we're all so different.'

Mellinger was silent for a moment. He was not entirely convinced, but there were other more pressing problems on hand. He moved into the firelight to warm himself and they stepped aside to let him through. Their hostility was gone, but something else had taken its place. Mellinger knew what it was. Dependency. They were depending on him. God help them, he thought. He felt as trapped as they did, as terrified, and as helpless. It was a grisly future for all of them, with one subtle difference – Kyle, if he was to be believed, had promised Mellinger immunity. Could he trust that bastard? Even if he could, it didn't alter the unarguable fact that he, and only he,

114

stood between these people and certain death. Across the hills lay safety. It was up to him to get them there. In his mind the doom bells rang – not for him, but for those who relied upon his protection. They made a sombre sound.

'We've got nearly eight hours till morning,' he said crisply. 'We'd better sit down and work out what we're going to do.'

'What can we do, for God's sake?' Mackey spluttered.

'Well, for starters, we can cut out this doom and gloom. If we're going to stand any chance against Kyle, we'll need all the positive thinking we can get.'

Goodman stared at him.

'You could escape,' he said suddenly, 'you're not chained. You could get out tonight, through the door, through the roof. We'll help.'

Mellinger shook his head.

'As soon as Kyle discovered I'd gone, he'd finish off the lot of you.'

The thought of that seemed to sober them. They stood in silence, the firelight giving their faces an eerie sheen. Mellinger's thighs twitched a bit from the exertions of the afternoon. He was glad to be here in front of this roaring fire. It was bitterly cold outside, and his muscles needed warmth and rest.

'Is he alone?' he asked, 'Kyle, I mean.'

They nodded.

'Naunton Huntley said he'd heard other voices.'

'That was probably us,' Jacobs muttered. 'We've talked together quite a lot. There's been precious little else to do.'

'So it looks as though Kyle is our only captor.'

Jacobs turned to look at him, frowning. His fleshy cheeks and scraggy eyebrows seemed unreal in the crimson glow.

'We could take him on hand to hand,' he said. 'There are five of us now.'

'I've thought of that,' Mellinger grunted, 'it's a possibility. Trouble is, you haven't seen Kyle in action and I

115

have. We might pull it off, but I can't be certain.'

'But if we all attacked at the same time?'

'Let's keep it in reserve, shall we? The way I see it, we've nothing to gain by trying to resist him at this late stage. If he's turning us loose in the morning, we might as well go along with it. That's open hill country out there – we stand every chance in the world of shaking him off. He might be an expert at tracking deer, but human beings can think for themselves. I believe we can trick him. The important thing is to stick together. We'll arm ourselves on the way – there'll be plenty of sticks and rocks up there – and if Kyle does manage to catch us up, we can try taking him on as a group.'

He was lying of course. Against Kyle, he himself didn't stand a chance, and one look at the others told him they wouldn't either. But he had to give them something to believe in.

Jacobs was nodding thoughtfully.

'Makes sense,' he muttered.

Mellinger took a deep breath.

'Let's look at the facts then. We don't know where we are, except that we're in the middle of a range of mountains and we've got to cross them to safety. Is there anyone here who's had experience in hill walking or mountaineering?'

They shook their heads in silence. Mellinger compressed his lips.

'That's what I was afraid of. So with the exception of myself, we're all absolute beginners. Kyle, on the other hand, can move across this terrain like a mountain goat. Hardly an even match, is it?'

'Once we get into those hills, we can hide,' said Goodman.

'That's true,' Mellinger agreed, 'or we can make a dash for safety. According to Kyle, the nearest village is nineteen miles.'

'What sort of a start do we get?'

'One hour.'

Mackey looked hopeful.

'That's not bad. We could cover five miles in that time, if we put our minds to it.'

'Don't kid yourself,' said Mellinger. 'Nineteen miles along a flat tarmac road and nineteen miles across wild hill country are entirely different things. In this kind of terrain I count myself lucky if I can keep up two miles per hour. In your case, since none of you are used to it, and let's face it, none of you are dressed for it either, I'd say we'll be lucky to manage one mile.'

Goodman's face filled with dismay.

'One mile? God, that's not much of an edge.'

'Not with Kyle.'

'We don't stand much of a chance then?'

Mellinger glanced from one to the other and felt his insides dissolve. They were dressed for the city, every last one of them. Suits, leather shoes, Mackey dammit was even wearing slippers. At least the girl, Marian Edwards, had on slacks rather than a skirt. But even without the threat of Kyle, they'd be lucky to last the day if the weather turned against them.

'I'm sorry,' he said, 'you're quite right. It's not much of a chance at all. We've no food and no decent equipment. You're inexperienced, and possibly out of condition. In normal circumstances, going into the hills like that would be lunacy, but we've got to give it a try, because the alternative is too horrible to think about.'

Their faces did not change. He hated what he saw there: trust, reliance. What did they think he was, a miracle worker? He sighed.

'Better get some sleep,' he advised. 'We'll need all the strength we've got in the morning.'

George Steiner took the train to Birmingham and found Detective Superintendent Brockway waiting for him at New Street station. Brockway was a big clean-cut Irishman with a bright cheery face, and hair so neatly trimmed that it always looked to Steiner as though it had been painted on as an afterthought. He had worked with Brockway some years before, and liked him immensely. Now, he returned the Superintendent's grin affectionately as the two men shook hands on the station platform.

'You're looking older, Commander,' Brockway said, 'that London smog's spoiling your complexion.'

'Never mind the compliments, Stan,' Steiner chuckled, 'just fill me in on our way to the nick.'

They passed through the crowd and strolled out to the taxi rank where the police car was waiting. The rain that had fallen all day had slackened off to a dreary drizzle, and Steiner could see the lights of Birmingham twinkling merrily through its haze. The road shone like polished tar, and the tall phalanx of the Rotunda building dominated the skyline.

Steiner settled himself comfortably beside Brockway in the rear seat.

'It happened by accident,' Brockway explained, 'a barroom brawl, nothing special, just a couple of tearaways taking it out on some poor kid who'd gone in for a drink with his girl. Then, after they'd been nicked, the pubowner spotted one of them slipping something into his plantpot. Well, he thought at first it was drugs, so he went and dug it out. And what d'you think it turned out to be but none other than Naunton Huntley's lighter.'

'So what did you do?'

'Turned the two of them out, good and proper. At first they weren't talking, a real couple of tough nuts. But when we threatened them with a murder charge, Henry Gardner broke down and blamed his partner. Said it was the partner who was responsible for the BBC shooting.'

'Who's his partner?'

'Young thug called Tony Renfrew.' He looked at Steiner with a tight little smile on his lips. 'Here's the interesting thing though. Both men were carrying wads of fivers, all hot.'

'Same job?'

'No. They came from a series of four bank raids over

118

the past three years. They denied them, of course. Said the money came by way of payment from a man called Frith.'

'Who's he?'

Brockway grinned.

'Don't be impatient, Commander. I hate to spoil a good story by giving away the punchline. Why not let Gardner tell it.'

At the police station, Brockway led Steiner down a maze of corridors to the interview room. A constable with a bandaged forearm gave him a cup of lukewarm coffee. Sitting in front of the desk, waiting, was Henry Gardner. Steiner had never seen Gardner before, but he knew the type. To Steiner's mind, small-time hoodlums looked very much alike. Perhaps it was that streak of similarity, or uniformity which kept them in the small-time. Gardner looked typical of a thousand others Steiner had seen during his years on the force : young, garishly dressed – and cocky with it, Steiner imagined, although most of his cockiness had drained from his sallow features and he looked, now, nervous, fidgety, anxious to please.

'Sit straight, Gardner,' Brockway commanded.

Gardner looked startled. For a moment, Steiner studied him in silence. The young thug tried to return his gaze, but gave it up in the end. Steiner felt cold, filled with a sense of inner certainty. The thing he had been waiting for had finally happened. The kidnappers had made their first mistake. Steiner knew he would get a confession out of this young man if he had to wring it out piece by piece. He knew, because the lives of six innocent people depended on it.

'You're in a right mess this time,' he growled acidly.

Gardner jumped as though he had been pinched.

'Me?' he echoed with feigned innocence, his voice thin and quavery.

'What a charge sheet. Kidnapping, murder, armed rob...'

Gardner leaned forward, his face bright with alarm.

119

'Now wait a minute . . . ' he began.

But Steiner wasn't in the mood for waiting. Gardner was close to breaking point, he could see that. Someone – Brockway probably – had frightened the living daylights out of him. All it needed now was a little more pressure.

'We're going to drop on you, Gardner,' Steiner hissed, 'from a very great height.'

'No,' whispered Gardner, his face turning slack with fear. He looked helplessly at Brockway.

'You promised . . . ' he moaned.

'Shut up,' Brockway snapped.

'But . . . '

'Shut up, you whining little prick.'

Gardner's eyes flickered. Steiner could see the fear in them now, could smell the scent of it emanating from Gardner's pores. Steiner sat silent, waiting. Sweat beaded Gardner's forehead, and his eyes filled with hopeless defeat. Steiner felt no sense of sympathy. Gardner was a thug, pure and simple. He had nearly kicked a boy to death that night before. If he was suffering now, he deserved it.

'Listen,' Gardner quavered, 'you've got to believe me. I didn't have nothing to do with them things, the bank jobs and all. And the shooting. That was Tony.'

'Tony?'

'Yeah, he done that. You couldn't blame him for it though. It was Frith. He was frightened of Frith.'

Steiner took out a packet of cigarettes and gave one to Brockway. He was watching Gardner intently, his mind sharp as a razor.

'Who's Frith?' he whispered.

Gardner's face looked ghastly.

'I dunno. I dunno who he is.'

'Does he have a first name?'

'Frith was all he called himself.'

Steiner slipped his cigarette lighter into his trouser pocket.

'Maybe you'd better tell me from the beginning,' he ordered.

Gardner sighed. His eyes were blank, and the muscles around his lips were beginning to tremble. He looked like a man losing control of himself.

'Tony and me,' he said, 'we're in this pub one night, see? It was the Nelson on the Bayswater Road. This geezer, this Frith, he comes up and says he can put something our way. Wages like, not a van job. That's how we begun the snatches, the first five anyhow. That last one, in Belfast, we didn't have nothing to do with.'

Steiner took the cigarette from his mouth and stared at Gardner through narrowed eyes.

'This man, Frith, what did he look like?'

Gardner shuddered.

'Like nothing you never saw before. He was built like a tank. And his face . . . Christ, you should've seen his face. It was . . .' Gardner ran his fingers over his cheeks, searching for the word. ' . . . it was like plastic, all smooth and glossy. He was bonkers, we both knew it, away with the angels, but he paid us on the nail after every job.'

Steiner nodded at the wads of fivers Brockway had laid upon the desk.

'With those?' he murmured.

'Yeah. We didn't know they was hot, did we?'

'You'll have a hell of a job proving that, my old son.'

Gardner looked indignant.

'Listen, I'm telling you everything I know, ain't I? That stands for something, don't it?' He waved at Brockway. 'He promised . . .'

'Never mind what he promised,' Steiner snarled. 'Start worrying about what I promise. Because I promise, Gardner, that you'll go down for life if you don't give me something a little more solid to go on.'

Gardner crouched back in his chair. Panic shone clearly in his eyes. He looked at Brockway. Brockway stared steadily back.

'Listen,' Gardner croaked, 'I didn't do no murder.'

'You had Naunton Huntley's lighter in your pocket.'

'What does that prove?'

'You've admitted you were there at the kidnapping.'

'But I didn't kill nobody.'

'Brumby Bayle was shot dead from the roof of All Souls' Church.'

Gardner spluttered helplessly.

'But that was Tony. He done the shooting. I was with Huntley and Frith in the car.'

'Can you prove that?'

'I'm *telling* you, for Christ's sake. Tony shot that geezer because he was frightened of Frith. You don't know what the guy is like. He's a nut case.'

'What about the other victims? Where were they taken?'

'I don't know. Frith had a plane. He flew them off some place.'

'What kind of plane?'

'How the hell should I know? Just a plane, for Christ's sake. He piloted it himself.'

'Where is he now?' Steiner snapped.

Gardner shook his head hopelessly.

'After the Huntley snatch he paid us off, and that's the last we saw of him. It's the truth, I swear it.'

Steiner sat back in his chair. He was thinking hard. Slowly, surely, it was knitting together. Frith. Something about the name disturbed him. He stared at Gardner. He was sure Gardner was telling the truth. The man was out of his mind with worry and ready to tell anything.

'Gardner,' he said softly.

The young tearaway looked up.

'This man Frith. You must know something about him.'

Gardner shook his head.

'Not a bleeding thing, except for what I've told you. He's bonkers, all the way. And strong as an elephant. He paid us in cash at the end of each job, that's all I know.'

'Where did he live?'

Gardner shrugged.

122

'Christ knows. When he needed us, he got in touch.'

'By phone?'

'Yeah, he rang Jimmy Blagdon in the pub next door.'

Steiner leaned forward again.

'Now think carefully, Gardner. Is there anything, anything at all you can remember about this man?'

Gardner's eyes were glassy.

'No Guv'nor, that's the truth, I swear it.'

'He must have told you something about himself.'

Gardner hesitated.

'Well . . . there was one thing like.'

'Yes?'

'It wasn't . . . I mean, it wasn't anything special.'

'Tell me, Gardner.'

'He did mention that he'd been in the S.A.S. You know, the Special Air Service.'

For a moment, Steiner just sat. The room seemed to freeze around him. Inside, he was hot, very hot, the heat moving through his body in a bright dissolving flash. As always at such moments, he cursed himself for having been a fool, for having missed the obvious, the one salient point that had been right in front of his nose; though of course such self-recrimination was ridiculous, for there had been nothing to divorce it from the mass of other unsalient points which had passed before his eyes and through his brain. Until now. He looked at Brockway.

'Stan, got any Scotsmen here?'

Brockway stared at him in surprise.

'Well,' he said, 'we've got Stew McCormack, but he's out on patrol.'

'Anyone else.'

'There's Jock Gallagher.'

'Where's he from?'

'Western Isles originally. North Uist, I think – somewhere like that.'

'Where is he now?'

Brockway looked at his watch.

'In the canteen at this time, I expect.'

Steiner pushed back his chair and got to his feet.

'Let's go find him,' he said.

Jock Gallagher was half-way through his lunch when they ran him to earth. He was a roly-poly sergeant with a jolly face and black curly hair. He grinned at Steiner over his steak and kidney pudding.

'Whit can ah help ye with, sir?' he inquired.

'Can you speak Gaelic, Jock?' Steiner asked.

Gallagher chuckled.

'Didna speak anythin' else until ah wis nine year old,' he said.

'Then tell me what kyle means in English.'

Gallagher frowned.

'A kyle is a slender stretch of water. Like an estuary.'

'Or a frith?'

Gallagher looked surprised.

'Aye, that's right. That's whit a kyle is. A frith.'

Steiner's heart was pounding as he took the lift downstairs. In Brockway's office he phoned London and asked for Barry Fawkes. When Fawkes came on the line, Steiner said crisply: 'Barry, did you check on that man Jonathan Kyle?'

'I've been working on it, Guv',' Fawkes answered, 'I got in touch with the S.A.S. central office, and they put me on to a Lieutenant Colonel Parker. He used to be Kyle's C.O. four or five years ago. Trouble is, he's off duty at the moment and I've had hell's own job running him to earth. His wife says he's at a regimental dinner at the Cumberland Hotel. I didn't think you considered it over-important, so I'd planned on leaving him alone until the morning.'

'Listen Barry,' Steiner said rapidly, 'get down to the Cumberland Hotel and pick up Lieutenant Colonel Whatsisname. I'm grabbing the next train back from Birmingham. Meet me at the station and bring the Colonel with you, right?'

124

'Right,' said Fawkes. He hesitated a moment. 'You think this bloke Kyle is our man then?'

Steiner smiled grimly as he lit another cigarette.

'Thinking doesn't come into it,' he said, 'I bloody know he's our man.'

TEN

They stepped out of the barn and into the open air, Kyle leading, Mellinger second, the others following in dribs and drabs. Overcome with the novelty of having their chains removed at last, they walked unsurely, like patients released after a long sojourn in hospital. It was bitterly cold. The rawness of it hit Mellinger in the chest as he stared with dismay across the bleak rolling landscape. Snow. It had snowed during the night – was still snowing, in fact. Fleecy flakes danced against his cheeks. As far as he could see, the land was frozen in a deathly hush of white.

'Christ,' he hissed through clenched teeth.

The hills looked unreal in the early dawn, creamy monsters which might, at first glance, have been storm clouds themselves; there was no clear division between land and sky, there was no depth or density, no colour or clear perspective. They were trapped in a world of unrelieved greys and whites, a world which chilled them to the bone and which, in Mellinger's fancy seemed about to swallow them up like a living force. The wind was slight, he was grateful for that. But in this weather they would leave a trail even a child could follow. That was if – and it seemed to Mellinger a big 'if' – they did not succumb to the sheer intensity of the atmosphere. There was snow everywhere, treacherous and yielding: good ground for tracking, good ground for a hunter like Kyle – but to the inexperienced, the ill-equipped, a death-trap. Mellinger's spirits fell.

'Snow,' he whispered.

Kyle grunted.

'Been falling all night.'

Mellinger thrust his hands in his pockets, shivering in the chill. He peered up at the brutish implacable face. In the thin light of dawn it seemed like the land, contourless, a pasty oval of nothing. The eyes looked purple. Had they changed, or was it a trick of the light?

'Surely,' Mellinger said, 'this throws a different complexion on things?'

'How's that?'

'Well, you can't send these people into the hills in weather like this. Dressed as they are, they'll never survive.'

Kyle shrugged.

'That depends on you. On how good you are.'

'For Christ's sake man, they're absolute beginners. Even the most experienced mountaineer would be hard put to stay intact in conditions like these.'

'Luck of the game,' Kyle grunted.

Mellinger scowled at him.

'You *are* a bastard, Kyle,' he hissed.

Kyle stared at him for a moment in silence. In the dawn air his face seemed somehow, for the very first time, to belong – as if that rigid flesh had itself been frozen, as if the eyes, cold and shrewd, were merely chinks of ice . . . He thrust something into Mellinger's hand, a small pocket compass.

'Your route lies due west,' he said simply, 'nineteen miles. You've got one hour's start.'

Mellinger tried one last time. It was a despairing effort, but one he knew he had to make. There was just a chance, a slim chance that somewhere within that impenetrable mask, a trace of human feeling still existed.

'Kyle, listen to reason. Don't do this thing, I beg you.'

No reply.

'Turning these people loose is nothing short of murder.'

'Retribution,' Kyle corrected.

'For what, for Christ's sake?'

Kyle shrugged. His face did not change. Watching him, Mellinger felt a shiver on his throat. It had nothing to do with the cold. It was the inexorability of this man. Nothing affected him, nothing penetrated that blank flesh-mask.

'I think, Mr Mellinger,' Philip Goodman put in anxiously, 'we are wasting precious seconds.'

Mellinger sighed.

'Kyle, for the last time, will you for God's sake change your mind?'

But Kyle seemed to be turned into stone. He stood motionless, his face as flat, as dead and as inscrutable as ever.

'Mr Mellinger, please,' Goodman pleaded, 'we're freezing to death here.'

'All right,' said Mellinger. He stared at Kyle, hate burning strongly within him.

'You bastard,' he hissed, 'I hope you rot in hell.'

There was no reaction and he had expected none. It had been an outburst, nothing more, a cry of frustration. He turned to the others. They were shivering in the stillness. Snowflakes clung to their clothes and hair.

'Try to keep in line,' he advised, 'and don't fall too far behind. If anyone gets out of breath, don't be heroic, call a halt. We've got to stick together. It'll be slippery up on the ridge, but if you keep in my footprints, we should be okay. Come on, let's go.'

They set off, shuffling forward, slithering in the ankle-deep snow. Mellinger felt glad to be on the move again, glad of any kind of mobility which would set his pulses racing and fan the fading body heat inside his belly. He watched the hills beginning to rise before him, saw the maze of valleys to the north and the lower snows which looked, in the thin light of early dawn, like the bellies of freshly-caught fish. The air was crisp, hurting his lungs, freezing the hairs inside his nostrils into tiny needle points. Snowflakes fluttered in front of his eyes, distorting vision, turning the landscape into a bleary bubble-like reflection, drained of life and atmosphere. He tried to restrain his impulse to set a cracking pace, remembering how out of touch they were, how inexperienced. Save energy, he told himself. They would need it later. They would need every ounce they could get.

The ground was rising rapidly, leaning upwards towards the ridge, a thousand feet or thereabouts. It would be a gruelling climb. He hoped they were up to it. God, they had to be. There were nineteen miles of this to go.

He squinted through the semi-darkness, picking out the hills which led to the spine of the ridge. It was the same ridge he and Kyle had followed the day before – was it only yesterday? Best to follow the contours, he thought. Too much upping and downing would wear them out in no time. They had to forget pain, discomfort, fear, forget everything except the need to go on.

The flanks of the nearest hills tumbled around them like billowing chiffon. Only their breathing broke the stillness; that, and the humph humph humph of their feet against the snow. He was grateful for the lack of wind. It was the one factor in their favour. Dressed as they were, a sharp wind could carve them up in no time, draining their bodies of the life-giving warmth which supported them, leaving them victims to the slow creed of hypothermia.

In the low colour of dawn, the hillside seemed to go on for ever, disappearing some inestimable distance above into a swirling sky. Mellinger paused, breathing deeply, and looked back. What an incongruous picture they made. Five people, dressed for the city, strung out across this deserted snow-strewn hillside. Mackey dammit was dragging behind. A long way behind. The little Cumbrian plumber looked in serious trouble. He was moving erratically, stopping every few yards to examine his feet.

Mellinger cursed and began to slither down the slope

towards him. Mackey saw him coming and squatted on a rock, waiting. He looked like an old man, face pale and haggard in the thin light of day.

'Come on Mackey,' Mellinger panted, 'we've got to stick together.'

'I can't help it,' the plumber said, 'my feet feel like lead.'

Mellinger looked at his saturated carpet slippers, and his heart sank. One glance told him they would soon come apart at the seams. They were obviously affording the plumber little protection as it was. Mellinger knelt down.

'Let's have a look,' he said.

He slipped off one of Mackey's slippers and examined the flesh. The foot felt like ice in his hands. He dug his thumb into the sole.

'Feel that?'

'No.'

Oh Christ, Mellinger thought. If Mackey lasted the day it would be a miracle. Those feet were done for. Another hour, two at the most, and he would be walking on chunks of dead flesh.

'Rub them with snow,' Mellinger advised, disguising the dismay in his voice, 'can't afford frostbite at this stage.'

'Sorry,' Mackey said, 'I hate holding you back.'

'It's not your fault dammit. But keep up as best you can, okay?'

The plumber nodded, and Mellinger set off after the others, feeling the snow curl into his shoes, feeling his socks, soggy as wet pastry, riding over his ankles, feeling, as he climbed higher, the first worrying currents of wind and thinking with a sense of unease that the higher they got, the worse conditions would become.

The hills rippled around them like a school of white whales. He could see the ridge now, clearly-defined at last against the gloom-laden sky, and beyond it more hills, much higher, erupting eastwards into clouds the colour of light lemon. It was cold and deathly. Move, he thought. On and up. Got to reach that ridge top. How long would the snow last? It looked set for the day, growing heavier by the minute, though not heavy enough, he thought sourly, to cover their tracks. No bloody chance. They were leaving a beautiful trail for Kyle to follow, and all it really depended on now was which of them was in better condition. That made it no contest, Mellinger thought, recalling Kyle's athletic scramblings of the day before. Unless a miracle occurred, they would none of them last till evening. But he put this from his mind as he shuffled past the others and gained the summit of the ridge.

Far below, he could see the valley dipping and twisting towards the west. The river was a spider's thread. On its banks he could see the copse of trees where Kyle had killed the deer the day before. He paused, sweating heavily, and looked back the way they had come. The farmhouse was almost hidden from view, obscured by an unending blanket of snow. The sky was brightening fast, casting slithers of light across bulging outcrops and stubborn clumps of moorgrass which thrust through the soft surface like blemishes on the creamy skin.

He studied the others. They were gasping from exertion, cheeks loose and putty-like, lips slack, eyes filled with a vague desperation. They looked done for, whacked out, finished. He could see defeat in the set of their shoulders, the looseness of their legs. Not yet, Mellinger thought. Not already. Jesus Christ, they had nineteen miles to go.

Philip Goodman was the first to reach Mellinger's side. The slender, normally urbane civil servant looked like a man near the end of his tether. His grey hair hung scraggily across his narrow forehead, and one hand clutched despairingly at Mellinger's sleeve.

'We've got to stop,' he gasped. 'We can't keep up this kind of pace, we're just not used to it. You've got to let us rest.'

Mellinger stared at him coldly.

'Rest?' he growled. 'How long d'you think Kyle will rest? It's taken us more than a half hour to reach this

130

ridge, and we're still not out of sight of the farm. There isn't time to rest, for Christ's sake.'

Goodman stood panting, staring at the snow, and something seemed to go out of him, something essential, some spirit or life-force went fluttering away in the greyness to leave him drained and defenceless on this frozen hilltop. Mellinger felt his anger soften.

'It's better to keep on the move,' he explained, 'not just because of Kyle. Once we stop, our blood temperature will drop, and in these conditions we could end up dying from exposure. You don't want that, do you?'

Goodman shook his head glumly. He was too exhausted to reply. Instead, he stood staring at the ground, still gasping in the frosty snow-filled air. Mellinger waited until the others had caught up. Their eyes, like Goodman's were demented with effort. Mellinger studied their faces, and felt the last shreds of hope desert him. They would never last the pace, he knew it. Deep inside himself he knew they were finished. Their inexperience, the cold, Kyle's unswerving determination to hunt them down – it was just too much to fight. But he would not admit it. Something within him clung stubbornly to the myth of deliverance.

'It'll be easier for the next mile or two,' he promised. 'The ridge bobs and dips a bit, but it's reasonably level; it'll give you time to get your wind back.'

They started off again, moving more freely now that they had gained their height. Mellinger began to feel hopeful. Perhaps he was wrong. Perhaps it had just been the initial climb that had drained them so. You could hardly blame them for that. It had been a damned stiff pull, almost perpendicular for the last hundred yards, formidable enough at the best of times, but this morning in particular with the hills wreathed in mist and shrouded by snow enough to daunt a regiment of crack pioneers. His little band of amateurs hadn't done badly at all.

But Mellinger's optimism was short-lived. Ahead, through the swirling flocks of cloud, he saw the ridge beginning to rise again, picking its way higher and higher into the mountain peaks. Goddammit, it would take them an hour at least to get up there. An hour? They couldn't afford it. Maybe he had made a mistake, an error of judgement. His pulse quickened. Of course. Following the ridge might make sense in mountaineering terms, but with Kyle after them it was far too obvious. The shortest distance between two points was the very route Kyle would *expect* them to follow. They ought to be boxing clever, zig-zagging, making detours, covering their tracks. They were playing right into Kyle's hands.

He stared into the valley. It meandered westward, going God-knew-where, with the river, the steep snow-crusted screeslopes, and the pinewoods cluttering its bottom. In the gathering light it looked strangely unreal, its depth lost in the wisps of drifting mountain mist. An idea struck him. He turned and looked at the others.

'Let's forget the ridge,' he said. 'It's time we took evasive action. As long as we're in the snow, Kyle can track us down without getting out of breath. But down there, we might be able to outfox him.'

The girl, Marian Edwards, looked dubious.

'Won't we be running ourselves into a trap?'

'Well, the valley meanders roughly westward. We'll have to climb out of it eventually, but for the moment I'd say we'd stand a better chance down there than up here.'

Something akin to panic shone in Michael Jacobs's eyes. He looked at Mellinger with an air of disbelief.

'You mean all this . . . the climb up to the ridge, has been for nothing?'

'Not necessarily,' Mellinger said, 'it'll help to throw Kyle off course. We've got to appear erratic. Once we begin following a clearly-cut plan, he can think ahead and intercept us.'

'But for God's sake,' Jacobs spluttered, almost in tears. 'That climb cost us valuable energy.'

'I know that, and I'm sorry, but if we're going to beat that bastard, we've got to play it by ear all the way.'

132

The girl watched him in silence for a moment. She was shivering, hugging herself for warmth.

'Do you have a plan?' she asked.

Mellinger shook his head.

'I wouldn't put it as strongly as that. But in the valley, I think we're more likely to shake him off.'

She grunted.

'That's good enough for me,' she said. 'Let's move, for God's sake, I'm shaking half to death here.'

They struck south from the ridge, leaving its jagged spine and taking a diagonal path down the steep precipitous snowbank. Mellinger had to slow his pace for fear someone – especially the girl – lost their footing on the slippery surface and went tumbling downwards all the way to the valley floor. It was tough going; sometimes, in conditions like these, clambering down could be harder than climbing up, but bit by bit they managed it, picking their way with the utmost care until they had reached the bottom of the hillslope. It was better in the valley. The wind currents had gone, shut off by the high mountain walls. Snow fell lazily about their heads, lining the tree branches with puffy white sleeves. Perfect setting for a Christmas card, Mellinger thought.

He surveyed his companions like a commander weighing up his troops. They still looked in a bad way. Their clothes, drenched with perspiration, were covered with snow. Their shoes, including his own, were completely waterlogged. Nelson Mackey was the worst hit. The little plumber's carpet slippers looked ready to dissolve at any second. Mellinger put that possibility from his mind. Right now, the important thing was to throw Kyle off the scent.

'How much longer do we have?' Goodman asked wearily.

Mellinger looked at his watch.

'The hour's up, I'm afraid,' he told them. 'Kyle started trailing us four minutes ago.'

Something like a chill settled on their faces. Their eyes,

already blank with the first hint of exhaustion, took on a glimmer of fresh fear. The air seemed heavy with menace, and the mountains which only a second before had felt comforting and concealing, became craggy monsters out to ensnare them.

'Don't look so grim,' Mellinger said, 'remember he's got to climb that ridge too.'

'Let's move,' Mackey whispered hoarsely.

'Take it easy. If we panic, we're lost.' Mellinger wiped some of the snow from his hair. 'We need something to confuse him,' he explained, 'to give us a breathing space. That's why we're going to follow the river.'

He waited for their objection, but they watched him in silence. He realised they had not fully understood.

'I mean follow it in the water,' he added.

'Good Christ man,' spluttered Jacobs. 'It'll be like ice in there.'

'That's right, but it's only ankle deep and it can't be any worse than the snow.'

Nelson Mackey stared at him with a sense of horrible expectancy.

'Mr Mellinger, I can't even feel my feet now.'

'Then you've nothing to worry about, have you?'

'But what's the point of it?'

'The point is,' Mellinger said harshly, 'snow leaves tracks, water doesn't. The longer we can stick it, the harder it'll be for Kyle to pick up our trail.'

In the ghostly daylight, they digested his statement. Goodman was the first to nod.

'It's the truth,' he admitted.

'I'm not saying it won't be unpleasant,' Mellinger told them, 'but it might give us the margin we need.'

They stared at him in silence. Their shoulders were hunched with fatigue, and for a moment he thought sheer misery would make them rebel. But then the girl, Marian Edwards, shook herself and, almost angrily, said: 'Oh, for God's sake, let's get it over with.'

Shouldering past him, she stepped into the freezing

water. One by one they followed her, gasping as the river
closed around their ankles. Then, shuffling along its shaly
bottom, they began to move with a sense of desperate
purpose towards the valley's head.

ELEVEN

At the farm, darkness hung stubbornly on in folds of
murky grey. The early sun cast a mauve flush across the
mass of storm clouds rolling in from the west, but did
little to illuminate the snow-covered plain or the twisting
labyrinth of valleys beyond. Kyle however scarcely
noticed the worsening of the weather; he was engrossed
in preparing himself for the job in hand. From the room
he had shared for the past three days with Mellinger, he
took his haversack, a small Karrimor and a steel frame,
and into it placed a few strips of dried venison and a handful of berries. No need to worry about moisture, he
reasoned, for there would be lots of rivers on the way, and
he could always eat snow if he had to. He put in his
Eclair film camera together with the image intensifier
lens, and three spare magazines. He rummaged around in
the loft until he found what he was looking for, a length
of nylon climbing rope, and coiled it neatly crossways over
his shoulder. Then he went downstairs, collected his haversack and checked his watch. Seventeen minutes to go.
The snow was coming in thick and fast, blotting out the
entire world beyond the dreary stretch of plain, blotting
out the hills, and the far-off eddying sky until it seemed
to Kyle he was alone on some primitive long-lost planet,
a solitary figure in a universe so desolate, so intolerable,
that its very existence was enough to plunge a man into
blank despair. But he liked it like that, austere and chill-

ing, a world which somehow matched his own soul, for he knew he owed no allegiance to the rest of mankind. People were a burden to Kyle. He did not understand them, and it was certain they did not understand him. The land however, was different. Here, in the raw terrain, he had found the only home he had ever known, the only peace he had ever known, and he was not, by God he was not about to leave its seclusion to become part of a society in which he knew he had no place. The land vitalised him and the land sustained him. He was at home here. He belonged.

It never occurred to Kyle to begin his pursuit before the hour was up. He had laid down the conditions, and he would stick to them impeccably. It had nothing to do with sportsmanship. It was simply that, having formulated the idea, he saw no reason to alter it now.

Kyle was not by nature an excitable man, but after the months of planning and preparation he would not have blamed himself for a little quickening of his pulse, a little stirring in his breast; there was, however, nothing, no excitement, not even hate. He did not hate those people. He knew they had to die, but he did not hate them. He felt no hostility, no pity, no regret or understanding. They were simply there, and they had to die. For the crimes they had committed, and for the crimes of others equally guilty he would hunt them down and destroy them. And the film – the film would be a warning. It would demonstrate to those others that he, Kyle, had declared war upon them, and they would tremble.

The snow whirled into his face, and he brushed it absently from his eyes. He had not expected this, the snow, though naturally he welcomed it for it made his job easier, the trailing, the destroying, all of it easier. He knew now that come what may, they could never escape. Even if he failed to catch them – and the thought of that was so remote he dismissed it as mere fancy – then the land itself would finish them off. He smiled thinly. There was a certain justice in that. He had wanted them to be aware of the land, to feel it as he did, to feel its power as he did, to feel it as a living force beneath their feet. He had wanted them to know its harshness, its barbarity, and its beauty too, and the way it could succour a man if he used it properly – but for the land itself to kill them . . . that was even better. For a moment Kyle considered doing nothing, of stalking them silently and watching them die one by one as they succumbed to the wet and the biting cold, but he dismissed the thought almost at once. The plan had been formed. He would stay with it to the end.

He went back to his room and rummaged around in the ancient dresser till he found a bottle of tablets the doctor had given him. It was almost full; he had used only two, and to be fair, only when the pain was beyond endurance. Thankfully, that didn't happen often. At the hospital, they had warned him that the attacks would increase with time, but at the moment it was not the pain which bothered him so much as the relentless weariness which seemed to lie in every corner of his body these days. He fought it doggedly, refusing to give in, and he would go on fighting as long as there was breath within him, but it seemed sometimes as if his insides had ruptured, leaving him open to the slow creeping spread of a dreadful paralysis. Kyle's thin mouth tightened as he thought of his last attack : he had doubled over in agony and rolled on the ground, his body convulsed by the sheer unbelievable strength of it. Blinding in its intensity, it had ripped through his insides like a ricocheting bullet while he lay helpless and gasping, waiting for the moment when the crescendo would pass. Kyle shook himself. This was defeatist thinking. He put the tablets back in the dresser. They slowed him down, made him stodgy, dull-witted, and he needed all his faculties for the job in hand. He would not take them.

He carried a tub of freshly-hewn logs to the farmhouse and topped up Naunton Huntley's fuel bunker. The Director General watched him in silence, his quick eyes noting the extent of the replenishment, realising some-

137

thing unusual was up. When Kyle returned several minutes later with a fresh stock of food, and then knelt down to examine the chain around his ankle, Huntley's suspicions were confirmed.

'You're not leaving me here alone?' he protested.

Instead of answering, Kyle took hold of the chain and gave it a quick tug. The metal ring on the wall held firm. Satisfied, Kyle rose to his feet.

Naunton Huntley watched him with an air of rising panic. If Kyle left and did not return, he, Huntley, would be done for. Once the food and fuel ran out, he would be doomed to a lingering death, trapped on his chain like a rabbit in a snare.

'You can't leave me fastened up like this,' he choked.

Kyle stared at him.

'You'll be okay,' he grunted, 'use the food and fuel sparingly. I'll be gone two, possibly three days.'

Huntley opened his mouth to protest, but without another word Kyle turned and left the room, locking the door carefully behind him.

He looked at his watch. The hour was up. With one final check at his packstraps, he set off into the snow, sliding forward easily, confidently, moving by instinct almost, for it was impossible to see more than twenty yards through that swirling whirling storm, and it was amazing how quickly it covered the ground, with what consummate ease it devoured grass clumps and boulders, peat hags and riverbeds, imbuing everything with the same unbroken disguise, a world where the entire outlook was white, white sky, white earth, everything drained of its colour and caught in the glacial grip of winter.

In his head, noises rattled like distant thunder. He knew those noises; they were wild geese flying high to nest in the snow covered mountains. The ground rippled and danced, its feathery blanket smoothing out each tiny landmark, destroying familiarity, perception, surrounding him with an immensity of emptiness. He moved at the double, not running exactly but shuffling Indian-style, shoulders hunched, head low, studying the trail which led steadily westward. Another hour, he thought, and those tracks might well have been obliterated, for the snow was lying fast. He had no particular feelings about the prospect of killing ahead. He had not thought of it to any real extent. Killing was killing; it came easily to Kyle, he had been trained for it, he did it well, and with the same professional air that a slaughterer might display at an abattoir. He did not enjoy it – but he did not particularly dislike it either. The fact that one of his intended victims was a woman made no difference whatsoever. He had killed women before. Male or female, he killed without discrimination.

The cold bit through the close-weave material of his anorak, but he enjoyed its crispness, its meanness : he liked the weather to batter him, as if it was a contest of sorts, himself against the elements, and somehow, whether by luck or by chance, he always seemed to come out on top. He had fooled those doctors at the psychiatric hospital, he'd fooled them all, fooled them or frightened them, he was never certain which. He frightened many people without meaning to. He had always been aware of that, always sensitive to the fear he saw in other people's eyes. He could recognise it even when they tried desperately to disguise it. At first it had worried him, that fear. He did not, in the beginning wish to appear intimidating. But the time had come when he began to realise that the fear he generated was a useful thing; it was good to frighten people, for with fear he could manipulate them. And with that realisation, a kind of truth, an elusive self-knowledge and self-acceptance had overtaken him, and he had never worried about anything again.

Kyle felt the earth begin to rise and he shuffled on without slackening pace, glad to feel the blood pulsing through his veins, glad to feel his lungs swelling and contracting, glad to feel the strain and stretch of his limbs again for he was into his second wind now, and it took him less than ten minutes to reach the spine of the ridge. Along the topmost heights, the wind was beginning to pick up, and here, the surface snow had been scoured by its force, leaving patches of grass and slabs of frozen peat. The trail was easily discernible, and he was able to tell, from the scattering of the tracks, that Mellinger was in the lead, that at one point he had retraced his steps to see to someone in trouble, probably Mackey (Kyle remembered the plumber's fragile carpet slippers) and that he was pausing from time to time, either to allow the others to catch up or to consider the route ahead. Then, without warning, the trail left the ridge and dipped sharply down towards the valley. Kyle slithered to a halt, puzzled. What the hell was Mellinger up to? After dragging them up to a height of a thousand feet or more, he was now leading them down again. A pointless time-wasting exercise unless – Kyle smiled thinly – unless Mellinger was trying to confuse him. That had to be it. Mellinger was playing a game of wits. Kyle felt a faint stab of respect. He had been wrong to underestimate that man.

Three minutes later, Kyle reached the bottom of the hillslope and found the spot where the tracks vanished into the twisting river. He frowned. The most obvious ruse of all – yet he had not expected it. Mellinger was trying to slow him down. Mellinger knew, as Kyle knew, that if he could hold him back long enough, the snow would cover their tracks for good. He might be a novice in the escape business, but by hook or by crook the man was giving a good account of himself.

Kyle glanced around. There were two ways they could have gone, either westward towards the head of the valley or back towards the farm. Surely not the farm. That would be madness, and Mellinger knew it. A simple shift in the cloud, a moment of clear visibility would have allowed Kyle spot them from the ridge above. Still, he could not ignore the possibility, and whether he liked it or not he would have to check it out. Kyle looked at the river and hesitated. Amazingly, after all these years, rivers – any river – had the same irritating effect upon him. He

140

hated to be near them, hated to immerse himself in their waters. Even now, he could see in his mind's eye the picture of Larry floating face down with his hair swaying in the current. Would he ever forget that? A sight engraved into his memory. Old Larry. His brother had been the one good thing in Kyle's life, the only person he had always known he could rely on. After the river episode, Kyle had felt for a long time as though the bottom had dropped from the entire world. That was a lifetime ago, he thought angrily, and with a conscious effort pushed it from his mind. Steeling himself, he stepped into the freezing water, oblivious to its chill, oblivious to everything except the irritating fact that Mellinger had succeeded in slowing him down. When he had satisfied himself that he was moving in the wrong direction, he retraced his steps and began to shuffle upstream, watching the banks for any sign, no matter how small, which would indicate that they had left the water. He tried to recall from memory how far the river went before it petered out. Four miles, he estimated. A lot could happen in four miles. From there, their route might be anyone's guess. Except that Kyle believed, was counting on it in fact, that sooner or later Mellinger would swing back to a westerly direction in the hope of reaching sanctuary.

It was now broad daylight, but the snow which whirled into his face shut off the sun to such an extent that it seemed like dusk. The river bobbed and twisted between thick clumps of woodland where branches, heavy with snow, straddled the water like an interlocking tunnel. Kyle moved quickly, though his legs were chilled to the bone and the current was running hard against him. His eyes flicked from one bank to the other. Sooner or later they would have to leave the water. Already, their feet must be frozen solid, particularly Mackey's. Not much further, Kyle was certain.

Suddenly Kyle slithered to a halt. He stood quite still, his face creased by a puzzled frown. Why had he stopped? Something had caught his attention, some detail that was out of place. But what? He peered around. The river slid over white shiny boulders. The banks, heavy with snow, showed no sign of footprints. The trees clustered close to the water's edge. Everything looked natural, undisturbed. Then he saw it. Although the forest was weighed down with snow, one tree branch, one overhanging limb was inexplicably bare. Kyle moved towards it, frowning. Some of its smaller twigs had been crushed, as though something – or someone – had handled it very roughly. He stared at the bank. It was virgin white. He clambered out of the stream and slid between the tree-trunks, studying the ground. Five feet back, the snow had been beaten flat by the impact of several pairs of shoes. Kyle's face broke into a smile of admiration. They had used the overhanging branch to swing themselves out of the river without leaving tell-tale marks at the water's edge. Mellinger again. That conniving son of a bitch had almost fooled him. Kyle looked up. From where he stood the trail led clearly west between the trees. Still smiling to himself, he set off once more in pursuit.

It was five hours later when Kyle caught his first glimpse of his prey. At two o'clock in the afternoon he topped a small rise and spotted just ahead, a lean stumbling figure weaving along the riverbank like a man clinging desperately to the last vestiges of life. Nelson Mackey. It had been clear to Kyle for some time that Mackey was in serious trouble. He had found, lying at the side of the trail, a piece of material which he recognised as a slipper heel. A little further on, he had come across the front portion and had known beyond a doubt, that Mackey would soon be within his grasp. With one foot naked, the little plumber had fallen well behind, and watching him, Kyle knew that Mackey was already close to death. Completely alone, he was caught in the throes of hypothermia, his body heat literally oozing out through his pores. He had already passed the shivering stage and his mind, disorientated, was conscious of only one thought, the need to push

142

on, to keep on the move. Unless Mellinger returned to collect him soon, he would collapse of exhaustion and death from exposure would be only minutes away. Kyle knew there was no longer any need to murder Nelson Mackey. He could let the snow do it, let the land finish him off, coldly and cleanly. But the killer instinct was strong within him. He wanted that satisfaction for himself.

He studied the land ahead through narrowed eyes. The trail led into a clump of trees flanked on one side by thorn-scrub and on the other by a small ravine. It looked a perfect spot for an ambush.

Kyle slid back and began to circle towards the left. He skulked jackal-like, low to the ground. Death was in him now, the stench of it in his nostrils, the taste of it on his lips. He reached the lip of the ravine and ducked swiftly through the darkened wood. He was sure Mackey had not seen him. He pushed his way through the suffocating blanket of branches, taking care not to mess up the tracks. He wanted Mackey to follow them blindly. Selecting the stoutest tree he could find, Kyle climbed it and straddled its lowest bough. Uncoiling the rope from around his shoulders, he began to tie a noose in its end. His fingers, chilled to the bone, tugged uselessly at the frozen strands. He cursed under his breath. He was taking too much time. Nelson Mackey was already approaching. Using his teeth for leverage, Kyle swiftly fashioned the slip-knot, widening the noose until it was large enough to drop over a man's head but small enough to be impeded by his shoulders. He could see the trail directly below.

He heard a soft footfall, a snort of pain as Mackey stepped on something sharp, and then the little plumber appeared, shoulders hunched, head bowed. He was swaying from side to side. Kyle dropped his haversack lightly into Mackey's patch. The plumber froze in his tracks, his brain numbed by the unexpected. Kyle saw his bald top-of-head gleaming through its sparse covering of hair, he saw the twin tendons which framed the thin man's neck.

He let the noose drop swiftly. Frozen by the chill air, the rope was heavier than he had bargained for, and its impact on Mackey's shoulders caused the small man to stagger. He looked puzzled at this strange thing which had dropped from the sky to encircle him, and one bony hand came up to brush at the frozen fibre. The fingers never got there. With a deft flick, Kyle jerked the noose tight and hauled Mackey, kicking and struggling, into the air. No sound came from Mackey's lips but his brain registered that he was dying, that his life-giving source of oxygen had been ruthlessly shut off.

Kyle wrapped the free end of the rope around the branch and tied it fast. He dropped into the snow and undid his haversack. His hands moved swiftly and efficiently as he laid out his equipment. Soon, the little corpse echoed to the muted whirr of the camera and the gentle creak of spruce boughs as Nelson Mackey, one foot naked and blackened with cold, kicked out his life with solitary desperation in the frosty snow-filled afternoon.

TWELVE

George Steiner got off the train at Euston station and found Detective Superintendent Fawkes waiting for him at the ticket barrier. It was early evening.

'Janie's been calling the nick all day,' the younger man said, 'she wants to talk to you.'

Steiner felt a stab of pain. Throughout the two-hour train ride he had been so absorbed with the job that his own problems had faded into the background. Now they came rushing back with uncomfortable force.

'What did you tell her?'

'Just said I'd pass the message on.'

'Okay, you've passed it on.'

Fawkes peered at him, frowning, as they shouldered their way through the crowds and headed for the street.

'What the hell's up with you, Guv'?' he muttered. 'You've been like a bear with a sore head all week.'

Steiner hustled on, not bothering to answer, noticing that there was already a hint of approaching Christmas in the air. Over the loudspeaker, Andy Williams crooned *Winter Wonderland*. A man dressed as Santa Claus stood by the door collecting money for the Save The Children Fund.

'Where's this Colonel Whatsisname?' Steiner growled.

'Waiting in the car. And not too pleased about it either. I had to haul him away from this dinner before the speechmaking.'

'Questioned him yet?'

'Thought I'd leave that in your delicate hands. You have such a winning way with you, Guv'.'

Steiner gave him a sour stare but did not reply.

Fawkes was right. Lieutenant Colonel Parker turned out to be far from pleased. He was a handsome slim-hipped man with a suntanned face and very black hair. He looked like a film actor, Steiner thought, or a professional model, and his good looks were emphasised by his precisely-cut dinner jacket and elegantly-laced shirtfront. Only his eyes spoiled the actor image. They were cold as ice and three times as hard. Sitting in the back of the car, he looked like a man controlling himself with an effort.

'Colonel Parker,' Fawkes said, 'this is Commander Steiner.'

The two men shook hands, but Parker's face did not soften.

'How do you do,' he said in a clipped voice.

Steiner settled himself in the front passenger seat. He nodded at the driver.

'Cruise around the block,' he ordered. 'Keep going till I tell you to stop.'

It was nearly nine o'clock and the streets were crowded

with traffic. They pulled out between a line of buses and swung left at the first set of traffic lights. Steiner clicked on his seatbelt.

'Sorry to tear you away from your dinner, Colonel,' he said. 'We wouldn't have done it if it hadn't been an emergency.'

'I hope not, Commander,' Parker growled. 'If I think you are wasting my time tonight, I'll make a point of seeing that you suffer for it.'

Steiner frowned. He was in no mood for histrionics. He glanced at Fawkes in the driving mirror.

'Didn't he call his Commanding Officer?' he inquired.

'First thing he did.'

'Colonel Parker, you've been instructed to co-operate, I take it?'

'Yes.'

'Then what d'you think we're doing this for, fun?'

The Colonel's thin mouth tightened. Steiner stared at him coolly. If Parker wanted a head-on collision, they might as well get it over with. Steiner had no intention of being intimidated.

After a moment however, the Colonel seemed to change his mind. He said apologetically : 'I'm sorry. But you can hardly blame me for being irritable. Tonight was rather a special occasion.'

Steiner's expression did not soften.

'A special occasion, was it, Colonel? It could be a special occasion for six other people I can think of. It could be their last night on earth.'

Beneath its tan, the Colonel's face went pale.

'Just tell me what you want to know,' he murmured, 'I'll help in any way I can.'

Steiner settled back and watched the traffic gliding by.

'Remember a man called Jonathan Kyle?' he asked.

'Very well.'

'I'm going back a bit, Colonel.'

'I know. But you don't forget someone like Jonathan Kyle.'

146

'Why?'

'Because he's . . . well, he's not like other men.'

'In what way?'

'He's mad,' said Parker.

Steiner glanced at him in the mirror and Parker gave an ironic half-smile.

'I mean it,' he said. 'He's a psychopath.'

Steiner sat for a moment, considering.

'What was a psychopath doing in the S.A.S?' he asked.

Parker took out a gunmetal cigarette case, opened it and offered one to Steiner. Steiner shook his head. Parker lit up himself, and sat inhaling thoughtfully.

'Commander,' he explained, 'spotting a psychopath isn't as easy as you might imagine. It's true that all our men, particularly those engaged in special duties, are given a thorough psychiatric screening, but a psychopath is not like a schizophrenic, or someone suffering from another type of mental illness. He shows no particular symptoms. He's neither withdrawn, depressed, nor in the habit of talking nonsense. Even to an expert eye, a psychopath often seems as sane as the next man. The difference is, he's capable of killing for no other reason than because his victim's mannerisms, or his hair-style, or even the colour of his tie have irritated him. Kyle was suffering from a defect of the mind which allowed him to respond to animal instincts in an uncontrolled fashion. He had no sense of right or wrong when it came to killing. Most men feel something, uneasiness, remorse, something at least; but not Kyle – in him, it aroused nothing but indifference. By the time we realised that, it was already too late.'

'Why?'

'We couldn't afford to lose him.'

Steiner was silent for a moment.

'Explain that, Colonel,' he said.

Parker's cheeks flushed. He said coldly: 'Look Commander, I'm willing to help you any way I can, but there are some things I cannot enlarge upon.'

Steiner sighed. He was aware that his patience was ebbing low.

'Colonel,' he said, 'somewhere six people are facing death tonight. Unless we can find them and find them quickly, your friend Kyle will be adding six new names to his death list. Now I know you've been trained to consider secrecy a number one priority, but unless you tell me what I need to know, I'm going to get on the phone to Hereford and tell them you're refusing to co-operate.'

For a moment, Steiner thought the Colonel would tell him to go to hell, but once again Parker's anger seemed to subside. He wound down the window and breathed deeply in the chill evening air.

'Kyle,' he said at last, 'was on special duties – operating in Ulster.'

'Doing what?'

'He . . .'

Parker hesitated. A taxi hooted as they dodged into its path. Their driver glanced into his mirror and gave an elaborate shrug. Steiner was still staring at the Colonel.

'Doing what?' he repeated.

'He wasn't playing boy scouts,' Parker snapped defensively.

Steiner was unmoved.

'Was it Kyle's job to murder people?' he asked.

Parker did not answer.

'Terrorists,' Steiner repeated. 'Was it Kyle's job to murder terrorists?'

Parker pressed his lips together. He looked stubborn and angry. Steiner let it go.

'He knew Belfast well then?'

'As well as anybody.'

'Well enough to know about a sewer complex when even the local police didn't?'

'It's possible.'

Steiner sat and thought for a moment. It was clicking into place. The more he learned, the more he felt convinced that Kyle was their man. However, one question

148

still puzzled him. Motive? Why had he done it?

'Tell me about his background,' he ordered. 'Anything you can remember.'

Colonel Parker looked at his cigarette. His forehead puckered in a frown of concentration. He was thinking back.

'He grew up in Scotland,' he said, 'in the border country, I believe. His father was a farmhand or a shepherd, something like that. He died when Kyle was quite young, crushed by a tractor; an accident.'

'What about the mother?'

'There was never any mention of a mother. Perhaps she died giving birth, or perhaps she left her husband when Kyle was too young to remember. At any rate, with the father gone, it was left to Kyle's brother, who was then in his early twenties, to bring the boy up.'

'Bit unusual, wasn't it? Why didn't the local authority take over?'

'God knows. We're not talking about the centre of London, Commander. Things are rather more basic in the borderlands. Besides, he made a good job of it, the brother; and he was certainly the only man in Kyle's life he was ever at home with.'

'Where is the brother now?'

'Dead.'

'You're sure?'

Parker nodded. He took another long pull at his cigarette, holding the smoke in his lungs for a moment before letting go. His eyes were reflective.

'It happened one weekend,' he said. 'It was early June. They'd taken some sheep down to Carlisle market. Kyle by this time was nearly nineteen. It was one of those very hot days, the first real scorcher of the summer. On the way home, they stopped to cool down with a swim in the river.' Parker paused as he wound up the car window. 'It was a sweltering day,' he went on, 'and the water looked inviting, so they just decided to take a dip. There were a number of factories along the bank, and in those days Commander, there weren't the industrial safeguards we enjoy today. That river was a steaming cesspool, swollen by the effluent from a half-dozen manufacturers. There were umpteen varieties of dangerous chemical flowing through it, including cyanide waste. Within ten minutes, Kyle's brother was floating face down on the surface, and Kyle himself just managed to reach the riverbank before he collapsed and had to be rushed to hospital dangerously ill. He was lucky in one sense. The cyanide which killed his brother never reached him, but lots of the other stuff did. His skin was burnt to a frazzle, particularly his face. They tried plastic surgery later, but it didn't take too well. Also, his hair fell out. I mean all his hair. It never grew again. Kyle doesn't have a single strand anywhere on his body, not on his head, his face, under his arms or between his legs. A man with no face and no hair makes a grotesque specimen, believe me. He ended up, for the rest of his life, a virtual freak.'

'Didn't he get compensation?'

'Oh yes. The factories which lined the river, while not admitting liability, clubbed together and made him a cash payment of five thousand pounds. I suppose to Kyle at that time it seemed a small fortune. He was beginning to pull through by then. He had always displayed an unnatural degree of strength. If anything, it was his strength which saved his life. But after the accident, he became obsessed with the idea of physical prowess. He began to build himself up, lifting weights, running, dieting, that sort of thing. He devoted himself to a training schedule that would have tried the devotion of a Trappist monk.'

'Perhaps he was compensating.'

'I'm sure he was. A man who looks mutilated can't help but feel vulnerable. At any rate, by the time he came to us, he had a fitness rating comparable with an Olympic athlete, and what was more, he had the strength to go with it.'

'How did he get on with the other men?'

'Not well, I'm afraid. He wasn't a mixer, seldom drank,

150

rarely went into town. He kept very much to himself. He was always conscious, I think, of his appearance. Few people could look at him without wincing. In those days, we did a lot of our training in the area around Mulgye in Scotland. It's very wild up there, almost uninhabited, and Kyle loved it. He loved wild country. He felt at home there. He was good at fieldcraft, anything to do with the outdoors.'

'Anything that got him away from people.'

'I suppose so.'

'What about his training?'

'The usual. Parachuting, intelligence, neutralisation ...'

'What?'

Parker looked at him.

'In your language, murder, Commander.'

Steiner grunted.

'Tell me something, did he ever learn to pilot a plane?'

'Can't say. He might have done. We did train some of our troops to be pilots. I couldn't be certain without checking his record though.'

'What happened to him after he left the S.A.S.?'

'He went back to Mulgye. He took over a derelict farmhouse we used sometimes as a billet, knocked it into shape, and literally went back to nature. He lived off the land, hunting for food, that sort of thing. Survival was what he had been taught to do, and without people around, it didn't matter what he looked like.'

'How do you know all this?'

'Because the local police got on to us three or four years ago. The Forestry Commission had moved in north of Mulgye. They wanted to extend their plantations in Scotland and had begun fencing off the land, building new roads, ploughing up the peat. That hadn't pleased Kyle at all. He'd begun smashing up their tractors, tearing out fences, destroying young shrubs. Then he went too far. He caught three of their men marking out a hillside and gave them a good going over, smashed all their legs.'

151

'Christ Almighty.'

'As I said, he's immensely strong, and breaking limbs is rather a speciality of his.'

'What happened?'

'We sent our psychiatric reports to the Scottish police, and he was committed to a mental hospital in Glasgow.'

'For how long?'

'I learned recently that he was turned loose after three and a half years.'

'With Home Secretary approval?'

'No Commander. Kyle was detained under section 60 of the Mental Health Act. That meant he could be released on a decision from a Health Review tribunal. The Home Secretary didn't come into it.'

Steiner drummed his fingers on his knee. They were passing Madame Tussaud's. Would Kyle, he wondered absently, become eligible for a place in the waxworks?

'Was there any reason for his release?' he asked.

'Yes, he was dying.'

Steiner turned to look at him, startled.

'What?'

Parker nodded.

'The chemicals which disfigured him all those years ago, never really left his system. They'd formed deposits in various parts of his organism which, despite his strength, eventually became malignant. In hospital, they tried radiotherapy, but only succeeded in making an even worse mess of his face. The doctors told him the truth in the end. Up to two years if he took things easy, less than twelve months if he pushed himself. Of course, by then, pushing himself was all Kyle understood.'

Steiner thought rapidly. Holy Jesus, was it possible?

'Barry,' he said, 'what do you make of it?'

Detective Superintendent Fawkes pulled a face.

'He must be an extremely bitter man, Guv'nor.'

'But could that be our motive, the link we've been looking for?'

'Pollution?'

'Does it sound ridiculous?'

Fawkes shook his head.

'I've heard worse,' he said. 'He wouldn't be human if he'd never thought of revenge. Hitting back at industries would be like punching a rubber ball – they're too impersonal. But people, they're different. Of course, you'd need to establish that each of the victims had polluted something.'

'That man Philip Goodman,' Steiner said, 'the one from the Department of Energy, didn't he negotiate a deal recently for the re-processing of Australian nuclear waste?'

Fawkes thought for a moment.

'I believe he did, Guv'. But what about Nelson Mackey? He's only a plumber. And there's the Edwards girl: she's a wig maker, for Christ's sake. What would they have to do with pollution?'

Steiner shook his head helplessly.

'I don't know,' he said, 'I don't know, but I intend to find out.' He glanced at the driver. 'Take us to the BBC Current Affairs studio at Lime Grove,' he ordered.

The BBC's News Information Department stands on the third floor of the rambling old building which once served as a major British film studio, and which, throughout the years, has been steadily expanding along the line of mundane terraced houses until, like a vast octopus, it now encompasses practically the entire street. News Info's function is to provide a cuttings service, so that journalists can study the backgrounds of stories they are called upon to report.

Steiner stood with the others amid the shelves of clippings files and watched the girls checking the list of names he had given them against the entries in their books. The first one was easy. Steiner had been right about Goodman. The Department of Energy man had indeed been at the centre of a recent environmental storm, and there were several newspaper accounts mentioning his name. The clippings bore such headlines as: BRITAIN'S NUCLEAR

153

DUSTBIN; GO AHEAD FOR AUSTRALIA'S ATOM JUNK; NEW DEAL ON NUCLEAR WASTE. What it amounted to was that as part of a new trade agreement, the government had decided to extend the re-processing facilities of its Windscale Nuclear Power plant to Australia, a decision which had resulted in uproar in the Commons. The negotiator, the man who had initiated and finalised the entire project was Philip Goodman.

Steiner slipped the clippings back into their file. They confirmed his suspicion that Goodman might make a possible target for a man like Kyle. He began to go through the others. There were three stories on Michael Jacobs, all relating to the same incident. As a Birmingham manufacturer of asbestos fibre, he had been prosecuted three months previously for allowing dangerous residue to be deposited on a Corporation rubbish site. Jacobs had made a natural mistake, not realising how dangerous the chemical was, and since there had been no accidents, the episode had not been widely reported. Nevertheless, Steiner felt his pulses race. For the first time, it was beginning to make some kind of sense.

It took slightly longer to dig out the stories on Nelson Mackey and Marian Edwards, but they too had recently featured in the national press. Nelson Mackey, as well as being a plumber, was also a local councillor in the little Cumbrian seaside town of Thelton. That July, he had been censored by his own committee for approving the site of a dangerous waste disposal tip on the town perimeter; it had resulted in two lorry drivers being hospitalised, and the tip closed by local health authorities.

Steiner felt his excitement growing. At last he had it. There was no longer any doubt in his mind. But the second cutting mystified him. It came from the women's page of the *Daily Mail*, and was a personality profile of six British ladies who had, in the paper's opinion, made a significant mark in the world of commerce during the past year. Marian Edwards was mentioned as a Sheffield hair and wig specialist who had brought out her own brand of hair-setting lotion, breaking the monopoly of the major corporations.

Steiner frowned. There had to be something else.

'Are you sure this is the lot?' he asked the BBC girl.

She adjusted her spectacles and smiled at him.

'Isn't it what you want?'

'It's a bit puzzling, that's all.'

Barry Fawkes peered over Steiner's shoulder.

'What's the problem, Guv'?' he asked.

'Well, at least three of our kidnap victims had something in common. They were all involved with chemical or nuclear waste.'

'So you think Kyle's some kind of crazy conservationist?'

'No, I think he's a psychopath out for revenge. Chemical pollution killed his brother, the only human being he could relate to. On top of that, it turned him into a physical freak. Years later, he learns that he didn't really escape that day on the riverbank at all, that he's destined to die anyway. A man like Kyle, who thinks in terms of direct action, would never be able to accept his fate as a simple act of God. He would need revenge, some way to hit back, if only to ease his frustration. So what does he do? He picks four names out of the newspapers. Four people involved in the same kind of activity which destroyed first his brother and which will eventually destroy him too.'

'You think it's possible?'

Lieutenant Colonel Parker coughed politely.

'With a psychopath, anything's possible,' he said.

Steiner drummed his fingers on the table with frustration.

'Except that the girl, Marian Edwards, doesn't fit,' he moaned. 'She's the outsider.'

They were silent for a moment, studying the cuttings. He *had* to be right, Steiner told himself. It was too much of a coincidence. Somewhere along the line, Marian

Edwards had to fit into the pattern, if only he could see where.

Lieutenant Colonel Parker sucked thoughtfully at his lower lip.

'This stuff she's selling,' he said, 'this hair-setting lotion, would it be poisonous?'

'No more than any other brand, I shouldn't think,' said Steiner.

'It'd be a spray, though, wouldn't it?'

Steiner looked at him as if he'd gone mad.

'Do I look as if I use hair-setting lotion?' he growled.

'Well, it stands to reason,' Parker insisted. 'If you want your hair to set, you've got to spray the stuff on, therefore it must be sold in an aerosol can.'

'So what does that prove?'

'Well, scientists have been worried for years about the number of aerosols in the world. The fluorocarbons which aerosols produce are steadily reducing the upper atmosphere's layer of ozone – that's a special form of oxygen. In other words Commander, the use of aerosols in a lesser-known, more insidious form of chemical pollution.'

Steiner took a deep breath. His heart was pounding.

'That's it,' he whispered, 'it's got to be. There's no other possible answer.'

'Okay,' said Fawkes, 'so Kyle's our man. But how do we find him?'

Steiner turned to Parker.

'Colonel, you know the way he thinks. He's kidnapped six people, where would he take them?'

'Mulgye,' Parker said promptly.

'You're sure?'

'It's the country he knows best. It's practically un-inhabited so there'll be no nosy neighbours, and if any of his captives should manage to escape he'd be able to track them down in comfort.'

'Tell me something, when you used it as a training area, did you build an airstrip?'

Parker nodded.

'We did have a small one,' he said, 'for bringing in supplies, nothing more. It's probably overgrown by now.'

'But big enough to land a Britten-Norman Islander?'

'Oh yes, those things can get in anywhere.'

Steiner's brain raced ahead, making plans. He turned to Fawkes.

'Get on to Stacey,' he ordered crisply. 'Mulgye's in his patch. Tell him we'll need at least five men, armed, the rest we'll bring ourselves. I'll contact the R.A.F. and see if they've got a helicopter base in the vicinity.'

Parker frowned.

'Just a moment, Commander. You're not thinking of going after Kyle with a handful of bobbies?'

'Why not?'

'I don't think you quite understand. Jonathan Kyle is a crack soldier, one of the most highly-trained professionals in the British army. He's skilled in every form of combat imaginable, and what's more he's operating in territory he knows like the back of his hand. Go in unprepared, and you'll be putting your necks on a chopping block.'

'I was thinking of using the D.11 Squad,' Steiner explained.

'Come on, Commander, what you've got is an ex-S.A.S. man. What you need are other S.A.S. men. Troops who think the way he thinks, who've been trained as he's been trained. Let me handle this. I can get you half-a-dozen top class fighters inside the hour. What's more, we've got our own transporter and helicopter service. We'll have you at that landing strip within three hours of daylight.'

Steiner thought it over.

'I can't call in the S.A.S. without Home Office approval,' he muttered.

'All it takes is a quick call, Commander. You know I'm talking sense.'

Steiner stared at him for a moment. Then he picked up the phone.

'Okay,' he said. 'You're on.'

THIRTEEN

The mountains huddled close. Their rutted slopes were
grey with ice. Darkness hung about their peaks like a dusty
shroud. William Mellinger sat outside the cave and
watched the sky resentfully. The snow had stopped. That
infernal bloody snow that had fallen all day, and on which
he had been relying to blot out their trail, had finally
bloody well stopped. That meant they were finished. At
Kyle's mercy. When the sun rose in the morning, their
route might as well have been signposted.

Mellinger shifted on his haunches. The slope where he
sat slid into a defile filled with crenellated ice. Its surface
looked almost blue in the darkness. There were deep ice-
troughs below and above the mountain wall, and immediately westward an outcrop of rock swelled into a
massive plateau of crusted snow. Mellinger thought : I
know you're watching us, you bastard. I know you're out
there, somewhere, crouched in the dark like a great bloody
tiger, waiting a chance to pounce. But come softly, come
swiftly my friend, or you will learn that even dead men
can bite if the need is strong enough.

Shuddering instinctively, Mellinger reached for the
heavy stick he had picked up in the forest that afternoon.
Against Kyle, it seemed a pitifully inept weapon, but who
could tell ? One good swipe, one well-directed blow dead
on target and perhaps even Kyle might fall. He was only
human after all, flesh and blood like everyone else. He
would find Mellinger a different proposition to poor little
Nelson Mackey. Mellinger blamed himself for Mackey's
death, blamed his stupid determination to put as much
distance between themselves and Kyle as possible. He had
planned to go back for Mackey later, but Kyle had out-
manoeuvred him. Poor bastard, poor helpless little

bastard. When Mellinger had found him hanging from the tree, outrage and horror had wrought a cry from his lips. Even now, each time he thought of the silent swaying body in the spruce grove, Mellinger's stomach tightened. There was something horribly undignified about a hanged man. It was not an ordinary kind of death. A figure, hanging, was an affront. It called attention to itself. It flaunted its mortality like a banner, demanding attitudes, reactions. It shocked and stunned with its presence.

Mellinger shifted uncomfortably in the snow. The cold slid into his vitals, chilling and disorientating. He felt his brain reel with the intensity of it. The great black shadows of night gathered between the hills until the whole earth seemed to lose its size and shape, leaving them helpless and cornered. Mellinger noticed that his right arm was rigidly locked, as though the blood in his arteries had frozen like water. In his fancy he felt like that, as if he had been absorbed into the cold hard earth, as if he had become a part of the bleak landscape with nooks and crannies, angles and edges, all solidified by the wintry chill. If Kyle did not get them, then the weather would. They had no food. They had no proper clothing. They could not cross the mountains in these sub-zero temperatures. There was no escape. They must, inevitably die.

Mellinger glanced at the cave where the others were sleeping. It was not a cave in the true sense but a deep fold in the rock which curled back on itself leaving a small sheltered place flanked by solid granite. He had built a small fire inside, and cupped as it was in the lap of the cliff face, it radiated a blessed circle of life-giving heat. It was crazy of course, to light a fire in such circumstances. A fire was a giveaway. Their position would glow through the night like a beacon. But they had no choice. Without it, sparsely clad and drenched to the skin as they were, they would have died from exposure.

And besides, though he had not mentioned it to the others, there was no doubt in Mellinger's mind that Kyle

159

knew exactly where they were. The ruse at the river had failed to confuse him. He had hunted Nelson Mackey down and strung him from a tree. If he had done that, then he had surely trailed them here, for their tracks had been clear enough for a half-blind man to follow. Mellinger had not told the others about Mackey. When he had returned from the wood, he had said simply that Mackey had disappeared. They knew, of course. They could see it in his eyes. But they had not pressed for details.

Mellinger glanced at the tangled line of scrub which ran from the point at which he sat into the mouth of the defile. In the stillness, it seemed frozen solid, a fossilised thicket from centuries back. Lost and forgotten in a world of misty starlight. Mellinger looked at his watch. He had worked out a rota system for standing guard. One hour per man. Not much. Not nearly enough. One hour, if you exempted the woman, gave each man only two hours' sleep at a stretch. But in this cold, an hour away from the fire was all a man could stand.

Mellinger gathered his knees against his chest, wrapping his arms around them in an effort to conserve his body heat. He wanted desperately to sleep. The rigours of the day, coupled with the lack of food, the constant fear and the shock of finding Mackey had filled him with a deep and dangerous lassitude. How blissful it would be, he thought, to sink back in the soft gentle snow and let slumber take him. That would be a sleep from which he would never awaken. The cold would finish him. Either that, or Kyle.

He heard sounds of movement from within the cave, and out of the entrance stepped Philip Goodman, his pale Scottish face slack with exhaustion. He looked done for, in spite of his rest. Every ounce of energy in his body, every tiny spark of life had been needed to sustain him through the day. Now his face showed the toll. He walked like a dying man, his cheeks riven with shadow. Where the eyes had been, deep craters hung like holes gouged out of splintered rock. They were all of them in a bad way, all close to breaking point. Goodman's breath left a vapour on the frosty air.

'Gosh, it's cold,' he hissed, his voice muffled in the silence.

Mellinger felt too chilled to answer. He struggled to his feet with an effort, wincing with pain as feeling returned to his frozen limbs. He had not believed that an hour could last so long. Goodman, despite his pitiable condition, looked suitably thawed at least, which was a blessing.

'Seen anything?' Goodman asked, peering at Mellinger's pinched cheeks with a worried frown.

Mellinger shook his head.

'Just stars,' he said.

Goodman rubbed his nose.

'Snow's stopped,' he muttered.

'Yes.'

'That's a good sign, isn't it?'

'It is for Kyle,' Mellinger grunted. 'It means our tracks won't be obliterated.'

Goodman's face fell, and Mellinger was sorry he had mentioned it. The man was under an appalling strain, not just physically but mentally too; they all were dammit, but somehow Goodman managed to appear a little worse than the others. Perhaps it was his country doctor's image, his air of vagueness and preoccupation. Goodman made you feel protective towards him, and Mellinger was strangely unwilling to move into the warmth and leave him alone to the cold.

'You'll be okay,' Mellinger whispered.

Goodman nodded.

'I've got my stick,' he said.

'Don't fall asleep. You'll have to watch that. Cold numbs the brain.'

'It's too uncomfortable to sleep.'

'You're wrong. Drowsiness is the first symptom of exposure.'

'I'll be careful.'

'Shout if you see anything. Even if it's just a shadow.

Don't worry about waking us up. Better safe than sorry.'

Goodman's mouth tightened into a grim line.

'I'll shout all right,' he promised. 'I'll bring the bloody heavens down.'

'Good,' said Mellinger. 'If Kyle does come, our only chance of survival is to stick together. Jacobs will be out to relieve you in an hour. It won't be pleasant, but you'll last out till then.'

Goodman hesitated.

'Mellinger,' he muttered.

'Yes.'

'I just wanted to say . . . ' He smiled with embarrassment. 'I just wanted to say thank you. For what you've done for us.'

'It's damn-all I've done for you.'

'You're wrong. You've pulled us together. You've given us hope.' He hesitated again. 'I don't suppose any of us will come out of this alive,' he murmured, 'but it's damn certain that without you, we wouldn't even have got this far.'

Mellinger stared at him in silence for a moment. The stars cast a sliver of light across Goodman's haggard face. He was smiling still, but the smile looked more like a grimace on a naked skull.

'We'll come out of it,' Mellinger said. 'The one thing Kyle didn't allow for was our will to survive.'

He turned and plodded across the snow, disappearing into the glow of firelight which beckoned welcomingly from its rocky fold.

Thirty feet away, Kyle crouched in the darkness, his pale eyes glittering. He might have been a statue, or a log left behind on some long-forgotten forest clearance. Not a muscle flickered. Impervious to the cold, he lay belly-flat on the snow, a mound of shadow. The minutes ticked by. He was in no hurry, Goodman was as good as in his hands already. How long would it take to cross that empty snowscape? Ten seconds? Five? Kyle would snuff him out like a candle, do it so softly, so delicately, that no one would know he had been and gone. Only his victim. And then, only for a moment.

Goodman was crouched in the darkness and his head was nodding. The exhaustion and the cold were beginning to tell. Sleep gathered in his brain, ready to lull him into oblivion. There was no sound from the cave itself. Mellinger and the others would be fast asleep. Not that Kyle feared discovery, but it seemed a shame to spoil things. He wanted them to die one by one, so that those left behind would have time to ponder. They could not know what they were dying for, no chance of that, but others would. Others like them, all those bastards who had collectively or individually defiled the earth, committed crimes against everything that lived. It was right that they should die here, in these surroundings, that they should feel the wrath of the land they had turned into an enemy.

The clouds parted. A crescent moon hung over the ragged summits, suffusing the earth with an ethereal glow. The mountains were still, frozen giants in an arctic universe. Mist hung between the peaks, pale and luminous. Gullies, filled with ice, rippled down their massive slopes. Goodman's chin was resting on his chest. It was hard to tell if he was asleep or not, but his eyes were closed. Kyle decided it was time to move.

He left the thicket and swept lightly over the snow. He was bent animal-low, his blunt head thrust forward like a battering ram, his haversack bulging above the bulky anorak. Philip Goodman had no opportunity to cry out. He had been lost in a wonderland of tropical sunshine where cold and darkness did not exist. In his mind, magpies danced amid soft summery ash trees. The first impact of collision hurled him backward into the snow. His eyes flicked open, bulging in terror as one massive hand fastened on his windpipe, pinning him helplessly to the earth. The dream was gone, and in its place a roaring tumult rang in his ears; it filled his brain and his jerking limbs, and he knew that death was near. Kyle held him, thrash-

163

ing by the throat, while with his free hand he carefully undid the straps of his haversack, took out the Eclair, and with slow meticulous movements screwed on his nightsight lens.

The thin scream brought Mellinger awake. Even without its signal, he knew that something was wrong. It was broad daylight. The fire was almost out. Why hadn't someone woken him, Goodman or Jacobs? But he realised the answer as he struggled to his feet and lurched into the open air.

There was a sense of peace in the early morning. The sun was already high, brightening the valleys, casting a rosy glow across the peaks and plateaux and the distant sheen of a mountain lake far to the west.

Standing on the brow, panting in the thin morning air, the girl, Marian Edwards, clasped both hands to her terrified face. At her feet, laid out almost reverently, was Philip Goodman. The snow around his thin aesthetic body had been beaten solid, and there were streaks of scarlet where Goodman's fingers had been grazed in his struggle for life. His face had lost its weary look. It was caught in a vision of complete aloneness, a face that had withdrawn, unmistakably, from the world. Poor sod, Mellinger thought, recalling how he had looked the night before, that tight smile, the expression of gratitude. Now he was gone, finished. One glance told Mellinger that his neck was broken.

Footprints led into the nearby bushes, and in a moment of absurd bravado Mellinger followed them, not knowing what he would do if he discovered Kyle there. It was with a sense of relief that he watched the trail twisting out of sight down the line of the nearby gully. He returned to Goodman, his spirits sinking. As he drew close, he realised the body was coated with a thin sheen of ice. The silver hair looked strangely brittle. Mellinger stared glumly down. Another name to chalk off Kyle's list. And how long had he been lying there, for God's sake? All bloody night, by the look of it. Mellinger looked around for Michael Jacobs. He saw him coming out of the cave, his eyes fixed hypnotically on the body in the snow.

'Goodman?' he whispered in a croaking voice.

'Didn't he wake you last night?' Mellinger asked.

'No.'

'You didn't stand guard?'

'Christ no, I must have slept through the lot.'

Mellinger was silent. Jacobs and him too. He had heard nothing : no scuffle, no cry of alarm, no grunt of pain. Exhaustion had lulled him into insensibility. His built-in alarm system, his sense of instinctive self-preservation had failed. But what was Kyle playing at? He'd had them all at his mercy, yet had left them to sleep the whole night long.

Jacobs stood staring open-mouthed at the body by his feet.

'How long . . . how long's he been like that?'

'All night.'

'What?'

'Since I left him at twelve o'clock.'

Jacob's eyes widened in disbelief.

'You mean he was lying here, and we were lying in there, and no one was on guard?'

'That's right.'

'Then why, for God's sake, are we still alive?'

'Only Kyle can answer that.'

Mellinger looked at the girl. She was in a mess. Her hair, long and ragged, hung across a white sickly face, her torso stooped in an attitude of deep fatigue. Her trouser knees were scraped and dirty, and terror hung plainly in her eyes. She was close to hysteria. Mellinger could see that. He took her shoulders in both his hands. For a moment, he thought she would scream again. Her lips parted, but no sound came, she seemed incapable of either speech or movement. He shook her gently, and something, a spark of sanity, of comprehension, came drifting back. She glanced at the body again, and he took her chin in his fingers and raised it.

'Don't look,' he ordered.

'But . . .'

'Don't.'

She began to cry. Tears issued from her eyes and traced the steep curve of her cheeks. He felt her shoulder shudder under the sobs, and decided, for the moment at least, to leave her be. If she could weep it out, so much the better. Michael Jacobs clutched at his arm.

'We've got to get out of here,' he whispered hoarsely, 'Kyle might be watching us this very *minute*.'

Mellinger felt ridiculously calm.

'He's probably been watching us since yesterday afternoon,' he replied.

Jacobs's eyes filled with panic.

'Then we've got to run.'

'Where would you suggest?' asked Mellinger drily.

'Anywhere, for God's sake. Away from here.'

'We need food,' said Mellinger, 'something solid in our stomachs. We can't cross the mountains in this cold without fuel for our bodies.'

'To hell with food. I'd be sick anyway.'

'You'll get it down and keep it down. Kyle will have to wait.'

But finding food was easier said than done. For Kyle of course, it was a simple matter : he knew how to hunt, he knew what to look for, he knew which berries to eat, which plants to pick and where to find them. Mellinger had spent a lifetime mountaineering, but had never, like Kyle, been obliged to live off the land. Besides, it was mid-winter. There were no berries, no plants, nothing edible to be found in ankle-deep snow.

They set off, sliding down into the mouth of the nearest valley. It was comforting down here, a deep and sheltered place. Around them, the ice-peaks glistened like diamonds, shining in the sun. Splashes of amber daubed the whiteness where rocky outcrops nosed through the snow like

166

inquisitive moles. Wind weaved creamy spumes along the breasts of the distant ridge, but here in the valley, the air was as still as the barren earth. A wide stream washed its way over shiny pebbles, curling obliquely across the valley floor. Mellinger stumbled along its bank, staring into the water. Memories of his wife danced inside his brain. Strange how you thought of those you loved when death was near – even stranger when they themselves had been dead for so long. His wife, his son. But they had never really died, he thought. As long as he survived, some part of them lingered on.

He stared at the river, stumbling blindly, crushed by the awful inevitability of their situation. Would they last the day? Jacobs was a heavy man, strong as a bull in some respects, but this slow ponderous battle for survival took more than mere strength. And the girl? Did she stand any kind of chance at all? Did any of them, if it came to that?

They needed food; not to satisfy their hunger – they were none of them hungry. Pounded by the cold and physical exertion, their stomachs had given up. No, hunger wasn't a problem, but Mellinger knew they had to get something inside them to maintain their body heat. Without food, they would not immediately starve, but they would damn soon freeze. They had to eat.

The river sparkled in the sunlight. Its edges were frosted with ice, and the boulders peeking through its rippling current looked shiny as wet glass. Beneath the surface, something moved, a shadow: it hovered, flitted, hovered again. Mellinger stopped, frowning. Yes, there it was. Good God, a trout. It was late in the year, incredibly late, but it was, undeniably, a trout. His pulses raced.

'Stand still,' he ordered, and slid soundlessly into the water. Its chill bit deep into his aching ankles. He stood, legs apart, cupped hands held motionless just below the surface, waiting for the unwary fish to deliver itself.

On the bank, Marian Edwards and Michael Jacobs

watched in silence, grateful for the rest. Their faces were without expression, beyond feeling, beyond – at least momentarily – even fear. A minute passed, two, and still Mellinger stood there, his spine stiff and aching, his bones frozen to the marrow. He longed to straighten, to leap out of this nerve-numbing water and prance around until his circulation was restored. But he forced himself to remain immobile, silent, waiting. Come on, you little bastard, he thought, over here. Gently now. Let me get my fingers around your pale glistening flesh. He watched the fish detach itself from a clump of boulders and dart inquisitively towards his outstretched hands. Its reactions were sluggish, befuddled by sleep. Just a little further, Mellinger thought excitedly. The fish paused, fins playing the water as it pondered the meaning of these strange elongated rocks. Mellinger stood motionless, scarcely daring to breathe. Come on, he thought: another foot, you can't bugger off now.

The fish came on, curious but cautious, its mouth opening and closing in a soundless rhythm. Its scaly skin bushed Mellinger's thumb, and with one swift movement he whipped it up and tossed it on to the riverbank. Jacobs whooped with triumph.

It was hardly a large trout, and would provide little more than a mouthful each, but it was better than nothing.

Mellinger borrowed Jacobs's penknife, cleaned the fish and gutted it, then cut the raw meat into narrow strips. The girl stared at them with distaste.

'Can't we light a fire?' she whispered.

'No time,' Mellinger grunted.

'But we can't eat it raw.'

'Try.'

'I can't.'

'Close your eyes,' Mellinger suggested. 'Forget what you're swallowing.'

They ate slowly, filling their mouths with the raw rubbery flesh, forcing it down in an effort to gain sustenance. For a moment, Mellinger thought he would be sick, but with a distinct effort of will turned the feeling aside. He had to hold the food within his stomach, had to. They needed it, they all needed it, something to give them life, warmth, energy.

Michael Jacobs grinned.

'Not exactly châteaubriand,' he said.

Mellinger shrugged.

'It'll help to keep you alive.'

The small man's face was smeared with dirt. His skin texture looked like melted wax.

'What I could do with,' he said, smiling thinly, 'is a little salt. I don't suppose you have any?'

'How about a bottle of claret to wash it down?' Mellinger suggested.

Jacobs giggled.

'And a glass of port and a thick cigar.'

Hysteria seemed ready to engulf them. Even the girl was smiling, a blank shapeless smile.

'Listen,' Jacobs said, chewing furiously, 'I owe you a meal.'

'Forget it.'

'No, no, I'll take you out to dinner when we get out of this.'

'Thanks,' grunted Mellinger.

'I know this lovely little spot in the country,' Jacobs said dreamily, 'the Cotswolds.' He turned to the girl. 'That's Laurie Lee territory, you know. We'll all go, the three of us. You'll love it.'

'Sounds good,' Mellinger agreed.

They went on chewing, trying to swallow the strips of dead fish. Mellinger's fingers felt frozen. He was grateful for the sun, but it was a wintry sun without much heat. He could feel the snow's chill through the seat of his pants. Jacobs stared thoughtfully at his last piece of trout, and carefully removed a sliver of bone.

'I ate a cat once,' he announced cryptically.

'What?'

'During the war. A cat. We were trapped in the air raid shelter, couldn't get out.'

'What was it like?'

Jacobs pulled a face.

'Worse than this. It tasted a bit like rabbit, but stringier.'

Mellinger began to laugh. He shook his head, giggling helplessly. He stared across the hillside, and suddenly his laughter died. Something had moved. He frowned. Sections of the nearest snowbank had detached themselves and were drifting across its surface. Good God, he thought, sheep. The hills were alive with them. Their woolly coats were scattered with snow.

'Look,' he croaked.

'What?'

'Sheep, for Christ's sake.'

Jacobs shrugged.

'What's remarkable about sheep?'

'What goes with sheep, you idiot?'

Jacobs shook his head, dumbfounded.

'Shepherds dammit,' exploded Mellinger. 'A farm. If there's sheep, there's got to be a farm.'

'No,' Jacobs murmured, 'they're hill sheep. Hill sheep can range for miles.'

'Like hell they can. Sheep never wander far from their holding, whether they're loose-ranging or not. What's more, they're blackfaces.'

'What does that mean?'

'It means,' Mellinger said excitedly, 'we must be somewhere in Britain, probably Scotland. Don't you see? Kyle tried to outfox us. He said it was nineteen miles to safety, and so it probably was if we'd followed his route, the route he wanted us to take. What he didn't point out was that there are farmhouses much closer, and farmhouses mean food, clothing, warmth, maybe a telephone, or a car to escape in, or possibly even a shotgun. Find the farm those sheep belong to, and we're saved.'

For some moments, they stared at him, their minds

170

unable to accept the shock of unexpected life ahead. Saved? Could they dare to believe it? He saw hope begin to dawn in their eyes. It was crazy, but true. Of course Kyle had lied. He had *wanted* them to follow that ridge. And they, however unwittingly, had fooled him. Mellinger felt the laughter coming again. That cold clever cunning bastard, they had fooled him, and now they were only a few miles from sanctuary, perhaps less.

'But for Christ's sake,' said Jacobs, 'the farm could be anywhere. It'd take weeks to explore these valleys.'

'Well, we know it's not behind us. It could be to the east or west, that's true, but my bet is they'd build it on the river. I'll lay fifteen to one that all we have to do is follow this stream and we'll wander right into its front yard.'

'Then what the hell are we waiting for?' Jacobs stammered, throwing down the rest of his fish and scrambling to his feet.

And as if on cue, from somewhere quite near at hand they heard the sound of a dog barking in the stillness.

FOURTEEN

The farmhouse lay in a broad saucer of land, a dirty smudge in a field of glacial snow and ice. Hardly a Christmast card scene, Mellinger thought: the building was squat and ugly, its granite walls built with more consideration to the weather than to architectural beauty. It had two chimneys, one at each end of a sloping roof, and their very uniformity seemed to add an air of drabness; its barn, corrugated metal, painted black, was an eyesore, but to Mellinger at that moment it seemed the most beautiful sight in the world. There was a tiny garden

171

out front, and beyond it, a narrow road went looping southward across the hills. There were no telephone wires, but Mellinger's heart beat faster as he spotted a Land-Rover parked outside the stone-walled garage. The monotonous chump-chump-chump of a private generator came clearly to their ears, dull and insistent even through the incessant barking of the dog. That damned dog. Didn't it ever stop? It had yelped continuously the entire way. In fact, it was the dog which worried Mellinger most of all, for it had gone on and on, not in any purposeful way, but with the same mechanical obstinacy of the generator itself, a rhythmless spiritless bloodchilling bark that had no sense or reason to it. Why on earth didn't somebody shut it up? True it had proved a saviour in one way, guiding them with its sound, leading them out of one valley and into the next. But its sheer persistence had frayed Mellinger's nerves raw, and more than anything, more even than food and rest, he wanted to get there and silence its din.

None of them talked much, needing all their strength for the trudge ahead, for even with the farmhouse in sight it was a breathtaking job ploughing through the shin-deep snow and Mellinger kept his gaze fixed on the narrow front porch, refusing to look away, as if to stare once more at those frozen hilltops would be too much for his body to take and would slide him back into a blank despair.

Keep going, he thought, and ignore the dog, what's a dog for Christ's sake? And then, as he drew closer, he saw the object of his discomfort, a black-and-white collie which caught his scent and mercifully quit its yelping, ploughing across the snow to meet him, its thin body shivering with cold or fear.

Mellinger reached down and patted its head. He was frowning. Something wasn't right. The dog was afraid. And there was no smoke from the chimneys, yet the house must be, had to be, occupied. After all, there were curtains at the windows, and there was the Land-Rover in front of the garage, and the front door was open wide to the walls, and – Good God, wasn't that a man sitting on the porch? It *was* a man, he realised, sprawled in a battered old chair, a man in wellingtons and faded army coat, just sitting there watching his approach. There was no surprise on the man's face, and he had made no attempt to stop the dog's whining. Mellinger felt his blood begin to turn cold.

He came out of the snow and on to the road where the Land-Rover's tracks had beaten the way flat, and in two or three steps had gained the front of the porch, knowing what he would find, feeling his heart thump in fear and anger, cursing himself for being so stupid for not thinking ahead. The dog sniffed, moaning softly, around the feet of the man on the chair. He was an old man, grizzled and grey, and his face, sharply pointed, had the wind-tanned weatherbeaten look of someone who had spent most of his life in the wilds. It was a face that must have grown old long before its time, drained of moisture, battered by the elements, chiselled by hard work, isolation and constant disappointment. The mouth hung open, the thin lips were drawn back to reveal toothless gums. The eyes stared steadily at Mellinger, neither friendly nor unfriendly. They were sightless eyes, beady eyes, eyes that could watch without fully comprehending, the eyes of the old, or the very young. The neck was broken. It was a clean break. There was no other sign of violence, no bruising, no scratching, even the man's expression looked peaceful. Kyle had done his neatest job yet.

Mellinger stood motionless, surprised at the calm he felt. If Kyle had been here, if Kyle *was* here, then surely fear should by now be crushing him in its grip. But Mellinger felt no fear. He was beyond fear. He was, he told himself, beyond sensation of any kind, even pain.

It took a moment or two for the others to catch up; they had dragged behind in the long haul across the snow-field, and now it was the girl who came first, her pale cheeks slack with exhaustion, her eyes fixed on the old man's body with undisguised despair. Her lips writhed like angry snakes but no sound came out. She looked as if

173

the last vestige of hope had finally deserted her.

Jacobs staggered close, sucking at the air as if he was holding on to life with only the most agonising struggle, and as his eyes took in the body on the porch, absorbed the meaning of it, Mellinger saw his face glaze over, actually glaze as though death itself was moving through his limbs, clogging his blood, clouding his brain.

'Jesus,' he hissed, and his voice, almost unrecognisable, sounded like gravel rolling down a metal shute.

'Kyle?' he whispered. 'He's been here?'

Mellinger nodded. He climbed on to the porch and stepped through the open door. It was a crazy move, he knew that. If Kyle was waiting inside, he was delivering himself, shorn and helpless like a sacrificial lamb, for he had no doubt Kyle intended to kill him too, did not believe, could not believe Kyle's promise of immunity. Yet suddenly he did not care any more, he had ceased to fight, ceased to struggle, was caught in a kind of blissful urge to drift, to be carried along, hoping that the moment of obliteration, if it came, would be swift and painless.

There was no hall, no passageway; the farmhouse, probably built centuries ago, had been designed for utility rather than comfort, and the door opened directly into what appeared to be a combined kitchen and dining room. It was stone-walled and bare-floored, and a large wooden table in its centre had been set for lunch, with place mats, glasses, a jug of water and an ornate pepper-and-salt set inscribed with the words: 'A Gift Frae Bonny Rothsay'.

The table was the only piece of furniture still standing. The rest lay scattered about the floor in wild disarray. There had been a struggle of sorts, and a spirited one from the look of things. Mellinger moved inside, his mouth dry, his gut tight. The place had that feel about it, the feel of something rotten, an air of menace as if something dreadful had happened here and he was intruding into the realms of evil. He felt no surprise when he discovered the bodies: he had sensed their presence, even without seeing them. They were lying by the gas cooker, two women, one young, one old : the younger one had been strangled, the older, a lady in her late sixties or early seventies lay with her throat slit from ear to ear, her blood already crusting on the cold stone floor. Probably done with a kitchen knife, he thought, though there was no sign of the knife now, Kyle had seen to that.

In fact, there was nothing, nothing at all, that could serve as a weapon : even the cutlery, with the exception of the spoons, had been removed from the table. The drawers in the kitchen unit had been pulled out, and the most commonplace household implements were missing, scissors, carving sets, even rolling pins, anything that might be used for defence. Mellinger felt rivulets of sweat trickling under his arms. Despite all that had happened, he was appalled by Kyle's savagery, his sheer lack of pity. Knowing they would find the farm, he had moved ahead of them, killing without mercy these innocent folk whose only crime had been to lie in their path. Mellinger knew without looking that the food would be gone too, and it was, every last crumb of it. The refrigerator shelves were bare. He went through the cupboards one by one, doing it on impulse almost, knowing as he opened each door that the inside would be empty. He found a packet of teabags and a tin of salt, nothing else. Kyle had taken everything, had coldly and calmly gone through the place with a toothcomb, removing anything that might help them on their way. But why? Why go to such lengths? Why murder harmless people when he could have killed them at his leisure inside the cave? There could be only one explanation. Kyle didn't want to kill them here. That wasn't his game at all. He wanted them to die in the open, and he wanted them to die slowly, one by one. That's what his crazy film was all about. Mellinger let himself relax. He knew now that Kyle was no longer inside the farmhouse. He had come here only to de-fuse it, to neutralise its usefulness, knowing that with nothing to help them, no food, no hope of sanctuary, sooner or later they would have to take to the hills again.

Mellinger stood breathing deeply, trying to think. The sluggishness of his brain bothered him. Fatigue, and lack of sufficient food was making him dizzy. That, and the shock of discovery : the old man on the porch, the bodies on the floor, the dried crusted blood, Kyle's rampage. He heard the others moving through the door behind him, but did not bother to turn. He had to think, had somehow to get hold of himself, try to plan ahead, work out what Kyle was plotting, outsmart him if possible. He was, after all, not infallible. Ruthless perhaps, cunning, immensely strong, but not infallible. He could be, he had to be outsmarted. First thing, check the house. He might have missed something, a gun, a knife, a tin of beans, something small; check the lot, room by room.

Mellinger stepped through the door into a sitting room of sorts, smaller than the kitchen but more lavishly styled. It had an old-fashioned fireplace that looked at least two centuries old. In front of it, on the hearth, lay the body of a man in his late twenties. He had sandy hair and a ruddy red complexion, and the back of his head was also red where the skull had been staved into a pulpy hollow filled with slivers of splintered bone. On the floor by his right hand lay a shotgun. Mellinger did not need to pick it up to see that it had been rendered harmless. The hammers had been carefully removed, and the twin barrels were twisted to the right. A second shotgun, similarly sabotaged, lay tossed upon the sofa. Kyle had left the packet of cartridges which had split open as the man fell, scattering its contents across the sitting room floor.

Mellinger stared down at the lifeless body. His mouth felt dry. Was there nothing Kyle was not capable of, no depth to which he would not stoop? How many dead now? Five, six? He did not try to unscramble them in his mind. Check the house, he thought again, forcing himself back to reality : there might be something, anything.

He went through into the back, blinking in the dark. There were no windows here, but there was enough light

176

to see that the back closet had been meticulously searched. He went on up the stairs to the second floor and checked the bathroom first. The cistern chain had been ripped away, and for some reason the towels too had been removed, but apart from that, everything seemed normal. Kyle, from the looks of it, had stopped long enough to take a wash. The soap on the basin had been freshly used. Probably cleaning off the old woman's blood, Mellinger decided. He moved on to the first bedroom. The wardrobe was open, but the clothes inside had not been disturbed. The discovery startled him. Kyle's first mistake. So he *was* fallible, after all. Mellinger felt hope returning. Warm clothing was just what they needed. Coats, jumpers, boots, wellingtons, anything was better than the useless sodden things they were wearing. At least they need not freeze to death. In spite of Kyle's efforts, their position was not quite so hopeless as before.

Mellinger was smiling thinly as he moved into the second bedroom, but the smile froze on his face and something in his stomach seemed to turn over, lying within him, heavy and leaden. That sense of evil he had experienced downstairs came to engulf him again, a feeling of death that was so acute he felt his heart flutter with the strength of it. He could hear the others moving about in the kitchen, and the sound saved him from panic, but the awful menace of the room held him like a vice. His vision blurred, and he blinked furiously, clearing it. Hold on, he thought, get a grip on yourself, for Christ's sake. It was not, he saw, a bedroom at all, but a children's playroom. The floor was scattered with toys. In one corner stood a crude doll's house, built with painful loving care and only recently painted, its paint already stained from constant handling. A bicycle lay propped against the wall, and an old-fashioned rocking horse that looked as old as the house itself was framed against the window. There were two children : a boy, not more than seven, Mellinger guessed, and a little girl, older, probably eight or nine. Kyle had not left them like the others, tossed haphazardly like bits of rubbish around the room. He had laid them side by side in gentle repose, as if even he had been bitten by remorse, as if — was it possible — even he had been appalled by his own savagery, and now the tiny bodies, positioned with such strange and unexpected reverence, might almost have been asleep. Except that they were not asleep. Mellinger knew they were not asleep. He knew the pallor of death, had seen it often enough before, in Vietnam, in Kurdistan — they were not asleep, by God. Oh, the bastard. The heartless fucking bastard.

Mellinger felt the anger coming from deep inside, felt it swelling like a cataract, heard its roar in his ears, felt its tumult in his throat. His heart pounded madly inside his chest. He had gone through too much to be moved by the bodies downstairs. It was as if some integral part of him had been blunted, rubbed insensitive by pain and suffering so that the sight of death had no more impact than the first glimpse of that whimpering dog. But now. Looking down at the sad helpless little figures, something happened to Mellinger. The anger came again, shaking him with its intensity, making his limbs tremble and his eyelids flutter. He was back in time, back to that awful day when the news had first come through — the crash, his wife, his boy, the dreadful finality of death. A sentence, a word, and pouf — they might as well never have existed. In the hospital they had looked like this, peaceful and unmarked, not scratched even — as if it was all some kind of squalid joke — they couldn't be dead, not really dead, could they? Where were their wounds, for God's sake? From which point had their life force been taken?

Mellinger felt himself sway. Dizziness blurred his eyes. Oh, that bastard. He did not deserve to live, could not be allowed to live. For the good of humanity, for the good of mankind he had to be stopped.

Mellinger fought for possession of himself. Slowly he calmed, feeling the giddiness leave him. He did not look again at the children on the floor. He kept his gaze at shoulder height, gulping air, tasting its chill freshness in his mouth, tasting the scent of snow and ice and wintry heather. Through the window he spotted Jacobs trying to start the Land-Rover engine. There was no response from beneath the bonnet. It would have surprised Mellinger if there had been. Kyle would hardly have gone to such elaborate lengths to block off their source of supply if he hadn't also destroyed their means of escape. Still, there might be something down there worth salvaging. Keeping his eyes averted from the bodies on the floor, Mellinger went back downstairs (ignoring Marian Edwards slumped exhausted in a kitchen chair) and joined Jacobs outside, who by this time had given up trying to start the Land-Rover and was poking about in its engine with a mixture of fury and despair.

'You're wasting your time,' Mellinger told him quietly.

Jacobs hammered the lid with his fist, almost weeping with frustration. Who could blame him, Mellinger thought? They had imagined themselves saved, had begun, almost fearfully, to believe in life again, and now this. It was too much to take.

'He's fixed it good and proper,' Jacobs choked. 'We'd never get it going in a million years.'

Mellinger ignored him. He felt completely in control of himself. Even the cold no longer bothered him. Not the cold, nor the hunger. He had come to a decision – not in a conscious sense, but a decision had been reached nevertheless, and it was there inside him, a strong motivating force, terrifying in its clarity. He nodded at the garage.

'Anything in there?'

'Just a tractor. He's fixed that too.'

Mellinger grunted.

'Now we know where Kyle's been all day.'

He stepped inside to the smell of petrol and leaking lamp oil. The tractor wheels looked huge in the confined space, their caterpillar treads clogged with dried peat and bits of grass. Mellinger poked about among the shelves which lined the walls. He found a screwdriver, a pair of pliers, a watering can. In the corner stood three or four

179

drums of petrol and behind them, an absolute gift, a rusty chopping axe. Kyle hadn't been quite so clever after all. The axe was small, but it could still be used as a weapon. Mellinger picked it up, turning it over in his hand, testing its weight. Not much, but better than nothing. All he needed was an element of surprise. One good swing, and wham.

The memory of the children returned and he felt the anger again, only this time it was different: a chill terrifying anger that filled him, not with fury, but with a relentless sense of purpose.

Jacobs followed him into the garage and stood staring at the axe.

'Where'd you find that?' he murmured.

'Behind the petrol.'

'Any food in the house?'

Mellinger shook his head, and Jacobs swore.

'Cunning bastard.'

'He's missed one thing though,' Mellinger said. 'There's lots of clothing. Anoraks, sweaters, rubber boots. At least we can die in comfort.'

Jacobs gave him a baleful stare.

'That's not funny.'

'No,' said Mellinger, 'take a look upstairs, you won't find that funny either.'

Something new was in him now, some element he did not understand. Not fear, the fear had gone, blotted out by the intensity of this unaccustomed emotion. He was no longer playing someone else's game. This was his game. His and Kyle's. It had become deeply personal, and nothing was going to stop him from what he had to do.

Jacobs rubbed his face with his hands.

'Listen,' he said. 'There's still a chance. If we follow the road, it's got to lead somewhere. Maybe there's a village just over the hill.'

Mellinger laughed without humour.

'That's just what Kyle expects,' he grunted. 'Can't you see? He's waiting for us, out there.'

Jacobs's face clouded.

'You can't be sure.'

'I'm sure.'

Hysteria entered Jacobs's voice.

'How are we going to get away?' he cried.

'We're not,' Mellinger smiled. He felt absurdly happy, wanting to laugh out loud as if the act of decision had given him a strength and power he could not control. He tucked the axe into the belt at his waist, picked up one of the petrol drums and thrust it into Jacobs's hands. The smile was still on his lips, a cold smile, cold and hard. He felt good, strong, confident, sure of himself. Nothing bothered him any more. He knew what had to be done and he would do it.

'We're going to kill him,' he said.

FIFTEEN

The roar of the rotors pounded Steiner's eardrums as their helicopter went into a steep curve, swinging east across the mountains. He hated flying, always had, but somehow the sheer breathtaking sweep of snow and ice down there made him forget his uneasiness, held him breathless with its beauty. The nearest summits seemed strangely distorted, so close, some of them, he felt he could almost jump into their laps, his fall cushioned by that great soft blanket of white. They looked like the Alps, he thought, or the Rockies. Not Scotland. He could not get over their wildness, or the way that, in places, some of their valleys were still green, curling up into the first powdery snow-patches and then on to the thick-coated blue-and-white tinged summits. Who would have imagined so much wilderness still existed?

Steiner shifted on his haunches. The sergeant had fastened him carefully to the hull with a canvas strap; a wise precaution, Steiner thought, since one sudden dip could send them all sliding through the open hatch like a bunch of graceless vultures. But perched there with the mountains below him, he almost forgot about gravity, distance, or the dangers of crashing to the rocks below. The helicopter swayed across the hills like a monstrous bird, and for the first time in his life, Steiner felt the real thrill of flying.

Around him, the S.A.S. men sat with bored expressions. They had seen it all before. To them, this was just another exercise, another operation, and the beauty of the mountains down there was not going to make up for the discomfort they would soon have to endure in ploughing through them. They were here to do a job and that was all.

Steiner stared at them thoughtfully. They were none of them young men, every one was in his mid-thirties. (Parker had explained that older men were favoured by the S.A.S. for their resilience and mental toughness.) They looked however, each of them, as fit as a trained athlete and as hard as stamped steel. They wore no recognisable uniform, just camouflaged combat suits and a variety of berets. (One was wearing a deerstalker, another an old canvas cap.) They carried no insignia of any kind, and the sergeant leading them wore no stripes. Even Parker himself, though he was a Lieutenant Colonel, looked just like one of his men. Just as tough and just as fit. He caught Steiner watching him, and winked. Steiner gave a thin smile. The night before, Parker had irritated Steiner: his manner, his attitude of quiet arrogance had been like a red rag waved at a bull, but this morning, dressed in his combat clothes, Parker looked like what he was, a man of action, and for the first time since their meeting, Steiner began to like him.

He felt someone nudge his shoulder and found Barry Fawkes waving a packet of cigarettes under his nose. Steiner took one out and showed it to Parker who nodded okay. Fawkes passed the cigarettes around, and soon they

182

were all smoking quietly as the mountains slid implacably by.

Despite himself, Steiner's thoughts drifted back to his wife. Sooner or later, he would have to make a decision about her, he knew that. Walking out wasn't enough, he had to make up his mind whether or not he had done it for good. Even now, he couldn't be sure. That night – was it only the day before yesterday? – things had seemed simple enough: a straightforward course of action, the only path open to him, and for the past day-and-a-half he had tried to put it out of his mind, to focus all his conscious thought on the problem in hand, the overriding business of finding Kyle and getting those hostages back alive. Yet somehow – inevitably, he supposed – the memory of Janie impaled upon that bed drifted hauntingly back, and it wasn't any use, he realised, sooner or later he would have to make the decision, to stay together or not to stay, that was the answer he must come to.

He loved her, of course. Still? he wondered. Yes, still. No point fooling himself. But she's made a monkey out of you, he thought. Pride, it always boiled down to that. What was pride? Steiner grimaced. Pride was what held a man together. When you hurt pride, you hurt much more than flesh and blood; sometimes you hurt so badly, and so acutely that the hurt could never be properly cured.

How could she care about him, to jump into bed like that with a total stranger? Well, not a stranger to her perhaps. How long had the thing been going on anyhow? A week, a month, a year? And his friends, they'd all known – or at least, hers had. Still, he had never cared much for her friends. That was the heart of the trouble, he supposed, in fact that basically they were different people, creating their own worlds, living in their own worlds, coming together – for what? Sex? Companionship? It was hard to put a finger on the answer to that one. But still he did not doubt, never had doubted that he loved her. He could go back, he supposed, cap in hand, but that would be capitulation. And of course she would do it all again. How could he blame her? He was never at home, his job saw to that. No, going back was out of the question. Divorce, then? Why not? She did not care about him, how could she? And yet . . . Fawkes had said she'd been ringing the station all day. That must prove something. Remorse, probably. Even Janie would feel the odd twinge now and again. He could always talk to her, he supposed : a phone call, not face to face. Just a talk, an airing of views. But sooner or later, it all came back to one thing. Decision. His decision, a decision that had to be made coolly and clear-headedly. Talking would only smudge the issue.

Steiner finished his cigarette and tossed the stub through the open hatchway. He sat back, pressing his spine against the hull, shivering in the chill. He was wearing a heavy duvet jacket which Parker had provided and a pair of heavy boots he used for working in the garden. The sun shone directly in his face, and along the line of distant mountains, their tops glistening like polished glass. There was a plateau down there, forged by converging ice streams into a blur of misty yellow light. Somewhere, perhaps directly below them, Kyle would be hiding. A madman. A psychopath. Crazed and desperate, capable of anything. But was he, Steiner wondered, capable of what they were attributing to him? It seemed so out-landish, so impossible to accept. He had heard of people killing for inexplicable reasons, but pollution? Steiner shrugged to himself. Anyone could be accused of pollution. Just by existing, you polluted something.

They had been flying for less than an hour when he noticed Parker waving downwards and peering out saw a long clearly-defined ridge in the snow which he took to be the disused landing-strip. Disappointment flooded through him : there was no sign of the aircraft, and no marks in the snow's surface to show that the strip had been recently used. Were they, after all, on the wrong track? He felt the helicopter dip as they swung into a steep curve, and saw Parker mouthing : 'We'll take a closer look.'

The ground came rushing up towards them, and watching, Steiner felt his heart jump, for there *was* something, there on the strip, something out of place, a heap of snow that should not be there, a lump, a shadow that needed to be investigated. He caught Parker's arm, but Parker had seen it too and nodded quickly as he barked into his radio mike.

It took them two minutes to land, and then Steiner was out with the others, forgetting for a moment to unclip himself from the hull, then sliding out into the snow and running with his head low beneath the swirling rotors, knowing they were far too high to catch him, but ducking anyway, cowed instinctively by their roar. The S.A.S. men had already reached the curious snowy hump, and Steiner felt his pulses begin to race – he'd been right after all – they were peeling back a camouflage net to reveal the blunt nose of a Britten Norman Islander aircraft, its shiny surface coated with ice, its windscreen misted over in the bright clear winter sunlight. Parker turned to grin at him, and his breath left a cloud of steam on the frosty air.

'This is how he got them here,' he said.

Steiner slipped in the snow, steadied himself and ploughed on until he reached Parker's side.

'Anything in the cabin?' he hissed, gasping for breath, still feeling the elation pumping through him, the feeling he always got at times like this when a simple hunch, a moment of wild intuition had paid off.

'We'll take a look in a moment. My guess though is that we'll find him up at the farmhouse. These windows are too misted; there's been no one in that cabin for the past twenty-four hours at least.'

'Where's the farmhouse?'

'Just over the rise.'

'Then forget the plane. We can check that later. Kyle must have heard our engine. We'd better get over there before he scarpers.'

'Right,' said Parker, suddenly all efficiency and purpose.

He barked an order, and the troops fanned out, skirting the rise with their rifles held chest-high. Steiner watched with wonder the way they slid through the snow. How could they do it, how could they go so fast through that lot? It was taking him all his time to put one foot in front of the other, but the S.A.S. men were moving at the double, and as far as Steiner could tell, not one of them was even out of breath. Parker looked at him.

'This is our game now, Commander,' he said. 'If Kyle's in that farmhouse, we'll root him out. You stay here, or at least on top of the rise. We'll give you a wave when it's safe to come in.'

Steiner nodded. He was in no mood to argue. The Colonel was right: this was their country, and their kind of operation. He was content to leave it in Parker's hands, at least until Kyle was taken. After that, the arresting procedure, the care of the hostages, the flight back to Glasgow and from there to London would become his responsibility.

He slithered with Fawkes to the top of the rise, and they lay in the snow staring down at the farmhouse which looked, from two hundred yards distant, devoid of life, except for a slender column of smoke which rose lazily from the chimney. So somebody was there. Kyle, it had to be. No hiker, no wandering shepherd would be out in this weather. And the farmhouse was derelict. It *had* to be Kyle. Steiner's heart began to pound.

He watched the soldiers moving in, marvelling at the ease and control with which they negotiated the snow. They had split into two groups, one party taking the farmhouse head-on, the other curving around the back to cut off escape from the rear. They moved in snatches, running and dropping, running and dropping, and always weaving to and fro to avoid the chance of being hit by an unexpected bullet. Steiner kept his eyes on the farm, watching the windows, the door, the little tool shed, looking for any sign of movement, no matter how slight (though what he would do if he spotted Kyle taking aim

Steiner did not know: a shouted warning from this distance would be as good as useless).

But he went on watching just the same, and it was with a sense of deep relief that he saw the first of the soldiers reach the door, kick it open and burst inside. The others followed, one after other, and for a long heart-wringing second Steiner waited for the stutter of gunfire. None came. A minute passed, two. He looked at Fawkes. Neither of them spoke. What was happening down there, for God's sake? Then someone appeared in the farmhouse door. It was Parker. He raised one arm, waving them in. Steiner clambered excitedly to his feet.

'Let's go,' he said.

It took Steiner and Fawkes considerably longer to reach the farmhouse than it had taken the S.A.S. men, but then they were less trained for it. By the time they reached the open door, both men were sweating freely and Fawkes's face was so flushed he looked as though he was about to burst. Steiner stumbled into the stone-flagged kitchen and through to the room where the fire was burning. His eyes took in the scene in an instant, registering with a sense of disappointment that Kyle was not there, staring instead in surprise and incomprehension at the man who squatted on the bed, a thin grey-haired man whose right arm was suspended in a sling around his neck, and whose left ankle -- Steiner's eyes widened at this -- was chained firmly to a ring in the wall.

Steiner had never seen the man in his life, but he recognised him from the photograph in his file: Naunton F. Huntley, the missing BBC Director General. One of the soldiers was down on his knees, picking at the lock with a narrow rod.

Steiner stepped forward, nodding his thanks to Parker.

'Mr Huntley,' he said crisply, 'I'm Commander George Steiner of the Metropolitan Police Serious Crime Squad. Do you know the whereabouts of the man who kidnapped you, or what he's done with the other prisoners?'

Huntley looked at him smiling, the relief at being

187

rescued plain upon his face. He shook his head.

'I'm sorry, Commander,' he said, 'I've just been explaining to the Colonel here, that until a moment or two ago, I didn't realise there were any other prisoners, with the exception of Mellinger, that is.'

'Then where's Mellinger?'

Huntley shrugged.

'God knows. I haven't seen hide nor hair of another human being for at least two days. Kyle came in the morning before yesterday, stocked up my food and water supply and left a fresh tub of logs for the fire. I realised he intended to be gone for some time, but Kyle isn't the sort of chap you attempt to question.'

Steiner sighed, feeling the excitement ooze out of him. He had thought it was over, had imagined – prematurely, he knew – that their chase had come to an end, and instead it looked as though it was only just beginning.

He seized a chair, drew it alongside Huntley and sat down, crossing his legs.

'I think, Mr Huntley,' he said, 'you'd better tell us your story from start to finish.'

There wasn't much to tell, it turned out, for Huntley had spent his entire captivity confined to this room, and apart from brief brushes with Kyle and the momentary diversion of Mellinger's arrival, he was totally disorientated – did not know even, until Steiner informed him, that he was in Scotland. Still, he was able to confirm one thing; Mellinger had been here, and Kyle was their man. The question now remained, where was Kyle now, and where were the other hostages? Steiner got up. He stared at the food on the table with open distaste.

'What is this stuff?' he wondered.

Parker chuckled.

'Dried venison,' he said, 'rabbit, couch-grass, ground-ivy, burdock and bilberries, all the things Kyle learned about in his survival training.'

Steiner picked up one of the plants and put it down again. He felt confused and uncertain.

188

'Now what the hell do we do?' he murmured.

Parker shrugged.

'No use trying to trail them overland,' he said. 'Whatever tracks there might have been will have long since been blotted out by the snow.'

Steiner gave him a cold look.

'What does the S.A.S. manual say for situations like this?'

Parker ignored the taunt. He answered evenly: 'The most sensible thing would be to use the chopper and spiral outwards from the farm. Sooner or later we'd be bound to pick up something. Trouble is, a manoeuvre like that takes time and plenty of fuel. Our tanks will be running low very soon and we'll need to return to base.'

'Can't we just radio for fresh fuel to be sent out?' asked Steiner.

Parker smiled.

'It's not that simple, Commander. Machines like the one we're using, burn up fuel at a rate of knots. If we had fresh supplies ferried out, it would involve a helicopter of at least similar size and that would mean, naturally, that the fuel carrier itself would then need re-fuelling. I'm afraid we've no alternative but to head for home.'

'But that could lose us valuable hours,' Steiner protested.

Parker stared at him, frowning thoughtfully.

'I've got a suggestion if you want to hear it,' he said.

'Of course I want to hear it,' snapped Steiner, hating himself for being unreasonable, knowing it was only the disappointment but hating himself anyway. Parker however, seemed unmoved.

'We know Kyle isn't behind us,' he said. 'He must be either to the north, south or west. Now we can't cover all the possibilities, but we can fly to the nearest farm and see if anyone there has spotted movement on the hills.'

Steiner stared at him.

'Sounds like an outside chance.'

Parker shrugged.

'It's the only one we've got.'

Steiner nodded, frowning. They'd lost him, he felt it in his bones. Against all the laws of reason, they'd managed to pinpoint his lair, and now, with victory in sight, they'd gone and lost him. Still, he wasn't ready to give up yet. Not by a long stroke. Parker's idea sounded hit-and-missy to Steiner, but it was worth a try, anything was worth that.

'Okay,' he growled, 'Leave somebody behind to get Huntley out of that contraption, and let's get back to the chopper. Every minute we hang about here we're letting Kyle get further away.'

SIXTEEN

Mellinger lay on the bedroom floor, peering through the window at the flush of wintry sunlight. The little garden – it was a cabbage patch, no more – lay smothered in snow, its surface so clean, so smooth and so bright it seemed to have no contours at all, as if nothing existed down there but a shiny white mirror which caught the sun and sent it shimmering back, diamond bright. Beyond the fence, the land undulated in a series of rippling cataracts, peppered with fir trees and rocky outcrops and merging eventually into a pale blue sky. Somewhere out there, he thought Kyle was hiding. Kyle. When Mellinger thought of the name, his stomach tightened. There was something new inside him now, something which made Kyle, who had until this moment been a figure of fear, become the object of his deepest hate. He intended – had sworn to himself, in fact – to destroy Kyle's existence. His fear was only secondary to that vow; even his own life had become in some demented way of less importance than the need to extinguish Kyle's.

190

They had a chance now at least. They were better off than they had been before. Still hungry perhaps, but comfortable and warm, having muffled themselves in the luxury of fresh clothes. Mellinger had instructed the girl to light every fire in the house and now there was not a room which did not have flames flickering merrily in its grate; currents of warm air rippled through the entire building. It was not, however, for their heat that Mellinger had ordered the fires to be lit. He knew the chimney smoke would serve as a signal to Kyle, a signal that they intended to stay put, that they had not panicked as he'd expected and were going to remain where they were until he decided to fight them on their own ground.

Mellinger had no clear plan in mind. He had started out with some vague idea about using the petrol. After carrying it into the kitchen in bucketfuls, he had made up a number of Molotov cocktails, using empty lemonade and beer bottles, half-a-dozen of which stood on the floor beside him, waiting to be hurled through the window the second Kyle showed his face. He had filled the bottles with petrol and stuffed their mouths with bits of old rag, but never having done anything like it before, had strong doubts that they would actually explode. The chopping axe lay on the floor at his side, but that was a pitiful weapon to wield against Kyle, for the man was capable of such speed and strength that Mellinger's chances of landing on target were, he knew, extremely remote.

No, it was Jacobs who, unexpectedly, had come up with their trump card. The man was a marvel. Using only the screwdriver and pliers, he had turned the children's cycle into a homemade shotgun, dismantling it carefully and using the hollow tubing as a barrel. It looked unwieldy as hell, for there was no way of separating the main tube from the rest of the frame, but Jacobs at any rate seemed convinced that it would work. He had taken the firing mechanism from the sabotaged shotguns (Kyle had not imagined they would have either the ingenuity or the expertise to salvage what he had left behind) had replaced the missing firing pins with a fence nail, and was sitting downstairs now, with the unlikely contraption poised and ready across his knees. They had the ammo, all they needed; Kyle, believing the shells to be useless had left them behind. Mellinger's real worry lay in whether or not the damned thing would work. A test shot was out of the question, for the noise would alert Kyle and lose them the element of surprise. No, it had to be a once-or-nothing job. That went for the gun, and the petrol bombs too.

Since they were not able to cover every entry, they had – and again it was Jacobs's idea – booby-trapped the doors and windows with stringloads of empty tins; it would be virtually impossible for Kyle, or anyone else, to get into the house undetected. For the first time in days, Mellinger felt blissfully safe. They could not be taken by surprise, of that he was certain. No matter how good Kyle was, there was no way in the world he could get in without their knowing. When the tins began to rattle, then they had him. As long as that gun worked. Everything – their lives and Kyle's obliteration – depended on Jacobs's skill and know how. The gun would work, Mellinger told himself: by Christ, it had to.

Behind him, the door creaked open, and Mellinger slithered back feeling his stomach bunch tight as a cauli-flower. But it was only the girl, Marian Edwards, muffled inside a heavy duvet jacket and clutching a long narrow tin with both hands. She smiled at him brightly.

'Sorry, did I startle you?'

He shrugged, letting himself relax, annoyed at having displayed his tension.

'Bit edgy, that's all,' he grunted.

She came and knelt beside him on the floor, and he saw for the first time that she had changed. She looked quite different from the way he remembered her. She had bathed, and done her hair, and put on fresh clothes, but it was more than that: the look of despair, of utter ex-haustion that had hung in her cheeks like the pallor of death had gone. Now she seemed composed, relaxed, a woman aware of her power and of her beauty. And she was beautiful, Mellinger realised with a start, seeing her almost for the first time. Not in the accepted sense. She was – Mellinger could not put his finger on it – not different, but . . . vital, that was it. There was an air of vitality in those pale cheeks and full lips and Mellinger felt uncomfortable having her here beside him, so close, when his thoughts and attention should be occupied elsewhere. She peered through the window at the flawless sheen of the garden.

'Seen anything?' she murmured.

'Snow,' he grunted.

She smiled at him.

'Here's something Kyle missed,' she said, pushing the tin into his hands. 'Oatcakes.'

Mellinger stared at the tin in disbelief. He had forgotten his hunger, had pushed it aside with a conscious deliberate effort, but now the prospect of food, even such a pitiful morsel as an oakcake brought back the hollow sinking ball to his stomach.

'Where'd you find them?' he breathed.

'Back of the cupboard, they were under the breadbin. They're a bit stale, I'm afraid, but they'll fill a hole.'

'What about you?'

'I've had my share,' she smiled, 'there were three each. Jacobs has had his.'

With trembling fingers, Mellinger pushed the flat wafer-thin biscuits into his mouth, feeling them crumble and mingle with his saliva to form a clogging mush. He swallowed hard till there was nothing left, his stomach rumbling at this unexpected intrusion.

The girl sat, legs curled beneath her, staring thoughtfully across the snow. He watched the sunlight on her face, the shadows dancing in her cheeks. It was a face of some strength, he reflected, not having studied it before; and she had displayed that strength in surviving this far, for the past day and night had been enough to crush them all.

'Do you think he'll come?' she whispered, not looking at him.

'I'll put money on it.'

'Supposing he just decides to starve us out?'

'He can't afford to,' Mellinger explained, 'Kyle may be a superman, but he can't last for ever out there, not without shelter. He's got to winkle us out, otherwise he'll be dead long before we are.'

He turned to smile at her, trying to hide his doubt in a show of confidence, but she was watching the garden, not him.

'Think we've really got a chance?' she breathed.

He felt the smile fade and let it go without a struggle. The truth was, he hadn't even considered it. Survival had become less important to him than destruction. His plan of campaign hadn't taken into account anything beyond Kyle's death.

'As long as that gun works,' he said, 'we've got the whip hand. What I mean is, we're in the warm and dry, and we're also armed. If you were Kyle, waiting out there in the cold, how would you feel?'

She shook her head.

'I can't imagine being Kyle,' she said. 'He's beyond my understanding. I mean, why should he want to kill us at all? I'd never seen the man before in my life – that is, I'd never seen him until he kidnapped me.'

'He must have his reasons,' said Mellinger.

'What reasons?'

'Oh, they don't have to be sensible ones. The man's mad, I realised that the first time we met. But I'm sure he has a motive, even if it wouldn't make sense to you and me.'

She was silent for a while, and he took advantage of the pause to study her more closely. Her hair was long and shiny as silk (she had evidently just washed it, for it was still dampish at the ends). Her face was sensual, sharply-sculptured, a face you could depend on, relate to – or step aside from, he thought wryly, he'd like to bet she'd be a tiger when aroused. Her eyes were studying the road, watching it curve along the ridge until it vanished from sight in a blanket of snow.

'Jacobs thinks we should run for it,' she murmured.

'What about you?'

'I really don't think I could take another step. I'm utterly whacked.'

He grinned.

'Dressed the way you were,' he said, 'it's a miracle you got this far.'

She laughed, and her laughter made him feel good, made him feel they were going to come out of this all right, in spite of their dilemma. When she looked at him, her eyes curious, he did not feel the instinctive retreat-into-himself that he usually experienced at moments like this.

'You were really at home out there,' she murmured.

'I was scared out there,' he said.

'You never stopped, not for rest, not for anything.'

'Resting makes your muscles seize.'

'You know the mountains well, don't you?'

'I live in them,' he admitted.

'Where's that?'

'The Lake District.'

'Oh God.' She smiled and shook her head. 'I went there once. Oh, the people.'

'Must have been summer.'

'July, I think.'

'Well, that's the height of the tourist season.'

'Don't they get on your nerves?'

He shrugged.

'I make my living by them.'

'Doing what?'

'I run a little mountaineering shop on the lakeshore.'

'Good business?'

'July and August, we're run off our feet,' he said: he

195

rolled on to his back, staring at the ceiling. 'You know, the marvellous thing about the Lake District is that there comes a moment every year – usually around the end of October – when you step into the street and for the first time in months find the pavements empty. The visitors have all gone, back to Manchester and Birmingham, back to wherever they'd come from, and then you begin to see your neighbours again, the hotel managers, the shop-keepers, the restaurant owners, all the folk who make their living catering to the tourists begin to emerge like rabbits out of burrows, and there's this wonderful sense of new-found freedom. The whole area takes on a fresh character, its real character in fact – it's one the visitor seldom sees, but it's there, it does exist, and it only comes to life in winter.'

He stopped talking, surprised at himself. As a rule, this was something he didn't bother to explain, why he liked where he lived, why he chose to live there. It was a per-sonal thing that he did not expect to make sense to anyone else, but the girl was watching him fascinated.

'I close the shop down when the season ends,' he ex-plained. 'For five months of the year, I do nothing but climb on the crags, root around in the hills, and drink in the local pubs.'

'Sounds a dissolute life,' she smiled.

'I have a great aptitude for depravity.'

'It's a beautiful country,' she said, 'I remember that much.'

'Timeless too. You get a feeling – well, it's hard to explain, but the past is never very far away.'

She shook her head.

'I couldn't stand it, I don't think. All those people.'

'You can lose them easily enough. In the hills, there's plenty of room to stretch out in. And it's different in winter. In winter you can still get that sense of being shut off, secluded, as though things haven't really changed much in the past two or three hundred years. And the people, the shepherds and farmers speak a dialect that

196

doesn't even belong in the twentieth century. They use words that went out of fashion generations ago. They're wonderful people.' He smiled. 'It's funny coming out of the hills in winter, coming down in the dark after a long hard day, with the lights of some farmhouse twinkling down below. You're lucky if you can get through that farmyard without being called inside for a drink and a chat. Never happens in summer – too many people around, I suppose. But in winter, it's a different world.'

She shifted on her haunches, moving her body so she could face the window without having to turn sideways.

'We've got hills where I come from too,' she said, 'moors and dales. They're not like this : they're smaller, softer, and there are lots more people around. Do you know Derbyshire?'

'Bits.'

'Funny, I never cared for it much. Even as a little girl, I wanted to get away.'

'Why?'

'Oh, the usual things : bright lights, excitement. There wasn't much of that in Sheffield.'

'And now?'

She peered down at him, smiling.

'I'm not like you. I don't want to shut myself away in some secluded corner. I've managed to build a world of my own that has all the excitement I can handle. Excitement – well, excitement can be self-generated. I run my own business too, and there's nothing more stimulating than being in the driver's seat, do you know what I mean?'

Mellinger put his hands behind his head, staring up at her curiously.

'Are you married?' he asked.

'No. Why should I? Oh, I'd like children all right, but not at the moment. I want to see . . . I've just got this hankering to see how far I can get. What about you?'

He shook his head.

'I've had all that, the big ambition bit. The running around, living fast and loose. I've got what I want, at

197

least for the moment, and I'd like to keep it intact.'

She chuckled.

'I meant are you married?'

He felt the familiar flash of pain; it was absurd that it should still affect him like this, but there was no sense fighting it: the memories came flooding back, as clear and forceful as ever.

'My wife is dead,' he said in a strained voice, and instantly regretted it. He could sense her withdrawal, the sudden barrier between them. It had been going so swimmingly that just for a moment he had forgotten the terror that bound them together. Now he had driven this stake between them, displaying his hurt, making her feel she had opened old wounds, and wanting to recapture that sense of closeness, that intimacy, he rolled on to his side and said: 'Do you still long for bright lights?'

She looked at him and shrugged.

'I go down to London from time to time.'

'Does that keep you going?'

'Satisfied, I suppose.'

'And home?'

'I never think of it like that. It's just ... well, it's just the place I've made my mark in.'

He smiled.

'You've got what you want all right.'

She was watching him closely, her eyes filled with an expression he could not decipher.

'Do you know what I really want,' she asked, 'right now?'

He felt his mouth go dry. The truth, the unbelievable realisation came to him in that moment, and not wanting to accept it, not daring to, he stared at her in silence, waiting for a signal. Was that why she had come, he wondered, were the oatcakes merely an excuse for the feeding of a deeper hunger? Was he, for whatever reason existed in her mind, preferable to Jacobs down there for performing the function she required – to provide a brief respite, to take her away, at last momentarily, from reality?

198

'I want you to put your arms around me,' she whispered.

She was crazy. They were total strangers, awaiting the approach of a lunatic killer. Things didn't happen like this. He knew the need that was driving her, understood the desire to convert her fear into the one thing that could offer release, but something deep within him, fashioned by a lifetime's conditioning, rebelled, and he felt a burning resentment as he realised that her interest had been nothing more than a desire for oblivion. But a new and disturbing force was in him now, one which had nothing to do with the need to display himself, to achieve that sense of closeness he had almost forgotten in his years of bachelorhood; this was something more primitive, more compelling, and it pulsed in his veins with a remorseless insistence. There was nothing to fear. They were safe, absolutely safe. Kyle couldn't get near them, not without firing off the whole damned alarm system, and Jacobs was sitting downstairs with his shotgun across his knees. They had nothing in the world to worry them. The girl was watching him with her lips half open, her eyes filled with that cloudy dreamlike expression he had been slow to diagnose, and now could not quite believe.

'I know it sounds silly,' she whispered, 'We don't even know each other . . . but I want to forget . . . just for a minute or two, I want to forget . . . what's out there.'

Mellinger reached up and pulled her to him, feeling her mouth against his, hot and moist and breathless, feeling the soft heat of her body beneath the bulky duvet jacket, and everything faded, the room, the wintry landscape, the thought of Kyle, they drifted from his mind, usurped by the taste of her, the thrust of her limbs against his, the clamour of her mouth on his face and throat, the long-deferred need that ripped through his body, ignoring reason, ignoring consequence. Was this what it came to, a breathless struggle on a bedroom floor, two strangers seeking, not fulfilment, but insensibility? He felt a sense of disgust welling up within him, for they were using each

199

other without conscience, not caring even for the standards that simple pleasure dictated, each bent on their own brain-throbbing path to nowhere.

His hand, rummaging beneath her jacket, found her breast, warm and soft, and as his fingers caressed the yielding flesh some semblance of normality came drifting back. The room steadied, and just for a moment he began to think again, but she hissed urgently into his ear: 'Don't stop . . . help me lose myself . . . for a moment or two . . . blot out . . . everything.'

There was no holding back after that, he had already gone too far to stop, and now he wanted the same release she did, to bathe himself in the illusion of security by the most timeworn escape route of all. Kyle couldn't reach them, not here, not in their secret refuge. How safe he felt with the warning signals posted all around, and Jacobs, armed and waiting, keeping watch below. In breathless haste, they stripped off their clothes, and then her limbs were wrapped around his, long and cool, burning him with their coolness. Her soft breasts were crushed against his chest, her hand, groping, found him, he saw the long smooth sweep of her spine twisting expertly as she struggled for position, then she gasped as he penetrated her body and began the long slow ride to freedom.

She was crying out at the end, and he remembered thinking, as reality came crowding back, that Jacobs downstairs must have heard the sounds and wondered what the hell was going on, then the room stopped spinning and they lay in each other's arms, breathless and lathered with sweat.

It was crazy, he thought, a crazy thing to happen, but a deep and soothing peace came over him, and clutching her tight he was filled with gratitude towards this unfamiliar organism which was pressing against his, for it was she who had brought him out of his nightmare and made him whole again. He peered over her shoulder, his eyes sweeping the snowbound landscape outside. It was so beautiful out there, so indescribably breathtakingly beautiful, and it was strange that he had missed its beauty before, had been too bound up with his own survival to see it, the hills, the trees, the little garden. He did not want to talk – would not have known what to say if he had – only to lie like this, warm and content, watching the world outside. The snow lay in patterns of wondrous white, dazzling in its intensity. Even the garden looked different. He frowned. Dammit, the garden *was* different. Something wasn't right down there, some small detail had altered, but for a moment, a long sweat-stinging moment he couldn't figure out what. The garden. What had changed inside the garden? Then it hit him. Sweet God in heaven. Footprints. Those footprints, he knew, had not been made by any of them. Only minutes before, that snow had been virgin and untouched. Fear pierced his chest, jolting him into panic as the truth formulated in his brain. During the fury of their coupling, someone had crossed the garden, and that someone could only be Kyle.

'He's here,' he croaked, wrestling desperately out of her arms, 'for God's sake let me up. He's bloody here, I tell you.'

SEVENTEEN

Mellinger was on his feet and out of the room in an instant, still naked, not even noticing the cold air against his fevered skin, seeing the open hatch in the ceiling the second he stepped on to the landing. Suffering Jesus, they had booby-trapped every door and window in the house, and Kyle had come in through the fanlight, had let himself in through the roof as calm as you please and was inside now, this very moment, there were traces of snow on the landing top, he was among them already, the killer

201

was among them. Mellinger tried to shout a warning to Jacobs, but only a croak issued from his lips. He tried again, and managed to stop himself in time. What was he doing? His shouting might warn Jacobs, but it would also warn Kyle, tell him where they were for God's sake. If they were to come out of this, he would have to use his head. Stealth, that was the answer. Play Kyle's game. If Kyle was in the house, then first they had to locate him. After that . . . Mellinger shuddered. He did not like to think about 'after that'.

Check the landing first, he thought. The bedroom at least was clear. There was the children's room though. He padded softly to the door, his heart pounding. How he hated it in there: ever since his discovery of the little boy and girl it seemed to harbour an air of evil that chilled him to the bone. They had moved the bodies out, all the bodies, laying them reverently in the toolshed at the back, but the absence of death had not diminished its influence, and death hung in this room like an odour.

The door swung open easily; he stood framed inside it, unable to control the hammering in his chest, feeling his knees wobble as panic crowded close. God, he'd left the axe behind. The petrol bombs too. He was naked and defenceless and it was too damned late to go back.

Shadows danced across the room; the rocking horse was still there, its blunt face watching him with uncomprehending severity. The toys lay scattered across the floor. The sun slanted through the window, casting shafts of light across the bare boards. The room was empty. Thank God. He felt himself breathe again, felt the tension ooze out of him in a soft exhalation. Now, double back. Into the bedroom and get the axe. If he was going up against Kyle, he needed something to even the odds.

The girl was half-dressed when he slithered in. Struggling into the duvet jacket, she turned to face him, her cheeks pale with fear. He put his finger to his lips and she nodded to show she understood. He scrambled to the window and picked up the chopper. As an afterthought,

202

he grabbed one of the petrol bombs too.

'Listen,' he whispered hoarsely, 'Kyle's somewhere inside the house. We've got to find him, then kill him, understand?'

She nodded, zipping the jacket shut, her eyes blank with the fear inside her.

'Stay close to me,' he instructed. 'Move when I move, freeze when I freeze, and whatever you do, don't make a sound : got that?'

She nodded again, and he gave her elbow a squeeze of reassurance. The bedroom was clear, so was the children's room; that left the bathroom, unless of course he was downstairs already, and if he was – Mellinger shuddered – that meant that Jacobs was probably dead by now, and the gun, their only real hope, would be in Kyle's hands.

He crept on to the landing, the girl close behind him. His ears strained for any sound, no matter how slight, which might indicate another movement, another presence. If he is in the bathroom, he thought, then he must have heard us by now, must be waiting, cool and collected, to carry out his dreadful business. Mellinger's fist tightened on the axe. He would go down fighting at least, would make Kyle pay for his fun. He felt sorry for the girl though. There was little she could do against a monster like that.

The landing creaked under his foot, and he froze, cursing inwardly. Bloody floorboards must be a century old. How could anyone move about in here undetected? Kyle had, however. That bastard. He'd slipped inside as quiet as a mouse.

All right, Mellinger thought, stop reproaching yourself; if he's here, you'll kill him. All you need is one good swing. Wouldn't that be a laugh? He could just see Kyle's face. All that planning, all that scheming, and just at the moment of execution : wham-bam – Mellinger's axe descending on his skull. It wasn't such an outlandish thought at that. Kyle was good, but not that good. Leaving the clothes and shotguns behind had proved that he wasn't infallible. And if he wasn't infallible, all they needed was a little more luck.

Mellinger nudged the bathroom door with his knee and it swung soundlessly open. The room was empty. Even the cupboards were empty. Mellinger closed his eyes for a moment. The throbbing in his throat softened, but only briefly. If Kyle wasn't upstairs then he must be down, and that meant – oh Christ, Mellinger thought – that meant he had the gun. Unless . . . unless he hadn't got to Jacobs yet. There was one chance. Maybe he was still poking around down there.

'Come on,' he hissed, seizing the girl's wrist. They ran down the stairs, taking them three at a time. What an idiot, he must look, Mellinger thought to himself, naked and sweaty, clutching a petrol bomb under one arm and wielding a chopping axe with the other. Like some half-crazed Neanderthal man on the warpath. He had to grin at that, had to chuckle as the first spasms of hysteria took hold of him.

'Jacobs,' he yelled, throwing caution to the wind. 'Look out, for Christ's sake, Kyle's inside the house.'

They reached the passageway and paused just long enough to check the downstairs cupboard. No one there. Kyle, thank God, was not crouching in the shadows waiting for them, and they padded on down the corridor, still too overcome with urgency to think straight, to pause and consider. Where the hell was Jacobs anyway? Why hadn't he answered? Was he dead already? Had Kyle preceded them, was he now sitting chuckling to himself as he waited to squeeze out their lives as he had squeezed out Jacobs? If not, why didn't Jacobs fire? Maybe he was taking aim at this very moment, cocking back that make-shift hammer of his. But what if the gun didn't work? Jesus Christ, if it didn't, they were done for, Kyle had won.

Breathless and sweating, they burst into the kitchen. It was empty. In the grate, the log fire crackled merrily away. On the table lay the screwdriver and pliers which

Jacobs had used to fashion his homemade gun. There was no sign of Jacobs himself. No sign of Kyle either. No sign of anyone.

Mellinger frowned, blinking the sweat from his eyes. If Jacobs wasn't in the kitchen, then where the hell was he? Had Kyle carried him off jackal-like into the snow?

'Where's he gone?' the girl whispered, her voice dry as brushwood.

He shook his head.

'God knows.'

They edged across the stone floor, expecting at any second Kyle himself to suddenly materialise god-like before them. Mellinger felt the adrenalin pumping into his stomach. He wanted desperately to turn and go back, but something pushed him on, and bit by bit he circumnavigated the entire kitchen, peering into nooks and crannies, pulling chairs aside, checking every possible corner where Kyle – or Jacobs – might hide. When he had finished, he looked at the girl, mystified.

'It doesn't make sense,' he said.

Suddenly something caught his eye, sending shockwaves exploding inside his brain.

'Christ Almighty,' he hissed.

The door, the cupboard door, the one damned place he hadn't bothered to investigate was swinging open. And there was somebody in there, for Christ's sake, somebody alive was in there, somebody crouching, ready for action. Jacobs, it was Jacobs. Mellinger, feeling himself break at last, screamed as loud as he could: 'What the fucking hell do you think you're doing?'

Jacobs fell on the floor in fright, his fat limbs entangled in the metal frame of his ridiculous gun. Seizing him by the ankles, Mellinger dragged him into the sunlight.

'Jacobs,' he grunted, 'what were you up to in there?'

'I thought you were Kyle,' Jacobs whimpered.

'But you were supposed to blow his head off, for God's sake.'

He got hold of Jacobs by the armpits and dragged him to his feet.

'Oh my God,' Jacobs hissed, 'I thought my time had come.'

'It damn well nearly has,' said Mellinger grimly, 'and it will, unless you can control yourself long enough to fire that thing.'

Jacobs looked at Mellinger, and his eyes widened with surprise.

'What happened to your clothes?' he muttered.

'I was feeling the heat,' Mellinger said dryly. He glanced at the girl. 'Bolt the door quick,' he ordered. 'It's solid enough to slow Kyle down, at least for a moment or two.'

He turned back to Jacobs.

'Listen to me,' he whispered urgently, 'Kyle's inside the house. We don't know exactly where, but he'll know where we are all right : we've made enough noise by now. There are only two ways he can get into the kitchen : through the door or through the window. Is the gun ready to fire?'

Jacobs nodded, his lips writhing convulsively.

'Give it to me,' Mellinger ordered.

Jacobs hesitated.

'Give it to me, for Christ's sake. The way you're trembling, you couldn't hit a bull elephant at three paces.'

Reluctantly, Jacobs handed it over.

'How does it work?' demanded Mellinger.

'You have to cock the hammer.'

'Like this?'

'That's it.'

'It doesn't have a trigger.'

'Doesn't need one. Just point the barrel on target, and push the nail up like this.'

'That'll do it?'

'Should.'

'Okay. Take the axe, and the petrol bomb. Know how to use one of these?'

Jacobs shook his head.

'Well,' said Mellinger, 'if I miss with the gun, set fire to the fuse and throw the bottle at his feet. Have you got that? Not at Kyle himself, but at the floor by his feet. And make sure you throw it hard enough to break the glass.'

'All right.'

'He's coming,' the girl hissed urgently, and Mellinger knew she was right. They heard a sound in the corridor outside, a soft shuddering creak, and Mellinger gripped the cycle frame tightly, taking aim at the heavy bolted door, knowing that would be the direction he would come from. *Crraack*, the door splintered on its hinges, swinging wildly inward, and Kyle stood framed between its massive posts, his monstrous head weaving from side to side as he took in the scene before him.

'Oh God,' Mellinger breathed.

He fought the panic inside his chest, forced himself to remain calm, waiting breathlessly for Kyle to advance into the room, and as the sunlight leapt across the shiny expressionless face, Mellinger slid the nail gently forward with his thumb. Nothing happened. God Almighty, the damned thing didn't work. The crazy contraption had let them down at last. Now there was nothing at all between them and Kyle, except . . . the petrol bomb. It was up to Jacobs. He was crouched in the fireplace, his beefy face bright with terror. Kyle had paused for a moment, staring at the cycle frame with a puzzled frown. He did not understand what it was. Mellinger could see that Jacobs had the bottle poised and ready, but for some reason – fright probably – could not bring himself to let it go. In another second, it would be too late. Kyle's hands would have fastened on his throat, and all the petrol bombs in the world would not save him. Still Jacobs waited, eyes bulging, cheeks ghastly. Mellinger caught the scent of his fear, felt nauseous at the strength of it, and the hair on his neck prickled as he watched Kyle begin to move forward again, the great hands reaching out, ready to crush and destroy.

207

'Throw it,' he shouted, 'Jacobs, throw it for God's sake.'

Jacobs threw. The bottle shattered at Kyle's feet, sending petrol across the bare stone floor. It did not explode however. In his terror, Jacobs had forgotten to light the fuse.

Kyle kept coming, closing in. Mellinger screamed out an ejaculation of hopelessness. It was over. They were done for.

His eye fell upon the bucket. They had used it to siphon the petrol from the drums into the bottles. It was standing on the hearth, still filled to the brim.

Mellinger moved. He scooped it off the ground in one sweeping motion and hurled its contents directly into Kyle's face. The unexpected shock of the pungent liquid stopped Kyle in his tracks. Petrol ran from his hair, down his cheeks, soaking into his bulky anorak. He was drenched with the stuff, and its strong fumes drifted into their nostrils, jerking Jacobs into life like an electric shock. As Kyle stood blinking in bewilderment, Jacobs seized a blazing brand from the fire and hurled it into the air. Dry-mouthed, Mellinger watched the fiery stick arc in slow-motion, trailing spark and twisting circles of smoke from its tip. Kyle too saw it coming and leapt back, but the table was behind him and he crashed into it, half-blinded and helpless. The brand caught him on the chest, just below the breast-bone. Mellinger, watching, thought for a moment that the petrol had not ignited, had been too damp perhaps, or that contact with the brand had been too superficial, but suddenly there was a flash of heat that sent them cowering back against the fireplace, and Kyle was engulfed in a rippling fountain of flame. Mellinger wanted to turn away, could not bear to look at this awful living inferno, but something held him transfixed, his throat dry as bone, his stomach tangled into knots.

Kyle was on fire, was smothered in it : he was the centre of a twisting column of orange flame. His head and hands and legs were blazing furiously, there was no part of his body that had been left untouched, and he turned help-lessly from side to side as though looking for an escape. No sound came from his lips, that was the awful part; his suffering was done entirely in silence, and as he swayed and stumbled, Mellinger felt his insides begin to lurch. Don't cough up, he thought; not now, not here.

The flames leapt and bit, licking their way up the massive trunk, growing stronger with every second. Fire billowed between Kyle's legs, cascading sparks into the dry frigid air. Black fumes leapt from his wig. He turned and darted for the window, crashing headlong through it, shattering the glass with the mindless desperation of a man half-crazed with pain.

They watched with fascinated horror as he threw him-self into the snow, rolling over and over in an attempt to smother the flames. Smoke swirled from his body as he kicked and twisted, and yet it was working, the fire was beginning to diminish. Unable to look any longer, Jacobs turned and began to vomit on to the hearth.

Kyle was on his feet again, engulfed in a canopy of smoke. His shape had lost its definition. He was like some figure out of hell. His clothing gone, his flesh singed raw, he staggered off across the snow, smoke still swirling around him. They watched him weave his way across the hill, through the trees and over the ridge, until at last there was only the scent of burning meat to tell them he had been there at all.

EIGHTEEN

'I'm going to kill him,' Mellinger said, and Jacobs shook his head in exasperation.

'Listen, it's over,' he insisted. 'If the flames haven't

killed him, the cold sure as hell will. This is our chance. There must be something along the road, – a village, a pub, a farm. Don't you understand? We're free. Leave Kyle to die alone.'

Mellinger shook his head.

'I made a promise,' he said.

'A promise to whom, for Christ's sake?'

'To me.'

'You're mad, d'you know that? You're crazier than he is.'

Mellinger pulled on his jacket and zipped it shut. What Jacobs said was true. He *was* crazy. Kyle was finished. No one, not even Kyle, could survive that incineration. If he wasn't dead already, then he damned soon would be, particularly out there, caught in the breathless grip of winter. A cold and chilly death, thought Mellinger, for those who die alone. There was a cruel justice in Kyle's dying out there, in the very land he had used to trap them. Justice, Mellinger thought. He was not thinking of justice. He was thinking of revenge. It wasn't enough just to escape. That would be easy. What he wanted now – what he needed – was the sight of that massive body with its life drained out, extinguished by the flames or by his own hand. He had to be sure, and until he was, the job was only half over.

He turned to look at the girl, sad to be leaving her, not wanting to go, surprised at his reluctance.

'Stay with Jacobs,' he said. 'Follow the road. I'll be along as soon as . . . as soon as it's done.'

To his amazement, her eyes filled with tears. None of this was making sense. Surely that breathless struggle in the upstairs room had been a need for momentary release, nothing more. I really am a bloody fool, he thought, jumping to conclusions. Old scars had opened up; they ached a bit, but not as strongly as before. Only hope was meaningful. Here he was, leaving her for an hour or two and they were practically in tears, both of them. What the hell?

210

'Don't go,' she whispered. 'He might . . . he might not be finished. What if he's waiting . . .'

'I'm counting on it,' Mellinger said, 'I want him to try and get me. I don't want to kill him in cold blood.'

She bit her lip.

'Is it really so important? Couldn't we just do as Jacobs says? Let the police handle it. Kyle isn't going anywhere, not in the state he's in.'

He shook his head.

'You don't understand,' he said, 'it's something I've just got to do.'

He bent and kissed her, not a lover's kiss, a brief peck on the cheek : was that for Jacobs's benefit, he wondered dryly, or was he afraid that anything stronger would melt his resolution. She was right in what she said : Kyle was a wounded tiger, and wounded tigers were the most dangerous of all. More than anything, he wanted to turn his back on all further thoughts of killing, to make his escape while the road was open. But the memory of those two little children came hauntingly back, and he knew beyond any shadow of doubt that he had to go through with it. Kyle must die. He had promised.

'See you later,' he whispered.

Without looking at her again, he picked up the chopping axe and stepped into the snowbound afternoon. Don't think of safety, he told himself : don't think of rest, or food, or succour. There could be no succour until he had done this job ahead; nothing else had a place for him now.

Kyle's trail was easy to follow. He had been too crazed with pain to make any pretence at covering his tracks. Mellinger moved easily, surprised at how well his body was responding after two days without food. Perhaps it was the prospect of the kill ahead, the thought of physical action, an end to it all. Nevertheless, he did not look back. He was afraid to look back. The sight of Jacobs and the girl making their way to freedom might well, he thought, destroy his determination. He took a firmer grip on the axe handle and squinted into the glare of the sun. Think of the job ahead, that was the answer. No side issues. No irrelevancies. Kyle, dead and dying. Kyle bleeding. Make him pay as he had made the others pay. The children – Goodman, Mackey . . . how many had there been, for Christ's sake? No, Kyle had to die and that was the end of it.

Still, it was funny about the girl. To react like that. After all this time, he had thought himself immune, dried-out inside. He smiled wryly to himself. Even dead men could twitch if the nerves were strong enough, he thought. Am I too old for Marian Edwards? Too staid, too methodical? He'd never thought of himself like that. Staidness had not been been one of his essential traits. Still, the years had passed, and he had left the real world behind, had run away in effect, so who could say what dull thoughts motivated him now. Perhaps she would like his staidness. Some girls did. They liked dependability. He could still go back, of course. There was television. He'd never cared for it much, but he wasn't bad at his job. They'd take him back, he was certain of it. No running away then. But what did he know about her? Was he hoping for too much, had it just been, for both of them, an instinctive reaction to terror and stress? Well, there was only one way to find out. Kill Kyle and go back. But what if Kyle really was alive, and not only alive but still capable of destroying him? What a joke that would be. The first time in years when he might conceivably have something to live for, and booomph – obliteration. Jesus. Mellinger's fist tightened on the axe handle. If there was any killing to be done, he thought, then he was the one who'd be doing it.

The trail vanished into a snatch of pine trees, and Mellinger worked his way to the left, moving slowly, not wishing to go into that tangle of shadows and branches – Kyle might be holed up in there, waiting his chance. move with caution; take it step by step. He smelled the crispness of the afternoon, felt the snow curl into the tops of his boots. It does seem sad, he thought, that in this blissful winter sunlight, I am bent only on destruction.

He breathed a sigh of relief as he rounded the wood. Kyle had left the shelter of the trees. His trail continued on towards the neck of the ridge. Not much further, surely. After being burned to a cinder, Kyle should, by the laws of normality, have already breathed his last gasp. But Kyle wasn't normal. Kyle was beyond the comprehension of normal creatures. Mellinger shuddered as he recalled that last frantic smoke-searing dash. No one, not even Kyle deserved to die like that. He begrudged him his pain. It was an improper end for any living thing.

The trail topped the ridge and Mellinger felt his heart jump in his chest – yes, there he was, Kyle, sprawled in the dip, his spine propped against an ice-glazed rock, his legs splayed out in front of him like a pair of charred logs. Dead? He looked it. Bile bolted sourly up from Mellinger's stomach. What an unspeakable mess. Kyle's body was shapeless. The head sprouted incongruously from the black mass of the torso. Where the nose had been was a shapeless lump, like a handful of melted wax stuck as an afterthought on to that flat expanse of the cheeks. The surface of the skull was shrivelled and raw, and the entire body displayed a texture like burnt porridge.

Mellinger circled cautiously, holding his axe at the ready. No movement came from Kyle, and at last, realising the man was beyond physical effort of any kind, Mellinger let the axe fall to his side and strode boldly in. Kyle was alive, he realised. The chest rose and fell as he strove desperately for air, and in the appalling darkness of his face, twin yellowish slits fixed themselves on Mellinger's approach.

'You took your time getting here,' Kyle croaked, his voice coming, it seemed, out of nowhere.

Mellinger stopped by his feet and frowned.

'You knew I would come?'

'Used my head. I knew.'

Mellinger squatted in the snow. The scent of scorched

meat filled his nostrils, bringing the bile back to his mouth. He swallowed it down.

'You're done for, Kyle,' he whispered. 'You know that.'

Something erupted deep in Kyle's chest. Incredibly, he was laughing.

'D'you want to give me a bloody lecture?' he murmured.

Suddenly he coughed. His whole body convulsed, and Mellinger heard him hiss with pain. Kyle's eyeholes were filled with pus. Mellinger stared at them, fascinated.

'I was wrong about you,' Kyle whispered weakly, 'that was my biggest mistake. I knew you'd be good, but I didn't believe you'd be that good.'

'That was luck. I was lucky.'

'No such thing as luck.'

'You deserved what you got, Kyle. You asked for this, you started it.'

'I'm not moaning. Now or later, what's the difference?'

Mellinger frowned.

'But you're dying. Nobody could save you now.'

'I've been dying a long time,' Kyle said. 'Half my life. Better to go like this than be eaten bit by bit till there's nothing left to weep over.'

Mellinger shook his head.

'I don't understand.'

'Stuff it.'

A pause. Something held Mellinger back. A need to talk, to know the truth, a desire to take this weight from his mind. Or perhaps he was putting off his macabre duty, stretching out time to its very limit.

'What would you have done with me?' he asked curiously, 'just as a matter of interest.'

Kyle looked puzzled.

'Done?'

'You couldn't have let me go.'

'Why not? That was the agreement.'

It was there then, that ultimate confirmation. Was there honour in Kyle? Humanity, even? Mellinger doubted it. Perhaps he would have survived after all, but that, he felt convinced, would have been due more to his usefulness alive than to his lack of it dead. He hesitated.

'Do you want to tell me anything?'

'Like what?'

'Why you did it.'

Kyle licked his lips. His moving tongue seemed incongruous against the blackened flesh. For a moment Kyle – God help him – looked comical, a clown wearing a clownish mask.

'The film,' he hissed. 'It was to be a warning.'

'To whom?'

'All of them. All those bastards who think they can ravage the land with immunity.'

Kyle coughed again, and Mellinger turned away, not wanting to look at the pain in his eyes.

'The land,' Kyle whispered when the spasm had finished, 'is all we've got. It doesn't belong to us; we belong to it. Destroy the land and there's nothing left.'

'And people? Aren't they important?'

'People come and go. The land remains.'

'You're crazy.'

Kyle smiled thinly.

'No,' he said. 'They are. The ones I was trying to destroy. They were ruining our world, Mellinger.'

'And did you think the killing of four helpless people would put an end to that?'

Kyle blinked. His shrivelled skull turned sluggishly as he peered into Mellinger's face.

'They were only the beginning,' he whispered. 'The first engagement in a holy war.'

'And the family at the farm. What were they guilty of, Kyle?'

Kyle sighed. His mouth opened wide, a pink fissure in a cavern of unrelieved gloom.

'I was sorry about that,' he said, 'but there was no alternative. They got in the way.'

Mellinger felt the anger rise inside him.

215

'The children too?' he hissed fiercely, 'did they get in the way too?'

Kyle looked at him. His eyes were lost. He was going fast, losing consciousness, going under in a barrage of exhaustion and pain. His chest struggled for air.

'Yes,' he whispered wearily, his voice barely audible, 'they got in the way too.'

Mellinger felt the fury ripping through him. He saw the little boy and girl laid tenderly side by side, their cheeks gripped in the rigidity of death. His heart pounded wildly. This was it then. The moment of truth, of sweet justice. The moment of retribution. No sense putting it off any longer. Now, while Kyle was still conscious enough to see it.

Mellinger rose slowly to his feet, keeping his gaze fixed on the top of Kyle's skull. He lifted the axe high above his head. The sunlight caught its rusty blade, turning it dull-red in the late afternoon. Somewhere far off, he heard the roar of a distant helicopter.

'There they are,' Steiner shouted, but the whirr of the rotors blotted out his words. He caught Parker's shoulder, motioning downwards with his hand, and Parker nodded back, giving the thumbs-up to show that he understood. On the road below, two figures waved frantically at the helicopter's approach. Even at that distance, Steiner was convinced the girl was Marian Edwards. He had studied the file so often, her face burned into his brain.

Gently, the pilot brought the 'copter down to rest, and this time Steiner scuttled out first, floundering through the snow towards the couple racing madly to meet him. The girl threw herself into his arms, sobbing hysterically: 'Thank God . . . oh thank God you've come.'

Only two, thought Steiner. That left three unaccounted for. He pulled her away so he could study her face.

'Marian Edwards?' he asked.

'Yes,' she said, half-crying, half-laughing. 'Yes yes yes yes.'

Steiner turned to look at the man.

'And you?'

'Michael Jacobs,' he murmured, and Steiner frowned. Jacobs did not look much like his picture. His cheeks were coated with beard stubble, there was dirt in his hair, and his beefy face was riven with exhaustion. Both of them were close to breaking point, Steiner could see that.

'Where are the others?' he demanded, holding the girl up with a physical effort.

'Dead,' said Jacobs, and Steiner looked at him with surprise.

'All?'

'All except Mellinger.'

Parker came trotting up, followed by his troops. His thin face looked sweaty in the sunlight. He peered at Jacobs, and then at the girl.

'They look half-starved,' he said, and turned to his sergeant. 'Fetch some food,' he snapped, 'and bring the cocoa flask.'

'Yes sir.'

The man scrambled off.

Steiner took off his jacket and laid it in the snow. Gently he eased the girl into a sitting position.

'Now,' he said, 'tell me what happened.'

She went through her story in fits and starts, and Steiner did not attempt to hurry her. At moments, she broke down altogether – then Jacobs butted in, prompting her along. When she reached the part where Mellinger had set out to track Kyle down, Steiner frowned.

'He's going to kill him?' he murmured.

'That's what he said.'

'Think he meant it?'

She nodded, and something seemed to choke in her throat. Steiner watched her with sympathy. She'd gone through a lot, none of them knew how much, but at least she'd come out of it alive. The sergeant came scurrying back clutching the cocoa flask, and Parker took it, unscrewed the plastic cup and thrust it into the girl's hand.

217

'Try this,' he said, 'warm you up.'

He filled the cup with steaming liquid, and she sipped it gratefully as Steiner rose to his feet. What a mess, he thought. Two of the hostages dead already, and now Mellinger – that bloody idiot – taking the law into his own hands. Who did he think he was, for Christ's sake – God? If he killed Kyle now, nothing Steiner could do would save him. He would be charged with murder, and that would be the end of it. Oh, there were extenuating circumstances of course, but no jury in the world would accept a plea of self-defence when Kyle was already at death's door. He might get away with euthanasia if he claimed he was putting the man out of his misery, but in any event he would have to stand trial. Steiner swore under his breath. He felt in some way responsible. After all, it had been he who'd involved Mellinger in the first place.

Well, he thought, he should have had more sense. Kyle deserved it, but it wasn't a jungle they lived in, not even here. Mellinger should have realised that, should have held himself in check. If he had done the deed, he would have to pay the price.

'Look,' Jacobs exclaimed suddenly, and following his gaze, Steiner felt his throat go dry. At the top of the hill, a figure was weaving drunkenly in the snow. At first, Steiner thought it was some strange creature from another universe, for it seemed too grotesque to be human, then he realised it was not one creature but two, one carrying the other across his shoulders.

'Mellinger,' Jacobs gasped, 'he's bringing Kyle in.'

They stood in silence, frozen into immobility at the strange sight which came stumbling down the snowbank. Good God, Steiner thought, look at the man go. He felt his stomach tighten, felt rivulets of sweat run down his back and under his arms as he watched Mellinger stagger clumsily on, legs dragging, lips swollen, gasping at the air. Was that Mellinger, the man they had sent into Belfast? He looked like a scarecrow, his pants in shreds, blood seep-

218

ing through the snow on his knees, his face ravaged by strain, vaguely demented. And that thing across his shoulders, was that Kyle? Sweet Jesus. Steiner felt his stomach lurch.

At the bottom of the slope, Mellinger finally collapsed, pitching forward into the snow. The sudden halt in his progress brought them out of their reverie.

'Come on,' Steiner shouted, and they ran towards him.

Steiner got there first. He tucked his hands under Mellinger's armpits and heaved him into a sitting position. Mellinger looked half-stunned. There was spittle on his lips, and his eyes were clouded, the eyes of a man on the verge of physical collapse.

Parker leaned over the charred senseless figure of Kyle, examining him closely.

'He's still alive,' the Colonel announced. 'Don't know how long he'll last though.'

The girl slithered up, crying, and slid her arms around Mellinger's neck. He turned to look at her, half-dazed, focusing his eyes with an effort. His lips parted, struggling for words.

'I couldn't do it,' he croaked, 'I couldn't even leave him there to die.'

'I know,' she sobbed, tears streaming down her cheeks, 'I know.'

She bent forward and kissed him on the lips, and watching, Steiner felt a sudden stab of pain. He rose to his feet and turned away, flinching as the chill wind bit at his face and throat. Seeing them together like that, Mellinger and the girl, had hurt him in a way he would not have believed possible. A vision of Janie came rushing to his mind. No sense trying to blot her out. She would not go away like a black cloud. Mellinger. Lucky bastard. For him, things were just beginning. For Steiner – well, for Steiner there was only the future, and the future looked drab and desolate.

He sighed, staring out across the blur of ice and snow. It was over, all of it. They had Kyle, they had the sur-

vivors. Now there was only the mopping up to do. Get
the living to hospital and pick up the bodies of the dead.
First things first, Steiner thought: they could leave the
second task at least until tomorrow. But now a great
emptiness seemed to engulf him. It wasn't much of a life
he had, he mused, not if he had to face it by himself. The
prospect of the years ahead, years alone, empty years,
chilled him. But what was the alternative? Take her back?
Would she come, he wondered? She'd always said he was
a bit of a deadbeat, unimaginative, insensitive. She was
right too. He was too wrapped up in his work, for one
thing. Still, he could always phone her, he supposed. What
was in a phone call? You could hardly call it a capitulation. After all, they were intelligent people. There was no
harm in talking things over.

He turned, stamping briskly to get his circulation going.
Two of the soldiers were carrying Kyle to the helicopter
on a stretcher. Mellinger and the girl were tucking in
ravenously to cheese and onion sandwiches. Jacobs was
sipping cocoa and chatting to the Colonel. There was an
air of optimistic bustle and efficiency. Steiner took out a
cigarette and put it between his lips. He felt better, he
reflected, now that he had come to a decision.

The Mighty All-Action Superseller from Sphere:

RAISE THE TITANIC!

Mightiest of ocean liners, the *Titanic* lies two-and-a-half miles down in the North Atlantic. And in her hold – perhaps the only amount anywhere of an incredibly rare substance that could make the free world invulnerable to foreign attack forever!

The Americans want it. So do the Russians. And the sea never gives up its secrets without a struggle. Which makes the task facing ace maritime troubleshooter Dirk Pitt one of the most stupendous tests of human courage and ingenuity ever . . .

RAISE THE TITANIC is the ultimate sea-adventure thriller, a spellbinding, breathtaking blockbuster of action and suspense that will grip the reader until the last page has been turned.
Soon to be a major film!

0 7221 2738 3   95p

Also by Clive Cussler in Sphere Books:
MAYDAY!
ICEBERG

THE CRASH OF '79

Paul E. Erdman

The countdown to the greatest economic disaster in history begins on the first page of this brilliant internationally bestselling thriller of power politics and high finance. . . . Against a background of oil riches, Middle East rivalries and the ruthless machinations of the world's top financiers who recognise no loyalties that can't be put on a balance sheet, THE CRASH OF '79 thunders towards its explosive climax.

A shattering masterpiece of exciting fiction, it could all too easily become tomorrow's mind-stunning fact . . .

'Riveting'   *Daily Telegraph*

'Paul E. Erdman has done it again . . . a bleak, exciting look at the very near future'   *Sunday Times*

07221 3349 9   FICTION   95p